These Treacherous Tides

Our Bloody Pearl

D. N. Bryn

Printed in the United States of America
First Printing, 2018

ISBN 9781721833412

For information about purchasing and permissions, contact D.N. Bryn at dnbryn@gmail.com

www.DNBryn.com

Edited by Courtney Rae Andersson with Elevation Editorial. Cover design by damonza.com

This work is fictitious. Any resemblance to real life persons or places is coincidental. Should the existence of siren in real life be established following publication of this book, that too is mere coincidence.

For Szilvia,
the first person to lay eyes on all my writing.

And for all nine hundred and eighty-two
H's in the scream you messaged me after
binge-reading the first draft of this manuscript.

OUR
BLOODY
PEARL

[1]

SWELL BEGINNINGS

There is one thing I know for certain:
We were right to hate the humans.

HUNGER HAUNTS ME like a bull shark. With every roll of the ship, the gunk inside my stagnant tub sloshes against my waist, stinging anew. The tight wooden room's stale air burns my lungs.

Steam whistles in the pipes that run along the walls, their copper gleaming in the dim ceiling light. My wrists throb where the metal cuffs locking me to the tub dig into my silver scales. The gill slits along my neck are clamped shut after a year without seawater and my head fins stick to my scalp like barnacles to rock.

I try to anchor myself with the memory of home, of fine sands and vibrant reefs, but I can barely recall the rush of the warm current or the thrill of the hunt. Even a single wrasse sounds like a feast now. *Or a few human fingers.*

At least I can still smell the sharp brine of the ocean. When the ship rocks, the small, circular window to my left reveals the sea rolling in an endless stretch of deep blue, begging me to return. The silhouette of an approaching vessel forms a blur on its horizon.

I squint at the hazy shape, but Captain Kian's roar of irritation from an upper deck makes me recoil. My captor's harsh voice is so loud it seems to shudder its way down my spine.

The new vessel leaves my sight as the ship I'm captive

on—the *Oyster*—turns toward it. The steam stacks clatter to life somewhere beneath me. Fabric and metal wings stretch out from the sides of the *Oyster*, and the ship bursts forward, riding just above the crests of the waves.

The sudden change in speed shoves me backward, tossing up my putrid water. As the liquid recoils, it grazes my largest tail fin, lying limp over the far edge of the tub. For all the pain I suffer, I nearly forget my tail exists, its iridescent gleam washed away by the filth and grime of the tub. It must still be impaired from the massive, anchor-like weight my captor crushed it beneath when she first locked me here. I can't bring myself to focus on its lifeless form for long. I wasn't meant for this.

I need the sea.

The ship tilts, turning again, and the ocean rises into view. The vessel from earlier reappears, skimming above the shimmering crests, much nearer now. A marauder's flag flies from its highest mast, a harsh scarlet with a crossed gun and sword, only a slight variation from the one the *Oyster* boasts. Just another pirate. Useless.

But this ship looks fancier than others the *Oyster* has fought. A series of small propellers spin in a blur along its scooping metal wings. Five main decks are visible, not including the levels piled at each end, all dark wood and silver finishings. Steam rises from four stacks sticking out of its back like mechanical dorsal spines. Its broad sails are in full bloom, pressed open like the stretched skin between an octopus's tentacles.

Wisps of smoke stream from the approaching ship's bow as its cannons fire. The *Oyster* rocks to the song of crunching wood. A rush of giddiness runs through me, and I tighten my hands around the edges of the tub. But then my stomach drops.

If the *Oyster* sinks, I sink with it, the metal weight trapping me inside this foreign container of wood until I'm crushed or I starve. A better death than what surely awaits me now, but death all the same. Not that my worries and hopes make any difference. The *Oyster* never loses.

The *Oyster* returns fire, its assault twice as powerful as the attacking ship. Before the cannonballs hit, a flash of light covers the sides of the enemy vessel, some form of translucent shielding unlike anything I've ever seen. I blink to convince myself it's there. The cannonballs deflect off it, plunging uselessly to the water.

With the attacking ship almost upon us, the *Oyster* fires again. This time it's not the harsh boom of the cannon, but a terrible, soft sputter. Purple light shoots from the *Oyster*, dividing and glowing like lightning. It hits the approaching vessel and engulfs it. Some of the crew jerk about and fall, near enough that I can make out their stunned faces.

The enemy ship loses speed until its hull hits the water, careening as it crashes into us. Its sturdier, propellered wings crush through the *Oyster*'s in a jarring twist of metal and fabric. Its hull slams against the *Oyster*, filling up my window and blocking out all but the faintest light. The tub rocks with such force that some of the foul water spills out of it, and pain shoots through my side as my ribs hit the edge. My chest burns, my heart rattling.

On the decks above, roars of attack and bellows of pain mix with gunshots and clashes of metal. *The Oyster . . . boarded?* The thought flounders through my mind as I struggle to process it.

Just overhead, the wood creaks under the weight of running feet. The sound dies in the bang of a pistol and the thud of a body. Slowly, a crack in the wood turns red. The liquid drips.

I lunge forward, catching the drop on my tongue. A soft, instinctive moan rises in my throat as the sharp taste spreads, hot and wonderful. The first fresh blood I've had in weeks. I open my mouth and let the rest drizzle in. What I miss trickles along my face, sliding down my neck and tinting the water pink. It's not the ocean, but it feels better than the air or the foul stuff in the tub. I would bathe in it if I could.

As the sounds of battle fade, the ships slip apart, revealing a stretch of sea and sky beyond the window. One of the *Oyster*'s small, flying dinghies races through the air. Steam blows from the dinghy's miniature stacks as a single massive propeller shoots it forward, its huge side fins providing lift. Captain Kian grips its sail, her dark hair pulled back in a low bun.

The sight of her drives a tremble down my spine, and I shrink back in the tub. She can't see me in here. She can't reach me. But even her gaze can hurt, the mere sound of her voice a tidal wave of silt and poison, stunning me from the inside out.

I force myself to watch her, because if I don't, I'll never truly believe she's leaving the *Oyster*. Her first mate sits beside her, shadowed by the mast. A cannonball shoots by them, but they vanish into the clouds, unscathed. The attacker's ship moves again, blocking the window once more.

I wait for relief to settle in. Kian's gone—gone with her fists and her raised voice. And she left me behind. But I can't feel her absence, not while the chains bite my wrists and the shouts of humans ring around me.

Beyond this bathtub room, the door to the main cabin rattles and opens with a bang. The thud of two sets of boots follow. A chill rises in my bones.

These new humans can be here for only one purpose: to learn how Kian captured my kind without succumbing to our songs. But what will they do with me? Kian held the other sirens she caught for a week or two, their voices echoing from the other end of the ship in choruses I can no longer create. Once we reached a harbor, they were sold to humans on shore. But through every cycle, Kian kept me.

I must have been the first she caught, the first anyone caught alive. I was her prize to herself for doing the impossible. My kind were untouchable—until Kian netted us.

Now, we're the humans' prey.

The hinges of Kian's chests squeak, followed by the scraping and banging of drawers. Someone curses, their voice deeper than Kian's. Their footsteps come nearer until they're just beyond the door separating my little room from Kian's large one. The latch opens with a ghastly click that jars my bones. Someone pulls the door outward.

I flinch away from the light that pours in from the large, ornate windows in the main cabin. Three orange shell lamps add to the radiance, glistening off the trinkets on the desk and accenting the golden embroidery on the bed covers. The gears of the hanging clock spin and click rhythmically.

Two humans stand in the midst of it all.

Both of them are broad of shoulder, with chests like mine, flat but with more muscle. The braided silver ring on the nearest one is something I've only seen worn in the right ear by the version of human they call a *she*. Her skin reminds me of the blotches of a flounder, patches of light and dark. Her straight black hair pools from beneath a broad-rimmed hat. The fluffy, blood-red feather tucked into the hat's ribbon bounces as she moves, matching her swirling cape and tight waist cinch.

"Get out," I tell her. I use the language of my kind, the words part vocal and part expression, with as much body signaling mixed in as I can manage, bound as I am. The humans understand nothing of it, but it feels good to speak in my own tongue. It's a language where you sing your soul bare, where words are concepts you define with your whole being.

Her thin eyes narrow as she looks me over, curving like dolphins in mid jump. "That bastard kept one," she mutters in the human speech, so rough and verbal and diminutive.

"I think you should close the cabin door, Simone," her companion adds.

Simone leaves my view, heading toward the front of Kian's quarters.

The one who remains must be a *he*, his earring on the opposite ear and made of something shiny and brown. His skin is the color of the wooden wall I've been staring at for weeks, a million little dark spots coating every bit I can see. Around his face, a mess of hair spirals in all directions, forming coppery, stormy waves.

He's tall for a human, but his light blue coat still caresses the back of his knees, the dark, rippling patterns on the edges contrasting with the deep golden vest beneath it. On his silken, brown belt lies both a pistol—which Kian once proved is good for three shots at close range—and a thin sword.

He whistles, standing in the doorway. "A live siren—can you believe it?"

My heart thumps like a fleeing fish and I hate it, but I can't force the terror away. What does he want with me? What could he want, but to do to me what Kian has already done? *Or worse.*

The main cabin's locking mechanism chimes and Simone returns. She leans against the wall at the other human's side. "They're smaller than I imagined. What do you think this one is, about eight feet long at most?"

"Their carcasses come in all different sizes," he replies with a dry grin. "But a *live siren*, Simone. Captain Kian was a lucky bastard." He steps into the little room.

I jerk away from him until the metal cuffs bite my skin. The bruises Kian left this morning show the reaction is worthless, yet some part of me still believes it will help, no matter how many times I'm proved wrong. But he doesn't move to touch me. Instead, he steps back.

"Find a corpse, would you? I think I'll be needing some entrails." A salty smile hangs from his words, a cutting sort of amusement.

Simone snorts, her nose wrinkling. "It would be a pleasure, Dejean." She sounds as though she means the opposite, but she makes her way back toward the door all the same.

"You're the best first mate!" Dejean shouts after her. "Never replacing you."

I stare at him. These are strange humans; Kian would have thrown a knife at her first mate on his way out. I shake the thought away. Dejean must not have enough blades to spare. Or maybe he's saving them for me.

As he creeps across the room, I draw a great hiss up the back of my throat, wishing with everything I have that I could sing. But my gills clamp to the sides of my neck like barnacles, dried to a crisp. *"I told you to get out."*

"It's all right, pearly, I'm just gonna sit here. No need to be angry." Dejean plops onto the floor, leaning against the wooden wall.

He doesn't reach for me, not with fingers or fists. But he's up to something. I don't trust him.

"Sneaky, vile human," I say. *"What's your game?"*

"What should I call you?"

"I don't want your nicknames." I have many already, all given to me by other sirens. But the humans won't comprehend them any more than they could understand the rest of my beautiful, melodious language, and I have no desire to be labeled with his rough jabber.

"Right then. How does Perle sound? You do shine like one."

I growl, leaning as far away from him as I can.

Dejean ignores the protest, humming. "Worth more pearls than I've ever seen in my lifetime," he mutters under his breath.

Baring my teeth, I hiss again. I'm no treasure to be hoarded or traded, no matter what Kian thought.

The scruffy copper hairs that ride over his eyes lift. "You know some of those words, don't you?"

"I'm not an animal." But it matters little what I say; he's just as dense as the rest of his barbaric kind. He'll never understand me.

Kian's cabin door opens with an ominous creak that makes me flinch even after watching her flee. The strong scent of blood precedes Simone's entry. She's pulled back her sleeves to her elbows, but scarlet from the fresh meat in her hands soaks the edges of them and drips along her breeches, staining the sandy fabric in splotches.

I've never felt so hungry before in my life.

"This is the most disgusting thing I have ever done. I do hope you're happy." She hands Dejean a liver.

He grips the organ with one hand and draws out a small blade with the other. "What about that time you fed a man's privates to a shark?"

"He deserved it."

"And the grave robbing expedition you took in search of cultist metal implants?"

"Skeletons don't bleed."

"I distinctly remember you shoving a woman's severed finger down her throat once," Dejean counters.

Simone huffs, moving out of view to bang around Kian's room. "That was a personal grudge and shouldn't be counted."

"Fair enough." With a shrug and a quick slice of his blade, Dejean cuts off a piece of the liver.

My mouth waters, and my stomach makes a noise I'm ashamed of. But when he shifts closer I jerk away, hiding my face.

"You can eat it. It's all right." His words are softened into what the humans seem to perceive as soothing.

I would much rather sink into a bottomless chasm, but I peek at him. He dangles the bit of liver just within my reach. It kills me to smell it, one snatch of my jaws away, but held by a human. I stretch my mouth toward the meat, so slow and cautious it's agonizing. The metal cuffs dig into my wrist as I lean farther. I catch the liver between my teeth and yank the food from him.

It saturates my mouth with a jolt of everything I've been

craving these last months and more. I devour it, far too ravenous to savor the sliver of blood-slick meat. I need the rest.

Dejean chuckles, cutting off another slice and scooting closer. He holds it out. His fingers look temping, but there's not much chance I'll be offered anything more if I bite them off. I take the liver out of his hand as delicately as my insatiable hunger will allow.

Oh merciful tides, it tastes *divine*.

Dejean scoots forward another fist-length, nearing the edge of the tub. Whatever his game is, he can keep playing it, because his offerings are the first fresh meat I've had in so very long. I should be embarrassed that a human could buy my trust with so little, but my stomach is larger than my brain will ever be. Most marine creatures are like that.

I savor the next piece, holding it in my mouth for a moment before scarfing it down like the rest. Dejean places a hand on the side of the tub. A hiss rises in my throat, and my subconscious screams for me to hide before he can hit me. I hide my face in my shoulder, a tremble running down my back.

"Perle?"

He doesn't sound as close. Forcing myself to look at him, I find he's leaned away. He holds a bit of liver over the center of the tub, though. I take it from him slowly, catching the juice and blood that's accumulated. It holds a different tang this time, as though mixed with the blood of another human. Cuts run along Dejean's fingertips.

I stare at them, the red slits thickening until a drop of scarlet trickles down. My teeth must have nicked him earlier, yet he hadn't made a sound. How odd. This is a very strange game, and Dejean is a very strange human.

He rises slowly onto his knees. I glare at him and fight the instinct to hide, but his gaze fixes on the metal around my wrists.

"Simone, you find a key yet?" he asks.

"Found eight keys." Simone pops her head back into the little room. "What sort are you looking for?"

"Small. Brass or bronze. I'm thinking two bits, maybe three."

"Here." She tosses him one that's the same color as my tub.

I flinch as he catches it, and it takes all my concentration just to steady myself. Whatever he needs the key for, I don't want to be caught off guard.

But then he slides it into the lock on the cuff around my wrist, and my heart stops. The metal unclamps with a click, and Dejean pulls it open the rest of the way. A rush of something hot and fierce pounds through me. I yank my hand out of the restraint, knocking my elbow into the tub's edge in my hurry. Yelping, I pull it toward my chest, but my arm stays locked in its half-bent state, pain shooting up to my shoulder.

No. This can't be. My arms are strong; not as powerful as my tail, but still sure and capable. I'm built for the water. The air should not hold me back.

But it does. My arm refuses to bend or straighten fully, locked in the same position. I swing it about, slamming it against the side of the tub. Knives of pain spring from the sore on my elbow, and I shriek a raw, hideous noise that grates my throat.

"Easy there! You'll hurt yourself."

Dejean's words sound distant to my ears, hidden in a rush like the crashing of the ocean, but the smell of the liver under my nose overpowers my fear. I snatch it between my teeth. He winces this time. I can still taste his blood.

He holds the next piece further out, but within reach of my freed hand. "Careful now," he says gently. "Go slow."

"*Slow,*" I grumble. I try it though. My arm tingles, tight and painful, and it shakes as I hold it in the air. But I can bend it a little more each time I move. I drop it back onto the edge of the tub, shifting my shoulder to avoid touching my elbow sore to the metal or my fingers to the restraint.

Dejean watches me, his gaze piercing. "You do know our language, don't you?" He says it slow and precise, as though that will somehow help me understand him better.

"Again, not an animal," I snap.

At least he has some level of comprehension. However small.

Dejean's brows pinch, but he nods, his lips turning up. He continues to observe me so intently that I want to pull deeper into the tub just to avoid his gaze. I prefer this to fear though; more cringing, less quailing.

"Would you let me touch your arm?" he asks.

"No," I hiss at him.

"All right, I get it." He holds his hands up, palms facing me. I have no idea what he means by the motion, but his expression is open, submissive. "I just want to look at that sore. I might have something I can bandage it with."

A bandage. Those are the white skins humans stretch over wounds. I don't know if their healing techniques work on sirens, but the sores are painful. It might be worth a try. I hold out my arm to him, glaring as I do, narrowing my eyes.

The rough skin of his fingers makes me itch, but he stays clear of my more tender scales. "You should know, I have not the slightest idea what I'm doing."

"Clearly."

"This doesn't look terrible. Sirens must be made of different stuff than humans." Dejean's finger brushes the edge of the sore, and I cringe, a growl burning up my throat. He lets go, handing me a chunk of liver. "Here. You did well."

I move my elbow more this time. The muscles tremble, but it bends easier with each motion, mending itself in long, aching strokes. As Dejean stands, I jerk away, lifting my arm to protect my face. My hand smacks into my face from the force of my motion, and I stiffen in shock.

Smiling weakly, Dejean edges around the tub toward the port side. "You don't have to go knocking yourself out to get me to slow down."

"I could eat you, you know!" It rises as a growl at first, but the words become a whine, the air contorting my beautiful noises into something almost as ugly and rough as the human's tongue. *"I will someday, when I'm stronger."*

Dejean's eyes sparkle. "That didn't sound very friendly," he chides, slipping the key into the lock of my other wrist restraint.

"I'm not friendly."

The metal clicks open, and I draw out my other hand, carefully bending my arm a few times to work out the tightness. I drop them both into the water, but the foul stuff stings my dry scales. Drawing in a breath through my teeth, I yank them back out. I want to murder Kian, each of her crew members, and everyone who ever set foot on this terrible ship. Instead, I hiss at the liquid and cross my arms over my chest.

"I'll be back soon." Dejean stands. He heads for the door, taking the rest of the liver with him.

I twist to face him, gripping the tub with my hands, and scream, *"Mine!"*

He stops. The metal lances my chest as I throw myself against the side of the tub, grabbing for the rest of the liver. I can't quite reach it.

With a dramatic sigh, he cuts off a large chunk of the meat and tosses it at me. "Go slowly. I don't want you getting sick in here." He waves the remaining half. "You can have the rest later."

Then he vanishes, leaving the door to my room open. Kian's cabin shuts tight and the lock clicks. Simone must have found the spare key to that, too.

I gnaw on the liver, trying my hardest to savor it. Some of the warmth is gone, but it's still juicy and tangy, and I yearn for more. Out the port window, Dejean's ship floats a fair number of dinghy lengths away. The nearest wing dangles, tilting the vessel slightly, and the steam stacks flicker with an odd light. They must be broken.

The glimpse of sea to either side of the ship stretches endlessly, tugging at me in a way not even the tastiest morsel can. If not for the weight pinning me to the tub, I could attempt an escape. But at least one door and two flights of stairs stand between me and freedom. With my arms so weak, I doubt my tail will be any better. If I stay where I am, Dejean may keep feeding me, and perhaps bandage my sores.

I huff to myself. What's he playing at? He can't be doing this for *my* sake. Maybe he means to sell me.

A shiver runs down my spine. At least as a captive on a ship, I can see the ocean, feel it rock beneath me, smell it in the breeze that comes through Kian's cabin door. If these humans bring me onto land, I won't survive.

The door thuds as it's flung open. Dejean's arm comes into view, but he turns away, dropping something off to the side as a new set of footsteps approach. Most of the light vanishes as he closes the door on me.

"I thought said I was not to be disturbed." His voice shifts away from the playfulness he takes with Simone and the thoughtful, soothing emphasis he uses on me. This new tone holds none of Kian's harsh cruelty, but it sounds forced, as though he pulls his joy from beneath layers of wet sand, the emotion coming through blunted and coarse. "What do you need, Chauncey?"

"Just a report, Captain." The crew member makes no mention of Dejean's stiffness. "We finished the search of the ship."

"And did you find them?"

"Not yet, but there are locked chests in the hull we're still opening. We've also cataloged enough provisions to last a full crew two weeks. The damages along the port are nearly patched, and we've pulled the wings up. What would you have us do with Kian's crew?"

"I'll deal with them later," Dejean says gruffly, even for a human. "You may return to the search."

"Aye, captain." Receding footsteps follow the words and Kian's door closes once more.

I try to make sense of the conversation, but a missing piece seems to drift too far out to sea. Dejean has more sides to him than Kian. And he's searching for something.

He opens my sliding door and enters, carrying a long tube, a stack of buckets, and absolutely no liver. He hands me one end of the tube.

"I can't eat this." I glare at him, but he only smiles in reply.

"Put it in the tub. I'll bring you the liver once we're finished."

I lower the end of the tube into the water, slowly, waiting for something terrible to happen. Nothing does.

Scooting closer, Dejean spreads out the buckets in a row. He pauses. "How long can you survive without water?"

"How long can you survive without air!" I shove the tube back at him.

Dejean scrambles to catch it. "Not long, I get it." He scowls at the tube, but the expression fades when he looks back at me. "I just need to know how quickly I'll have to refill the tub after the bad water's been drained."

Suddenly, I feel very small. Creeping my fingers over the side of the tub, I snatch the tube and shove it into my filthy muck.

"I guess that's my answer?"

I nod, sinking away from him with a scowl. If I had any dignity left, I would try to maintain it, but Kian bled mine out, every last blistering tear.

Dejean sticks his end of the tube in his mouth, sucking on it until water siphons up. He drops it into the bucket, hacking out a mouthful of revolting liquid. "That is foul stuff."

Humans are so strange. Though I suppose the way he holds his chest as he coughs and the wrinkles that form around his nose aren't all that different from a siren. I focus on the water draining instead, listening as he shifts the tube to a new bucket in steady intervals.

Despite the rancidity of the water, it still feels wrong to draw it away. Prickles run across my scales, up to the point where the weight presses down on me and I feel nothing at all. The little translucent fins along the side of my tail droop as the water drops beneath them, matching the state of my largest fanning fin where it slumps over the tub's edge.

I flinch as Simone sets down two fresh buckets of seawater. The fresh, salty smell floods my senses. I coo at it in adoration.

"Noisy creature," Simone mutters.

"I'm not opposed to eating you, too," I mutter in return.

A small smile tugs at Dejean's lips, but he shakes his head. "They're just talkative."

"Be glad they can't serenade you right now." Simone picks up two of the dirty buckets and carries them out.

The tube gurgles as the last of the old water siphons up, and Dejean sets it to the side. He pours the fresh bucket in. I want to sing, but I only manage a weak moan. Cupping the water in my hands, I splash it onto my face, letting it drip down my chin and across my clamped gills. *Bliss.*

Dejean fills the tub until it reaches the center of my chest, leaving just enough space that it won't slosh out as the ship rocks. After the muck I had before, I prefer the fresh water to any meal. I can't cover myself in it as I wish to, but it saturates my tail and my lower torso, relieving the itching that's cursed me for months. I pour it over as much of my shoulders and arms as I can, letting my body soak.

As Dejean wraps my elbows in his mystical bandages, I avoid looking at him, avoid flinching every time his hands move too suddenly. If nothing else, the weird white skins seem to work as a decent padding against the metal. He finishes up the second one and moves toward my back.

Twisting, I snarl at him, my sharp teeth bared.

"I haven't hurt you yet, have I?" He points out softly.

"*Maybe not, but you will.*" If I don't eat him first. His aid only means he wants me healthy for whatever he's planning. The healthier I am, though, the easier it will be to escape.

When he tries to edge around me once more, I give him a pointed look, tightening my round eyes. Very slowly, I lean forward. He slips as far as he can into the small space between the back of the tub and the wall, until I can see nothing but the fringe of his curls. My instincts send me mixed signals: scramble away or attack, hide my face or bite his off. But I ignore them. Staring at my fingers, I run them through the water. They glide, long and spindly in a lovely, deadly sort of way, pointed nails drawing no resistance.

Dejean pauses from his work. "Why can't you sing?"

Curling away from him, I growl a warning. He must want to keep me mute. He's afraid that if I could sing, I'd soothe him with my voice and eat him while he's mesmerized.

I would, but that's not the point.

"Did Kian do this?" A mournful tone seeps into his softened voice, distant and pensive: the sound of a somber memory. "Did she remove something of yours? Some kind of vocal cords?"

The sincerity in his reply stuns me and my brain goes numb. I shake my head. His melancholy still echoing through me, I reach up and brush my fingers over the gills on my neck, sealed tight from being exposed to the air for far too long. The flaps themselves hold no hypnotic ability; that power lies in the oscillating chamber they open to. No siren knows how it works, only that with it, we make a vibration that subdues any land creature. A beautiful sound; the song of the ocean.

I yearn to create that melody, but with the chamber hidden beneath locked gills, I can do nothing but growl and click and whine. I yank my hand down, hissing at Dejean for good measure.

He hums under his breath. "I understand, it's very personal." His fingers brush my shoulder as he wraps the bandage around my upper back. I scowl, but again, he catches me off guard with his words. "Maybe we can get them working again, once you trust me enough."

He can't know what he's offering me.

Simone appears in the doorway to my little room. "Excuse my saying it, Captain, but you're as dumb as they come. You shouldn't be giving a siren any advantages. That creature will eat you the moment they can sing again."

She's not wrong.

Dejean chuckles, finishing with the bandage and standing. "Just as many humans want to stab me through— should I live in fear of adding to that list? At least Perle isn't planning to dump me overboard for the minnows."

"Crabs, not minnows." I mimic a pair of crab pincers with my hands, baring my pointed teeth at Dejean.

He returns the motion, baring his own teeth in a way far more annoyingly friendly than I had. "Does that mean something? A lobster?"

With a scoff, I make the pincers less rounded.

"Crabs?" Dejean looks at me with so much elation that I barely manage to hide my amusement. After a nod from me, he repeats it louder, testing out the hand motion once more. "Crabs!"

Sighing, Simone shakes her head. "You'll need to watch out for Kian." She leaves the doorway, vanishing into the farther reaches of Kian's cabin. "Especially since you're playing with her pet."

"This siren isn't Kian's anymore," he snaps, though his bitterness seems directed elsewhere. "That monster's not touching Perle again."

"I'm not yours either," I object. The thought of a future without Kian brings me some comfort though, as terrible and misplaced as Dejean's beliefs about me may be.

Simone reappears, nudging around the puzzle of connected metal shapes Kian would spend hours detaching and then reconstructing in the dead of night. "They're more intelligent than I anticipated."

"It's reasonable, isn't it?" Dejean bobs his head, as though agreeing with himself. "Sirens *are* very similar to humans, physically."

"They're like an ocean monkey then?"

"A very bright ocean monkey, I think."

I cross my arms over my chest, grumbling a noise between a hiss and a gurgle. *"If you humans were any smarter than a bright monkey you'd know how dumb you are to believe that!"* At least they seem to be learning, though. If they keep this up maybe they'll be halfway intelligent someday. Dejean grins at me, and I snort. *"As though you have any idea what I'm saying."*

He clearly doesn't, but he continues smiling anyway, the expression only fading when Simone asks another question.

"Why are you doing this, Gayle?" Her brows crease and she stares at him in a way far too siren-like, with genuine worry and affection where gruff, selfish human nature should be.

Dejean avoids her gaze. When he speaks, his words come out in a hush. "I'm passing down my debt."

"You know the sort of compassion you owe is lost on animals, even bright ones."

"I like them better than people." He cuts the rest of the liver in two, tossing me half of it.

"We agree on something!" Taking small bites, I savor it, the growl of my stomach mellowed somewhat.

Simone barks a laugh. "That murderous creature will eat your liver just as soon as the one you're offering. Your debt is wasted on them."

Again, she's not wrong. Though with the weight still pinning me down, I would rather be handed free liver by Dejean than eat his only to have Simone starve me as punishment.

Dejean shakes his head in response. He leaves for a moment, but when he returns, he carries what looks like a big square sponge.

"Do you think you can lift your hips into the air for me?" he asks.

I figure he means to put the weird sponge under me—at least, the part of me not weighed down by a hunk of metal. I would prefer sand, but anything is better than the harsh grinding of the tub. Gripping its sides, I push myself up as far as I can, straining against the weight.

Dejean slips the sponge into the tub. It takes time for him to ease it into place. Having his filthy human hands in my water does not make me the least bit happy, but for this, it might be worth it.

"Hurry up," I yowl at him. *"I bet I could eat a little of you and get away with it."*

He makes that ridiculous cheerful laugh he seems so fond of. "Almost—there!" He pulls away.

The sponge stays in place as I sink onto it. Where I can feel it, the soft, squishy material cushions me nicely. Not like sand, but a worthy alternative.

Dejean hands over the last piece of liver. I savor it, sad for the loss. If there are any other viable livers on this ship, I hope he brings me them soon. He's not like Kian; he seems to enjoy the aid he provides. Though why he would bother still troubles me.

He joins Simone in Kian's cabin, but again, he leaves the door open. Out the large starboard window, the sun sinks into view. Both humans move deeper into the cabin, out of my line of sight.

"Did you find them?" Dejean asks, his voice low and grim.

"I broke open every damn chest in here, and the crew has searched the rest of the ship, but they haven't turned up," Simone replies, just as harsh. "They may not be here at all."

"No schematics either?"

Silence follows, which must have included a head shake from Simone, because Dejean groans. The ship creaks, and far above someone shouts a command across the top deck.

The stacks roar to life, and smoke trails into both windows for a moment before the vessel surges forward. Out the port side, some of Dejean's crew still stand on his ship, waving us off.

"What if there *are* no blockers to stop the effects of a siren's song?" Simone asks. "What if Kian was lucky, and found a way to catch them without making direct contact?"

"I don't think so. As far as I can tell, Perle believes they can't sing as a side effect of something wrong with their gills. I doubt Kian could have known that going into the hunt."

"Then she took whatever blockers she had with her." She leaves Kian's cabin, Dejean following in her wake. "This attack has been for nothing."

"We found Perle, and we took the ship intact."

"One siren and a ship." Simone snorts. "Perle is a prize on their own, but with the cost of repairing the *Tsunami*'s shield and Kian out there, likely vengeful . . . What good does one siren and a ship do us in the long run?"

"Maybe none." Dejean's next words are lost as he locks the cabin door.

He's just looking for investments. Of course, that is the way his kind function. No honor, only greed and cruelty. I can't trust the humans. But as I'm left alone with my thoughts, relaxed against the funny sponge, licking the last traces of liver off my nails, I realize something.

The pain is nearly gone.

[2]

SIREN SQUALLS

The sea calls to me;
> *In the tow of the tide and the salt in the breeze.*
> *But it calls loudest the moment the storm hits.*

DEJEAN COMES IN with the dawn. Eyes tired and face slack, he looks like Kian after she's stayed up two consecutive nights to write notes and yell at her crew. He carries a human stomach and a bag of pungent smelling fish. I huff at him, crossing my arms, and turn my attention away. Outside my little window, the sun rises as a dim haze through approaching clouds.

"I just got here, and already I've done something wrong."

"You existed." But I don't mean that. If not for him, I wouldn't be crossing my arms or complaining about food. His existence benefits me. Though, he could do a lot better; even his freshest meal lacks the excitement of the hunt, and this tub is a tight prison when compared to an equal-sized tide pool.

He sighs and leans against the wall. "What is it now?"

Glancing at him, I grumble under my breath. *"Everything."*

"I've no idea what you're trying to say." With a groan, he moves back toward the door. "If you need something, I'll be asleep in the cabin." He shakes my meal at me a couple times, taunting me to take it before he leaves.

Ignoring the foul meat, I point at him and make the crab claws.

"I'm crabby, I know." His lips quirk in a lopsided grin that makes him look a little less tired. The baggy shadows beneath his eyes darken as his expression drops. "Or do you just want to eat crab? I didn't think sirens would know that sort of slang . . ."

I motion to the ship around me. *"I learned it here."*

Dejean nods, but then his brow creases. "How long have you been here?"

Too long. Months, maybe even a year. But I reply with a shrug, clicking for his attention.

"I want . . ." I say as I point to myself, then cup my hands, palms up, and pull them toward my chest. Next, I form my fingers into a circle, squeezing them twice before pausing, repeating the motion once more. *Lub-dub. Lub-dub. "Heart."*

"You want . . . to . . . strangle me?"

"Every other minute." Bringing the motion to the center of my chest, I repeat it. *"Heart."*

"A heart. You want the man's heart?"

I nod, waving him away again.

"If you say so." But Dejean chuckles as he leaves, taking the rejected food with him. Barely a minute later, he returns, a heart in hand. Though chilled and long dead, with a slight hint of decay, it bleeds when I slice my nails through it.

I pick it apart. Dejean plops down against the wall as I eat, his gaze fixed on the dark clouds approaching. The ship tips farther than usual, revealing the harsh, dark peaks of wind-whipped waves in the port window.

"What do sirens do during storms?" His voice sounds distant.

Setting the rest of the heart to the side, I form the waves with my hands, and myself beneath them, riding the fresh currents, giddy in the turbulence.

"You want to be out there." At first I think surprise lifts the pitch of his voice, but his lips turn down and his glare drifts away from me. *Guilt.*

I nod, wistful sounds building in my throat. *"More than*

anything."

"Maybe someday you will." He speaks with a confidence that can't be sincere. He keeps me locked here, the ocean a wall of wood away. He cannot mean to free me . . . can he? Maybe Dejean truly wishes to let me experience the sea once more. Maybe he's kinder than most humans. Or maybe he simply believes he is.

Finishing the rest of my meal, I wave for his attention. I point to him, then make the gesture I used for *heart*, adding in a modified *want* motion and pinching my cheeks in the typical siren emphasis for a question. Together, my body asks *you - have - heart - ?* though the humans would phrase it in a longer, clunkier way. *"Do you have a heart?"*

He stares.

I repeat myself, both in my own tongue and with the series of motions. *"Do you have a heart?"*

Realization creeps over his face. He chuckles. "According to Simone, only for fish in bathtubs."

I'm not a fish any more than I'm a whale or a human, but I'm not going to bother explaining *that* to Dejean. I point to him again, then to my head, twirling my finger once before popping it away, cheeks once more pinched. *"What do you think?"*

"Me? Am I crazy? I'm thinking . . . What *do* I think?" He makes the think gesture and laughs, a sharp, harsh sound. "I don't know, Perle. I'm using strange hand motions to talk to my kind's natural predators, yet this is easier than any conversation I've had with another human in a long time," he says dryly. "I threw Kian's crew overboard last night, you know—well, all but one. He wishes he were with them."

That explains the screaming.

"You tell me. Am I heartless?"

All humans are. But he and Simone have been different from Kian and her crew. Even within humans, perhaps some variety exists. Dejean looks at me with such a soft, worried gaze that I almost can't picture him hiding deadly siren traps in the shallows. *Almost.*

I make the gesture for *heart,* but I shrink it as far as I can while still making it beat. *"A small heart."*

His smile reappears. "That's better than nothing, I guess."

I need to ask something specific, but I don't know how to show it. After a bit of thought, I motion him over.

He looks surprised, but he kneels beside the tub, so close that I could bite him. I don't. I still need him.

I point to him and then make the same cupping and drawing motion I used with the heart. Brushing one hand up my throat, I open my mouth as though I'm singing. For the last motion, I clasp my hands over his ears. I try not to touch him as I do it, but my fingers brush his hair by accident. *"You want the instruments Kian created to block out siren songs."* And the obvious addition: *"Why?"*

Dejean pulls back. "I . . . don't know what that means."

But he does. He proves it in the darting of his gaze and the drop of his brow. I hiss at him, and he scoots away, averting his eyes.

A purposeful knock comes from Kian's quarters, and Dejean stands. He ignores my scowl as he closes the door to my little room. After the lock's click and the swing of the main cabin door, a shuffle of steps echo, too indistinct for me to tell how many have entered. Only one voice follows.

"Here he is, Captain, as promised." The speaker sounds like the crew person who interrupted Dejean yesterday. *Chauncey.*

"He certainly looks terrible." A blunt lack of emotion leaves Dejean's voice hollow.

The smell that hits me confirms his words, the sharp tang of blood overwhelming. Whatever they inflicted on this human Chauncey brought in didn't bode well for him. He makes the low, pathetic noises of a wounded creature. Maybe I'll have another liver soon.

"I'm not a cruel man, Flavien. If you tell me where Kian keeps her siren song blockers, you are free to leave at the next port," Dejean says, each word precise and monotone.

Flavien; third mate of Kian. I flinch. If I had held any sympathy for this pitiful, whimpering prisoner, it would have left me in that instant, replaced by the feeling of his fingers digging into my scalp and his fists cracking my ribs.

"Kian told me nothing!"

Dejean's boots make a distinctive thud as he walks, his pace more erratic and heavy than most humans. "This is your last chance. Choose your words carefully."

Flavien yelps, his shout turning into a soft, sputtering sound and a blubbery cry. "I don't know! She never told me where she locked them up."

"Then you have no use to me."

Flavien's screams slice through the cabin, and then returns to a faint sobbing.

"Throw him over; dead or alive, I don't care." Dejean's voice catches on the last word, whether from frustration or something more, I can't tell.

In some ways, he shows all the harsh, insensitive traits of the humans I've known, of Kian and Flavien, and even Kian's second mate, Theirn, when she pressures him. But his actions toward his own crew, though distant, seem far from cruel. He is not kind, yet a part of him is *good,* somehow.

The shuffling returns as Chauncey and his silent helpers take Flavien away. Not until the lock of the cabin door clicks does Dejean open my little room. He carries a long, flat, pink muscle with him, one end oozing red. A tongue.

My stomach grumbles.

"You're still hungry then?" He offers it to me.

"I'm always hungry." Snatching it out of his hand, I split it open with my nails and chew on the bloody meat.

Another clatter of boots interrupts my meal, and the cabin door clicks once more before flying open. Simone sprints in. The wind comes with her, a stormy gale carrying salt and brine.

"We picked up siren vibrations, ten minutes out." A

sudden pounding of rain against the port window rumbles beneath her words as the clouds break.

Sirens! I grip the sides of the tub, my heart lifting. Breathing deeply, I search for the mark that tags our territories. Even locked in this stinking box of wood and metal I find faint whiffs of the soft, floral scent.

Dejean ignores me, rising to his feet in an instant. "Are you sure?"

"The meter is steady at fifty em-trons. There's a whole pod of them coming."

"At least we have fair warning this time. Get everyone below deck," Dejean orders. "Aileas reported secure locking mechanisms on the first and second storage units. I want the entire crew there in five minutes."

"But the storm? With no hands on deck . . ." Simone walks back toward the cabin door, Dejean following her closely.

"We'll secure the ship as best we can, lock the helm away from land, draw in the sails and wings, and stoke the stacks to full," he says. "I won't sacrifice my crew for the well being of a stolen ship. We only need to survive the siren attack, then the quick jaunt home."

Their footsteps pause, and Simone speaks again, softer, more urgent. "Be careful. Your call to the seas has always been deeper than most. I don't know what that pet of yours will do to you when you lose it . . ."

"They haven't hurt me yet." Dejean resumed walking, his voice growing muffled as he passes beyond the main cabin door.

"They haven't had this sort of chance before . . ." Simone continues talking, but the creak of the ship masks her distant words.

Sinking back against the tub, I tap my fingers on the rim. Killing Dejean now would do me little more good than it would've yesterday, whatever state he might be in. But I might still gain something from this storm.

Under Kian's watch, a siren attack had been a horror, the screams of my kin echoing through the hull of the ship for days after. But Dejean and his crew have nothing to block our song. The humans aboard this ship are the prey once more—the world turned right again.

The rain continues to pound, and crewmates shout somewhere above me, heavy feet pounding against the wood. Simone returns to the cabin first, hiding a piece of paper between a stack of Kian's books and leaving again. Not long after, another human comes in, closing Kian's door with a series of clacks, like an intricate lock sliding many bolts into place.

Dejean meanders into my little room, giving me a wary glance. He drops to his usual position, sitting against the wall across from the port window, tense and alert. He digs his fingers into his arm, tapping his foot erratically. His motions slow, and he closes his eyes.

All goes quiet as the happy rhythm of the siren's song reaches me. My chest flutters. It can't be heard yet, the vocals still too far off to make out, but our power lies not in sound. It comes from something even the humans can't describe, something they can only monitor the vibrations of with their strange technology. It rises in me like it does in all sirens, drawing from our love for our home, our desire to protect it, and our ability to thrive within it.

I want to touch the ocean now more than ever, with the ship keeling beneath me and the song flooding my veins. My scales shiver for it, my heart thumping in longing and excitement. It tears me apart just as it builds me up.

Finally, I can hear their voices, a soft call in the distance.

"It's so beautiful, you know?" Dejean sinks against the wall, loose and relaxed, a crooked grin on his face. "It sounds like life, like a brush of warm seawater on my bare toes, and the sand slipping away as the wave rolls out. Like the little fish diving into the coral, and the dolphins leaping in the distance." He sighs, his gaze distant. "It's peaceful and

[27]

colorful. And real . . . so real."

If I agree with anything a human says, I prefer not admit it. But he's right. It is beautiful. *"It's our love song."* One *that's taken the lives of many human intruders.*

He nods, though I doubt he has any idea what I've said with no hand motions to explain it. "I wish I could live there, deep down, beneath the waves. No humans, no nightmares. No fear. Just fish and whales and a long, eternal stretch of water."

The singing resonates from just beneath us now, pounding through the ship more violently than the howl of the wind and the piercing of the rain. A bucket's worth of my tub water splashes out as the boat tosses to one side.

Dejean staggers to his feet, wobbling before steadying himself. "I need to see it." He bobs his head, glazed eyes drifting through the window. "I have to be there."

"If you get eaten, I'll laugh." I watch him closely, though. In this state, I could rip him to bloody shreds and he would barely whimper. But he might just as easily hurt himself without my help.

Dejean leaves the little room, and the cabin door rattles as he tries to open it. "Locked," he mumbles. Clanks follow, and then a curse. "A combination. I need a combination."

He moves into my view once more, stumbling backward as the ship careens over a wave. His eyes don't quite focus on Kian's desk, but he makes for it anyway. "Simone. Simone said she'd bring one by . . ."

He grabs for a drawer, but misses, pulling off a paper weight instead. The stack of books comes next, then a decorative shell Kian's first mate brought her. He doesn't find what he's looking for.

Flinging himself back at the door, he shakes the knob more vigorously. "No! Let me out. Let me out, let me out." His voice cracks. "I need . . . *need* to be there."

He's so desperate for the sea. It's not the mindless greed I once thought the humans turned to, but the same desire I share, the same love for the wild ocean, increased until all rational thought is lost. It pulls him like a riptide, ever toward destruction.

I snap my head around at a bang on my little window. A gray siren clings to the wood, peering at me through the glass. My heart billows, and I grip the sides of my tub, pulling myself as far as I can manage.

"Help me!" I shriek. *"Let me out."*

Gray flings themselves at a hand hold higher up and bangs their tail against the glass. The wood around the window creaks, but it holds. They pause from their song to call for aid. A deep teal siren with black accents appears. A blue one leaps up beside them, grasping unsuccessfully, and plummets back into the waves.

"What have they done to you?" Teal hisses into the glass. Their gaze flashes from me to Dejean.

He stumbles into the little room. His unsteady feet carry him a step back for every two he takes toward me. He reaches desperately for the little window, toward the raging ocean, but he slips. Arms outstretched, he falls against the tub.

I grab onto him, my teeth bared. His head lulls, the hollow of his neck vibrating as he breathes heavily. Within his chest, his heart pounds a frantic rhythm. A heart so near, so vulnerable, I could rip it free between beats.

Liquid wells in the corners of his dark eyes, and he shifts against the tub, as though fighting an invisible weight. "I need the ocean, please," he whispers. "Please, let me go to it."

I tighten my grip. Even if I had my freedom in reach, I couldn't eat him, not while he's like this, crying the same words that are on my lips, mangling them with his human tongue. In one great heave, I shove him away, my weak arms trembling from the effort.

He stumbles back to his feet. Scooting his way around the tub, he flings himself at the window. "Please, let me out!" he cries hoarsely, banging his fists against the glass.

The little lock holding it closed rattles, but he ignores it, pounding all the harder. Teal and Gray tilt their heads, pressed so close to the glass that they can stare into his eyes. They grab the edges of the window, shaking it.

Please, please.

But the window's lock holds. The ship tilts, tossing Dejean backward. He lands heavily and knocks his head against the tub. Chest heaving, he collapses into a heap on the floor.

Teal screeches at Dejean's limp form, a vicious sound born of hate and pain. Their voice turns to a mournful melody as they turn their attention toward me. *"I am sorry."*

You did all you could. I can't bring myself to utter the words, so I use my body to convey them, sloped shoulders and forehead lifted, the tiny fins along my arms quavering twice.

They nod and shove themselves off the side of the ship. Through the rain, I see others doing the same farther along, leaping from the main deck. Watching them leave rips a hole in my chest larger than any I could take from Dejean. But I expect no more from them. They can't reach me, and I can't reach them. They are not my pod. They bear me no allegiance to the death. So long as Dejean keeps me down here, I'm doomed to this life.

The song fades away, leaving the pounding of the storm and the creak of the decks as the ship tosses in the waves. Dejean lays still. As the pain of the pod's departure fades into a miserable ache, I find I can't look away from Dejean. My hands tingle and I reach for him.

He moans. Rolling over, he shoves himself onto his elbows, a small patch of his copper curls tinted red.

My arm still hangs over the side of the tub and I brush a finger against the blood, sticking it in my mouth. Its sharp, wonderful taste eases the throb in my chest.

"That's rude," he grumbles, his words ragged and sloppy, but he doesn't move from the floor.

"You weren't going to use it."

He looks up at me, expectant. I point to him and make a motion that doesn't really symbolize the word *use*, but I have nothing better.

"I . . . should work on?"

I shake my head to interrupt him, glaring with all my boundless annoyance and disappointment.

He tries again. "I didn't need it?"

I shrug. *"Close enough."*

The ship rocks violently, and Dejean braces himself as water sloshes out of the tub, dousing his flamboyant coat. "Perfect," he grumbles, peeling off the fabric.

I point toward the door.

Confusion tugs at his eyebrows, and then he scrambles to his feet, falling into the wall as the ship tips again. "Dammit." He rubs a hand across his face, glancing out the little window. "I have to be sure the siren pod's gone before I release the crew. If they come back while we're on deck . . ." It must pain him to wait, because he taps his fingers aggressively.

"If you're not leaving, you could tell me where we're bound." I make the motions I think fit best. It takes him a series of guesses to get it right, but once he does, he makes me repeat each gesture on its own until he can imitate them.

"We're headed to the island of Falaise," he replies finally. Slumping back onto the ground, he leans against the tub.

"Your names mean nothing to me."

There is no need for signing, as he picks up on my frustrated expression with ease.

"Falaise. It has high cliffs around three sides, with an extensive reef to the north, overwhelmed by stingrays. It's dense with jungle, and the only port is on the east side, though it's a good harbor in a storm," Dejean explains. "It's a wonderful place; wild and peaceful. I have a house on a north-facing cliff. It overlooks the ocean for miles."

Wonderful, yes. The lack of people and the reef,

particularly.

"That sounds like . . ." I give him my name for it, but like all my kind's tongue, it's more than a word. The term is a complete concept, expression and vocals and motions combined to create something insightful and honest, spoken with the whole being.

"Are you saying you know it?"

I nod. For a few seasons, I lived two days' swim south of there, my pod roaming between a string of three small, uninhabited islands. That feels like lifetimes ago, not mere years.

Beyond the port window, the clouds look brighter, the rain slowing to a light drizzle. The ship sways, but none of my water splashes out. Dejean accidentally knocks the back of his head on the tub, and he rubs it with his palm, scooting away to lean against the wall.

"What will you do with me?" I make gestures to the best of my ability. When he hesitates to answer, I'm not sure if it's from lack of understanding, or an unwillingness.

Finally, he sighs. "I have a mechanic who might construct something bigger for you once we're on Falaise; something you can swim in while you regain your strength."

A bigger tub. This seems to be his way. He'll offer me something far better than Kian would, though never what I truly want. But a tub at a house means he'll need to carry me out of the ship somehow, and to do that he'll have to remove the weight from my tail. He just might end up supplying my freedom by accident.

With a groan, Dejean pulls himself to his feet. He sends me a weak smile and heads for the cabin. In my doorway, he pauses, glancing over his shoulder. "Earlier you asked about the blockers Kian created . . ." His voice softens, little wrinkles appearing on his brow. "Following Kian's footsteps and capturing sirens to sell—whether alive or dead—would make me a bigger fortune than even I could imagine. That was my plan."

Part of me burns like dry sand in the summer, but the way he holds himself, his tall form so small and vulnerable, quenches my rage.

"When I took this ship," he continues, "I had never met a siren before, just seen the blood smeared across the deck and mourned the loss of good crewmates. My heart may be small, but trading in such intelligent creatures, it . . ." He flinches like he's been hit by an angry captor. "I can't do it." His gaze shifts back to Kian's cabin. "Still, those blockers would be invaluable. Even if we never sell a siren, they would save many of my crew's lives, and chests worth of gold in repairs. I'll get my hands on them if I can manage it."

If he lies, I can't tell, but I know better than to accept his words as truth. Still, my voice rises in weak crackles. *You aren't going to use them to catch more of my kind?"*

Dejean's smile returns, soft as moonlight on the waves. "I'm not sure what you said, but . . . thank you for not being upset with me."

"I am upset," I grumble, but my heart burns as I say it. I wasn't expecting this. I don't know whether to be upset or overjoyed, forgiving or furious. By logic, I should be happy. If he really does tell the truth, it means he's a far better human than I assumed. Yet my chest still aches, worry and residual pain refusing to leave its harbor.

He lingers in the door for another dip and rise of the ship, looking at me with that frustrating smile. Then he goes to the mess of supplies and decor he knocked off Kian's desk, digging until he finds the paper Simone hid there. He reads through it once and moves to Kian's door, unlocking it with whatever combination Simone left. I hear no more from him.

The familiar heavy footsteps and shouts from deck return soon after. The rain lets up, though the clouds remain for the rest of the day, fogging the setting sun. When Dejean returns with two buckets of seawater to replace the ones I lost, he tells me the ship is in less than optimal condition, and the fuel for the stacks is heavily depleted. Without favorable winds, we won't reach his home in a reasonable time.

I think he just needs someone to complain to. He moves twice as slowly the next time he appears, the circles beneath his eyes darker and the slump of his shoulders more pronounced. Stupid humans, why don't they ever rest?

I point him toward Kian's bed, wiggling my fingers, and make a motion for sleep.

"I'm getting there." With a yawn, he draws out a forearm-sized fish from the ice box beneath Kian's bed, bringing it to me. It smells as though it's been chilling there for two days. My nose wrinkles from the stench, but it seems the humans smell too little to notice.

"What is it?" He asks, glancing at my dinner. "It was from the captain's personal stock, marked as caught the day before last."

Making a face, I do my best reenactment of those silly round things the humans tell time with, along with the reverse of the gesture I used to represent things done in the future. *"It's old."*

Dejean sighs. "I guess I'll see if I can catch something fresh." He moves to put them back in his fish bag.

Stretching with all my might, I snatch it out of his hand. I've eaten plenty of worse meals under Kian's care, and I don't trust him to fish in this state. He might get snagged by something big and stumble overboard, leaving me with no one but Simone. Who knows if she'll try to move me off the ship at all.

"Are you sure?"

I make the *future* motion, and then rise the sun with my hands, before scowling and pointing at him.

"Tomorrow morning then. Your breakfast will be better, I promise. Fresh out of the sea." He steps out of my little room, but pauses. "Goodnight, Perle." He makes up a motion to go with the words.

On some crazy instinct, I repeat it back to him. *"Goodnight."* It feels weird saying such a friendly thing to a human. I shudder. Maybe being out of the ocean for so long has begun to addle my brain.

Dejean puts the leftover fish back and drops onto Kian's bed. I lean as far as I'm able, but I can see only his feet, boots still on, none of those strange cloth squares the humans call blankets. Closing my eyes, I settle back. The gentle rock of the ocean relaxes me, and I wish it came with the brush of the water and not the creak of the ship.

I sleep well for a captive in a tub, but I'm accustomed to it, and the care Dejean has given me makes it easier. I wake before dawn and wash myself as best I can. Regular intervals of water running over my exposed areas keeps the cracking at bay, though my arms ache by the time I finish.

Dejean fulfills his promise and brings me fresh fish as soon as the sun rises. As the days go by, a routine sets in. I douse myself with clean water, my scales happy, though my gills refuse to open. Dejean fishes for me. He rambles while I eat, accompanying his words with hand motions he calls *signs*.

I'm hesitant to accept this. It's too ordinary, too affectionate. I won't be here long enough to need a language to communicate with him. But there's something in the way he talks that makes me think he has no one else he feels comfortable around, except maybe Simone. I give into this new language, adding my own signs to it. Like the human speech, it does not hold the depth and beauty of my own, but it comes much closer. Dejean seems to love it.

Convincing him I want to be friends works in my favor. This way, he'll be caught off guard when I made my break for freedom. Besides, this is nothing like the begging and flinching that molded my life with Kian. I would flee from Kian with everything in me, but the escape I plan now is a desire for the ocean, not a need to be rid of Dejean. Existing without the sea remains nearly impossible, but at least talking with him is becoming easy.

". . . And then," he says, "there was this time, years ago,

when Simone and I fished with a little dinghy out off the south tip of Seival. We had a nice catch at the end of the day, so I thought it would be great to throw one back out on the line." He chuckles, closing his eyes as though picturing it. Never having seen a fishing pole from that side of the lure, I can only imagine. "Whatever caught hold of that fish dragged us for ages before we managed to cut the rope. I swear, it had to be a siren."

"Sirens aren't that dumb."

"Siren's heads aren't . . . No, not heads." He stares at me for a moment. His eyes light up. "Stupid. Sirens aren't that stupid." He nods. "Simone always thought it was a shark. A siren would've sang. Or tipped us."

"Tipped you and eaten you. Humans should know better than to fish in a siren's territory." I don't sign the last part. I do tell him my frustration with his love for anchovies, because it's ridiculous to hunt something so small, and I motion him through a list of the best places to find nurse sharks when he gripes over never spotting them during the day.

After resting soundly the first night, he tosses and turns during every sleep that follows, waking with shouts and pacing the cabin beyond my vision for long portions of time before finally returning to bed. We drift by islands on both sides; small rocky ones out my port window and a long, blue haze on our starboard horizon. Two days later we pass so near an archipelago that I can see the break of the water over the reef.

Dejean tells me each of the island's names, and I offer my own versions, more beautiful than his human voice could ever pronounce. His expression softens when he hears them. We each have memories to go with the names, and I wonder if I ever saw him walking along the shore, or watched him skirt the edges of my pod's territory as his ship pulled away from the isle.

When Dejean comes in for dinner, five nights later, he's

grinning like he's just caught himself a great white.

"We're home, Perle," he says.

"Home," I repeat, in my own language. With my hands, I add, *"Why are you taking me home with you?"*

He startles, his brow shooting up. "Why wouldn't I?" The glare I send him makes his gaze drop to the floor. "I suppose I've felt different since I found you—better. I enjoy your presence. But I can't give you the space you deserve on this ship, so my house is the better option right now." He shrugs and turns back to Kian's cabin without another word.

I lean back in the tub, watching the ocean roll outside my window, waiting for the first signs of the harbor to appear. I must be ready. Whatever kindness he's shown me in the last week doesn't mean nearly enough. I'm going to escape these bonds—whatever it takes.

Sirens belong in the sea.

[3]

THE UNDERTOW

Which is worse:

> *Pain, the epitome of feeling;*
> *Or the complete lack thereof?*

"HOME." I SIGN the shape of the standard human houses I've seen peeking over beaches, their high, scaly tops colored like coral, shadowing long, crystalline windows.

Dejean repeats the sign, his grin sparkling in his eyes. "Home. But you'll need to stay on the ship a few more days while I have something built for you. In the meantime, I'll be here as often as I can." He hands me a pair of small croakers, which smell as though he caught them just minutes before. "There'll be fresh catches at the morning market; Simone or I will buy you whatever you'd like." His grin never once fades as he walks through Kian's cabin. He pauses to wave at me before disappearing from view.

Sinking back against the tub, I bite into the first fish. The island takes up most of my window, brown cliffs and sandy, golden beaches, with leafy, green trees and thick brush covering most of the soil. In the distance, the port town sits beside the harbor. Small boats float on the water, and a single three-deck ship is docked at a long wharf. Steam rises from the houses, vanishing into the clear sky. We seem to be heading away from the port, toward solitude.

Hiding.

I shudder. I have little faith in Dejean's ability to conceal a massive vessel of wood and metal. Every hour I remain on the *Oyster* is another hour in which Kian might return, might cut off my escape for good. I yearn for the sea—the light rippling against the sand, the rush of the currents—but I yearn also for the wide, free waters where I might flee until my gills grow weary. Until I am far enough from Kian that she will never find me.

Over the next few days, I do little but stare at the waves and check the horizon. Dejean talks to me less, constantly busy with one thing or another. He sleeps off-ship. I don't miss his presence, or his nightmares, and I certainly don't miss his stupid grin. But I feel a loss of something.

Sirens are not the cluttered creatures of Dejean's kind, but we still desire the protection of a close-knit group. But even if my old pod escaped Kian, there may not be a place for me with them after so long away. I am utterly alone.

By the time Dejean returns for a proper conversation three nights later, I've gnawed my smallest fingernail to a bunt in anticipation and worry. A scattering of lights poke through the darkness to reveal the harbor town asleep, the rhythmic swaying of the boat absent for once. Dejean smiles, broad and eager. He carries a huge piece of fabric, which he lays down outside my tub.

"Are you ready?"

I huff, motioning to the weight still holding down my tail.

His face darkens. "I know. Simone's coming to help."

The moment the words are out of his mouth, in she walks. "I still think this is a bad idea," she says. "That weight might have—"

"We don't know that for sure," Dejean cuts her off.

"What?" I wave my arms at them, but Dejean only pats one of my hands with his rough fingers.

"Let's get this weight off you," he says, moving around the tub.

Squatting, he and Simone apply some odd arrangement of straps across the block of metal and around their shoulders and backs. My heart beats frantically as they stand up. They pull the weight along with them, shifting until it's out of the tub.

I wait.

I wait for it to feel different. For the life to return to my tail. For some hint of my old strength to come back. If I wait long enough, feeling will arise, from the water or the tub or the twitch of flexing muscle.

But nothing comes.

I try to lift it, but it remains limp and inert, a gaping hole in my senses. The same deadness swirls in my chest, crushing my lungs. I choke. Struggling backward, I grab the sides of the tub and throw myself out, away from this impostor attached to my hips. The scales along my hips and upper tail rub painfully against the copper rim. Then, nothing; nothing but a dead weight, a block of limp flesh as useless as a heap of metal.

The floor rises up to meet me. I dig my nails into it, screeching.

"Perle!"

Dejean's voice sounds odd, distant. The ground swirls, boots and walls and my own shriek twisting into one. Dejean's soft words come again.

"Perle, look at me."

I force my eyes to his, though everything inside me yearns to bury my head and hide from the world. Air burns in my lungs, and my vision steadies.

"Just like that, Perle." He speaks with a strange calmness, the metal block discarded off to the side. With one arm, he holds Simone back as she clutches a knife. They both watch as though waiting for me to lash out, posture stiff, eyes narrowed. But I don't have the strength.

Trembling, I sink like a rock onto the floor.

Dejean lets Simone go, coming to my side. "What do you need?" he asks.

I motion to my tail, but I don't have the signs to tell him. *"It's wrong. It's all wrong,"* I cry, shoving my nails into a crack between the wood.

Wood. Wood is easier to think about. Wood is odd. I've stared at it for months, but I've touched little besides metal. Free of that copper cage, I run my hand against the deck. *I'm out of the tub.*

Only a small movement, but one I thought I'd never experience.

This isn't the end, but the beginning. My tail is just taking its time. My arms needed to recover, and their lock was hardly as confining as the weight Kian placed on my body. Once I'm in the ocean, I'll keep to the shallows and hunt in the reefs along the coast. The feeling and mobility in my tail will return, if I give it time.

"Are you sure you're all right, Perle?"

"I'm fine."

"Your tail—"

"I'm. Fine." I make the signs large and firm, my fingers copying the fierce look I give him. *"I just need water."*

He changes the subject. "Exactly how long can you stay out of it—the water, I mean?"

I make a rough guess, based on what I've been told by other sirens and the pain I experienced the first day Kian caught me, before she moved me to the tub. *"One of your human hours."*

"We'll have to hurry," he mumbles. "Can you roll onto the blanket?"

I rock my hips, swinging my shoulders around. It feels like I'm leaving my tail behind, as though it's nothing but a heap of someone else's flesh bound to my torso. My fins droop oddly, the once rigid silver rays now limp and transparent.

Dejean picks up my tail and places it inside the line of the fabric. Emptiness replaces the rough callouses of his hands. I doubt I would've known he even moved it had I not been watching. The thought sends another rush of panic through me, and I force my attention away, watching Simone instead.

She scoops a bucket of water from the tub and pours it over me. It rolls soothingly across my scales and drenches the blanket, but I don't need it. I won't be with them long.

"Don't go making any noise now, you hear?" Simone says. It takes me a moment to realize she's talking directly to me, perhaps for the first time since Dejean took the ship. I refuse to care. After the next few minutes, I'll never see her again.

"The more humans who know you're here, the more trouble it'll cause us all," Dejean adds, holding the fabric up around my head. He waits for me to nod before wrapping it over my face and torso. The world goes dark and muffled.

"If Kian finds out . . ." Simone says.

"She won't. We'll be careful." Dejean counts to three and the blanket rises, a little unevenly. It rocks as they move, like the gentle sway of the ocean.

"I hope you're not planning to tell my fiancée."

"Our dear Murielle? Not on my life." Dejean snorts. "I love her to pieces, but she can't keep a secret for all the treasure in the sea. Or all the pipes in a junkyard, for that matter. I can't imagine what she must think the massive saltwater tub is for."

"She knows you're equal parts eccentric and insane. Eccentric, insane, and not flying with all stacks."

"Be careful who you call an idiot," Dejean says. "I am giving you the *Oyster*, after all."

"You're giving me *command* of this stolen ship so I can race away from my fiancée and hopefully beat Kian to your malfunctioning vessel still floating in siren-infested waters, while you play with your new pet. I'll call you what I wish. Though that doesn't override the fact you *are* an idiot."

"I'm only trying to help Perle recover—" His words turn into a grunt as I jab him in the stomach with my finger joint. "Poke her, not me! I was defending you!"

"Quiet," Simone hisses.

The world tips as they ascend the stairs to the top deck. I hold back a squeak, gripping the fabric to keep from sliding.

After two flights of steps, we reach open air. The smell of the ocean fills me up, sharp and salty and wonderful. It calls to me, begging me to throw off the fabric and breathe it in. But I can't, not until I'm ready to flee.

This might be the last chance I ever have to escape; I'll have to make it count. I press my fingers against the sides of my neck. Had I not panicked, I would have submerged my head properly beneath the water to force it into my mouth and through my gills, but now I'll have to hope they unseal in the harbor.

My position shifts again as Dejean and Simone carry me down a long plank that must connect the ship to the dock. As they reach the bottom, the sound of their boots on the wood turns deeper and fuller, mixing with the soft patter of tiny waves. *It's now or never.*

My heart throws itself into my throat as I launch out of the blanket. My elbows knock against the dock. I dig my nails into the gaps between the hard planks and pull myself forward, but the fabric tangles around my tail, yanking me back.

"Perle!" Dejean drops the blanket, reaching for me. I snap my teeth at him and he recoils.

"I told you—" Simone whispers, but her words turn to a hiss as I swing my hips with all my might, dragging the fabric out of her hands.

The rough wood scrapes me as I roll toward the side of the dock, toward the dark water that ripples just below. My tail slams into a post. I flip over the edge, twisting as my face hits the water.

The fabric catches again, leaving me hanging with only my shoulders in the sea. Sitting up, I yank desperately at anything I can reach—the blanket, the wood, my own fins. My arms shake and my muscles protest. The dock creaks and the fabric slips before tightening further, lower this time. Dejean appears over the edge of the dock. He grabs me by my hips, catching hold of the blanket.

I shriek as he pulls me upward. With all my strength, I toss my body toward him, biting his shoulder. He grunts and jerks away. My tail slips out of the fabric. He snatches my wrist as I fall into the water, his nails digging into my scales.

"If you truly want to go, I'll let you." He breathes heavily, a small bloom of scarlet appearing where I broke his skin. "But I don't think this is best. You belong in the sea, but you're still recovering. If you rush this, you'll hurt yourself."

My entire body resists his words. He's known me for a week, and I've known myself my whole life. I need the sea.

"Is this really what you want?"

A pathetic noise rises through me, and I nod, struggling. The night shadows dim his sorrow, but I can still see it, pinching in his brows and tucking down his lips. He releases my wrist.

The water accepts me. It cradles me like a long-lost child, caressing my scales and seeping into my soul. It feels blissful, perfect.

Then it begins to strangle.

I draw in the sea, pressing it against my gills. A tiny slit opens on the right side of my neck, but the rest remain sealed, forcing the water into my lungs. I choke. More water follows, gripping me from the inside. I fight to stay afloat, but the weight of my tail drags me down.

Air! I need air. Tossing my hips, I push toward the surface with my arms. But I continue to sink. The water rushes in, constricting, terrifying, consuming. I thrash.

My wrist smacks into the post supporting the dock. Frantically, I grab it with both arms. I close my mouth, refusing to choke myself further, and pull upward. The wood tears at my softer spots, but I make progress. My arms tremble from exertion, already pushed far past their limit. Each movement is a battle all its own. My vision wavers, my chest burning.

The tips of my fingers break through the surface, the air greeting them, sharp and pure. But my other arm slips along the post, pulling me back under. No. *No, no, no.* I struggle upward again, darkness closing in. One more touch of air graces my hand. My muscles seize. The post falls away, an inky, suffocating world surrounding me.

Then nothing.

Through the haze, a pair of calloused hands breaks the water, grasping my wrist. Another, smoother set follows, and I'm dragged upward. I breach the surface with a gasp. As they pull me in rough, frantic bursts onto the dock, I choke. Water comes out, more water than seems possible, but my chest still feels raw and chafed, like the sun burning me from the inside.

I collapse against the dock and my head lands on Dejean's leg. He doesn't move, but I hear Simone stand, and a moment later the blanket settles over me, part of it still dripping. After the senseless panicked minutes trapped in the water, I can finally string together proper thoughts.

The sea betrayed me. My sea, the one place I knew I would be home. *I've been rejected.*

I wail, the sound almost an elegy of its own, dark and hoarse and fearful in all the places a proper song is beautiful and passionate.

"Perle," Dejean says, the smell of his blood almost overpowering. "I know you're hurt, but we need to move you." He reaches for me, then hesitates.

The rushing of the waves jeers. *What can you do,* they chide. *Why would we keep you if you cannot even sing?* They continue to laugh, until sounds from the *Oyster* mask their taunting.

"Perle?" Worry creeps into his voice. "My house is still open, if you'd like to come—as a guest, not a pet. It's a decent tub, I promise." He falters, but his next words are strong and sure. "Or somewhere else. A proper beach, maybe? Somewhere with shallows? Anywhere you'll feel safe."

I see it in his gaze: the same flash of pain that ran

through him the moment he let me drop into the water. Something new appears there too, a strange mix of determination and vulnerability. *He'll let me go.* He's giving me the option to choose the sea, and what's more, he'll help me get there.

And I want the sea, not a tub, not him. Brine runs in my veins and my heart echoes the pounding of the waves. The mocking voice of the water beneath the dock rises again, pressing a smothering hand to my chest. I draw a ragged breath, releasing it in a sharp, grieved sound.

I want the sea, but the sea doesn't want me.

I make the sign for his home. It has no word in my tongue, and even its motion in this halfway language we've created seems too beautiful to be connected to any human house. It's not what I want, not what any siren would ever want. But if I can't return to the sea, then can I even call myself a siren? As I sit near the taunting of the waves, the privacy of Dejean's home holds an appeal no other place currently offers.

"You aren't giving up." Simone shakes her head at Dejean. "You really are a stubborn idiot."

"Perle needs—"

"It's cute." She sounds amused for once. "Shut up and help me carry your *guest* to the wagon before your entire ship comes out to watch."

Propping myself into a sitting position, I stare at him.

"May I?" He asks.

I shrug, impassive, but an instinctive squeak leaves me as he wraps me in his arms, lifting me up. His warmth hits me first, then the buttons on his coat as they press annoyingly against my side. His hold is comfortable, secure in a way that provides support without feeling restrictive. His torso is much larger than mine, in both size and bulk, but my tail reaches twice the length of his legs. Simone comes to lift it, keeping it from scraping against the ground.

She stares at me with her usual annoyed expression, but

her lips do the little quirk she gives Dejean after he says something ridiculous. "I expect him back in one piece."

"I can't promise anything," I grumble, tucking my face into his shoulder to hide my embarrassment. I shouldn't care what a human thinks of me. But if the sea won't accept me, then I have to rely on these land-stunted creatures for a little longer. That's all this is. Self-preservation.

With my nose pressed against Dejean's coat, I can smell the blood from the bite I gave him. My stomach rumbles, though it shouldn't be time to eat yet. Dejean laughs, very quietly, his chest bouncing. He lowers me into the back part of some metal machine, with small walls around me and the open sky above. I wiggle to one side so Simone can fit my tail in. I try to ignore the frightening way it bends, the emptiness stretching out beyond my hips.

Simone lays the blanket over me, covering all but my face.

From the direction of the ship, Chauncey shouts, "Why're you catching reef sharks at this time a night?" He sounds like he's trying to yell without waking anyone. "Need any help?"

I had forgotten how terrible human vision is in the dark. It's amazing they've survived this long.

"We're done now, thanks!" Simone calls. She lowers her voice. "I'll try to bring the ships back here, but only if I'm far enough ahead of any trouble Kian stirs up."

"I don't plan to leave the house, so things should be quiet here," Dejean replied. "You do whatever is safest. I'll live even if I don't get my ship back for a season, so long as you feed my crew and don't let Kian blow you all up."

Kian. If Simone takes the *Oyster* away, then I might be safe here long enough for my tail to heal. But the sooner I leave, the less anxious I will feel.

My worry turns to anticipation as Dejean's machine roars to life, puffing billows of steam out its sides. The vapor rises to cover the sky while we idle, clearing in an instant as the machine bursts forward. The hunk of rumbling metal doesn't go nearly as fast as a ship flies or a siren swims, but the smallness of the craft and my inability to control it makes me anxious.

Dark buildings rise on one side, waves jeering on the other. After some time, Dejean turns the machine inland and uphill. Each bump of the uneven road jars my shoulders, my back, and my hips, the pain reminding me I can feel nothing lower. My head grows lighter with each jolt, my heart trembling. I concentrate on my arms, tightening and loosening their muscles. My tail just needs time. It'll heal. *It will.*

Above me, large leafy trees block out most of the stars, the occasional vine hanging so close that I could grab it if I reached far enough. A steady ocean breeze rises the moment the trees vanish, pricking along my drying skin. The blanket holds some moisture still, but it makes my scales itch, and the places it doesn't cover sting.

The machine slows and stops. It rattles as Dejean gets out, the gears grinding to a halt and the stacks making a soft tinging noise.

Dejean leans over the little walls that hold me in the machine. "How are you doing?"

"I feel like I'm dying, but at least the stars are pretty." I have to make up a couple of the signs on the spot, so I don't think he quite understands.

His brow pinches, and he quickly wraps up my tail in the blanket, handing me the end. He lifts me in his arms. My tail knocks into the little wall around the back of the machine, but my grip on the blanket keeps it from dragging along the ground once it's over the side.

Dejean's warmth bites against my dry flesh. He carries me along a stone path with a small grassy area to the right that fades into thick trees. The land to my left gives away, dropping into the ocean far below. I can hear the waves cracking against the cliffs, but the noise is subtle, muted by distance and a light breeze. The water stretches out along the horizon, each beautiful crest dipped in starlight.

I turn my face away, focusing on Dejean's house instead. Every part of it seems to point upward, as though it reaches for the sky. The wooden panels along the walls are the color of sea-foam, the pointy top boasting dark red-brown accents. The windows are all masked by hanging white blankets, the glass shut tight.

Dejean ascends the steps in front of the door. He props me against his hip, leaning awkwardly as he unlocks it. He closes it behind him, bolting it again.

"Welcome to my humble home. Your home too, as long as you need it."

"Is this what humans call humble?" I mumble in soft clicks, unable to sign with both my hands still holding up the fabric that supports my tail.

The entry room is even fancier than Kian's ship, filled by couches and little tables. It overflows with large shells and spyglasses, maps and globes, human figurines and model ships. Books are piled on shelves and a paper animal with wings hangs from the ceiling beside a metal contraption with churning cogs.

I don't get a good glimpse of them before Dejean carries me through an archway into the next room. This one is larger than the first, but equally cluttered by strange, colorful items, though they've been cleared away from a structure that takes up the entire far end. It must be the tub he's spoken of, though only the shiny metal plating reminds me of my spot back on Kian's ship. This square tub is at least twice as long as I am, and embedded into the ground. On the far side, it appears deep enough for me to sit up and still hold my head under the water. It butts up against a pair of long windows and a back door, thin fabrics drawn to reveal a view of the sea below. A machine chugs away beside it, pipes pushing water back and forth. The salty liquid smells as though Dejean's brought it from the ocean just hours before.

In its own way, it's almost beautiful, like a tiny reef cove made of metal instead of rock.

Dejean lowers me down, slipping me into the water. I unwrap my tail and together we wring the blanket out. He hangs it on a hook on the wall.

"What do you think?" he asks, signing his words instead of speaking.

"I have to test it first." I scowl, because if I smile he might realize how much relief the tub brings me, the little crevice of water comfortable and natural without reminding me too much of the ocean. Taking a deep breath, I close my mouth and push myself off the little ledge he's set me on, submerging fully into the water. It soaks into me, relieving the pain in an instant. The short, stringy fins on my head float, and the tips of them glide in my peripheral, translucent and shimmering in the artificial light.

I explore the tub. The metal is fused together, the seams barely visible. Little handholds stick out of the floor in the deeper parts, and I use them to help me move, my tail floating stiffly behind me. The lack of feeling and the sight of it dragging makes me grimace. I must ignore it for now. I must ignore it and believe it'll get better.

Strapped down in the shallow edge of the tub is a soft sponge pad the length of my full body. I can't figure what Dejean's aversion to sand might be; I'll have to get it out of him later. I slide onto the sponge, leaning my chest against another pad placed along the tub's rim.

"It's not terrible, I guess." It's no ocean, but it lets me swim without drowning, and I'm thankful for that. *"Better than Kian's."* I try not to act too enthusiastic, but the smile that lights up his face makes me want to duck my head under the water to hide the rush of heat through my cheeks.

He tried hard. I don't know why. Maybe he really is just an eccentric idiot, like Simone claims. But he tried to give me something that I'd be happy with, and I don't know how to fault him for that.

"Good." He sits at the edge of the tub, still grinning. "I

would've had to pay a heaping chest's worth of something shiny if Murielle hadn't agreed to do it for me."

Murielle? I have no way to mimic her name, but I whistle the same fluctuation he uses when he says it. *"She is Simone's . . ."* I can't remember the word he used, any more than I know what it means.

"Fiancée."

"What is that?"

"It's someone you love. Someone you're dedicated to being with, usually romantically and sexually, but not always." He looks at me expectantly. "Do sirens do that?"

"Sometimes." I shrug. *"Usually there's a handful of us to a territory, and we move between pods many times in our lives. But if two or three sirens work well together, we might create a new, smaller territory."* I don't sign all those exact words, my motions dictating something that in his tongue would translate to, *normal ten, fifteen, big area swim. Switch many happening. But small area swim create if two, three sirens . . .* I fumble then, not certain how to convey the next word.

"Love?" Dejean asks. He holds up his fingers to his mouth and then lowers it to his chest, pumping them in and out like a heartbeat.

". . . Love." Maybe that's what it is. I wouldn't know; I've never felt it for other sirens. I sign what I do know: *desire them not hurt, want them near;* and *future* with a much longer, greater motion than Dejean and I normally use. *"For a long time. Maybe forever."*

"Did you have one of these smaller groups?"

"No." I ignore him in favor of the windows, trying not to care what he thinks of this.

He says nothing for a moment. Then he asks, "What is it like, living in a pod?"

"Good. Safe," I answer. *"We work together, hunting as a group through a territory we set. Sometimes there are fights with other pods, if the water is very good, or the prey very scarce. But never death. We don't kill other sirens."*

Dejean lifts a brow, his jaw tightening. "You only kill humans, then?"

"*Of course not.*" I huff. "*All intelligent creatures are bound by honor to stay out of our territories, unless given permission. We kill those who refuse, and what we kill, we eat. Whales and octopuses respect this. Dolphins too, often.*" I drop my speech to a hiss, separating my motions so each is blunt. "*But never humans.*"

"Of course we don't!" His voice rises and he blurs his signs. "We have no idea where your territories are!"

"*They're very clearly marked!*" I growl, my hands fast and abrupt.

"To a siren, maybe!" He throws his arms out to the side, speaking with only his voice now. "My people—pirates, yes, but also innocent merchants and passenger ships—we take wild guesses based on spotty predictions, and half the time we're wrong. You sirens pick us apart for it!"

"*What?*" I don't sign either, my head spinning. All creatures smart enough to create a language of their own understand our borders. The smell and sound of a full pod is obvious to anyone looking for the signs. A few individuals pass on the exact placement of the border to the rest of their kind.

My stomach turns. Perhaps in some ways it makes sense. Humans are not of the sea. But they also would have little reason to share information with each other, not the way we do. They wound and kill their own kind more often than dolphins, and with just as much vengeance. Even Dejean.

"*Why do you defend them? You kill humans too. You all kill each other!*"

"We aren't perfect." The words fly from his lips, his face pinched. "But some of us try. They don't deserve to be eaten because of an honor code they don't know exists and territories they can't find the borders to!" He swings his arms once more, leaning forward this time.

I recoil off the edge of the sponge, the memory of a fist in my face bringing a hazy sort of pain with it; not quite real, but still terrible and harrowing. Whimpering, I struggle to pull my tail back up.

"I'm sorry." Dejean draws back, tucking his elbows close to his body. His gaze drops to his lap and a heavy breath leaves him. "It's not your fault you attacked us. You didn't know . . ."

I didn't. None of my kind did. I want to snap at him, to bare my teeth and fight him through it, to prove that his stupid humans caused all this. Last week I would have. Now I know it would be a lie. My kind are smarter and less murderous than the humans, but we made a mistake. We hold some of the blame for this.

And the way Dejean brushes a hand under his eye makes me think his own pain lurks deeper than mine, closer to his heart. Slowly, I brush my fingers against his leg, asking for his attention. When he looks up, I make the sign for *understand.*

"Thank you." A weak smile stretches his lips, but his eyes remain clouded, sad. He resumes his hand motions. "Pods sound nice." It's an odd regression in topic, like he's trying to distance himself from the talk of territories and death.

"They are. They're a family." I don't sign the last part, not sure what to use for *family.* Fondness? Safety? Home? Even creating a new hand motion feels wrong. Nothing can portray the ache in my chest when I think of the sirens I knew in the past, any of whom might die by a human trap or Kian's song blockers.

"Do you miss it?"

"Constantly."

Now it's his turn to look away. With a sigh, he stands and removes his coat, draping it over one of three chairs rimming a cluttered table. "I'll catch you something in the morning. There's a little tank around here somewhere I could stock . . ."

He moves into a hallway leading to the back of the house,

but I stop him with a whistle before he can ascend a flight of steps there.

"Yes?" His brows lift, his expression hopeful.

"Goodnight, idiot." The last sign is a tap to the head, wiggling fingers, and then a throwing away motion. I like to think it's a symbol of Dejean's hair.

He chuckles. "I'll be back down," he pauses, then adds, "If you don't mind. I sleep best in sight of the ocean. And—" With a shake of his head, he moves up the stairs. "I'll be back down."

As soon as the creaking of the wood fades, I settle down to stare out the window, waiting for him. Or perhaps I'm waiting for myself. Waiting for my mind to return so I can go back to loathing Dejean for the human he is, waiting for my tail to move and react as it should, waiting for the ocean to accept me as its own once more.

Waiting, and worrying that none of these things will ever happen.

I can live like this for the moment, but what will happen to me if I let it become the rest of my life? Maybe pain is better than emptiness. If my choices are to die in the ocean or waste away here, which option will I pick?

[4]

RIPPLES

If many soft waves tear through big rocks,
then many weak fists break strong hearts.
But many small smiles piece them back together again.

IN THE EARLY ocean mornings, light would dance through
the waves, soft and tender, coaxing the world to life. I lie at
the bottom of the tub, breath held, wishing Dejean's house
could replicate the effect. What it does give me isn't terrible—
golden light ripples across the copper metal and shimmers
my body into a multitude of hues—but it's not home.

I pretend that it could be. Closing my eyes, I try to forget
the human dwelling enclosing my tube, my space so pitifully
cramped compared to what I once had. I ignore the metal
brushing against my back where sand should be and turn
the humming of the water pump into the rush of distant
waves.

It still feels wrong.

I sit up, drawing in air. It's such a normal action that it
takes the subtle sting in my chest to remind me that it's not
my natural way of breathing. I almost drop back into the
water, but Dejean shifts in his sleep, and I turn my attention
to him.

He lays beside the tub on the largest sponge rectangle I've
ever seen, blankets and pillows covering it. Unlike his
sporadic naps on the ship, he's taken off his boots and belt.
A single slip of flowing cloth takes the place of his usual
billowing shirt and tight pants. It's still far more fabric than I

would ever want to wear, but at least it looks comfortable compared to the clothing humans normally don.

After tossing throughout the night, whimpering and crying out, he finally looks restful. His curls lay flatter on one side, frizzing up on the other, and a lock of them twists into his mouth, trembling as he breathes. In the light that pours crookedly through the front windows, his brown skin seems to glow, making the million little darker spots spread across his cheeks look all the more prominent.

He stirs in his sleep. His shifting holds none of the sudden jerks into wakefulness I've seen from him during the night. Instead, they're little, graceful movements: the fluttering of lashes, the curling of fingers, the rise and fall of shoulders. Slowly the heavy movements of someone in a dream drift into the lazy stretching of a waking person.

Snapping my eyes closed, I float on the water, pretending to nap. He pauses for a moment, as though waiting for me to breath. Once I do, he moves toward the other side of the room.

I peek at him, the world blurred and twisted into a tiny sliver. He rummages through a pile of clothing. His slip of night-clothing hangs off one of the chairs to his right. Little black sun-speckles cover so much of his dark skin that the unmarked regions look almost strange in comparison. I have just enough time to wonder why humans grow so much hair between their legs if they have plenty of it on their heads already when he shoves on a pair of baggy brown pants and turns toward the door.

I feign sleep once more. A series of shuffles follow, and he leaves wearing his heavy, chunking boots. The back door clanks behind him. I sit up to watch him walk toward the cliff, one of the human's thin, rod-like fishing contraptions swinging over his shoulder.

He whistles. It contains none of the beauty and soul of the ocean, but it's not an unpleasant sound either. He reaches the edge of the cliff, and the whistling dies as he jumps off it.

On instinct, I burst forward, coming as close to the window as I can. A little boxy machine of wheels and belts pokes out over the cliff. From the edge of it, a long metal beam extends, like those the humans use to lift cargo off their ships. A rope runs through the center of it, its length releasing over the side of the cliff. Dejean must be holding to it while he descends. The water may be a liquid, but I have seen sailors leap from flying ships for my song, and they are always dead before I reach them. Dejean is too smart to attempt that.

Probably.

As I sink into the water up to my chin, my little flap of unsealed gill opens for a moment. I draw in a deep breath of stinging air, clinging to a bit of the sky when I should be embraced by the water. I let the air out and dip my head just beneath the surface.

Fear holds me there for a moment, but I force my mouth open, taking in the water. It pushes against my gills. When it seems as though it might press through, the feeling of the harbor dragging me down wraps its terrible fingers around my neck. The water rushes the wrong direction. I burst over the side of the tub, clinging to the edge as I cough out searing liquid. Trembling, I lower myself back down.

Something feels different; the temperature around my gills is a bit colder, my neck a bit less stiff. I submerge my head again. If I don't try now, I know I won't have the courage to try at all.

When I open my mouth, I let in as little water as I can manage. Instead of assaulting my chest, it pushes through the crack in the side of my top left gill. I repeat it, again and again, feeling the gap widen. My head feels light by the time another crack forms, but I keep going, giddy at the progress.

My gills all come loose at once, clarity returning to my vision in an instant. Laughter bubbles out of me, ringing off the sides of the tub. I tear through the water, using the handholds built into the floor to aid my still immobile tail. My arms quickly start to ache, but it's the good sort of ache that tells me they're regaining muscle.

I can't wait to show Dejean.

The instant the thought pops into my mind, I wish I could take it back, but the excited smile that will consume his dorky, speckled face makes me cling to the desire all the same. Slowing, I break the surface.

The back door rattles. I prepare to whistle the tune of Dejean's name, but the sound dies in my throat as the door swings open. A human far shorter and rounder than Dejean appears.

Their coiled red hair is piled on top of their head, held up by two pens and some sort of tool humans use on machines, with curls springing out at erratic angles. The human wear a piece of clothing that looks like pants, but it comes all the way up their chest and buttons at their shoulders. Something tight around their waist holds it in place. Swirls cover one of their arms, like the chaotic but beautiful lines of a reef, drawn in brilliant colors against their near-black skin.

I slink beneath the water, pressing myself against the side of the tub. No one can know I'm here. Dejean I can accept, but if someone else steals me away . . .

Footsteps echo ominously through the metal of the tub. I don't move a muscle. The water above me stills.

Go away. Go away! I shout in my mind, as though somehow Dejean will hear my thoughts and return.

The human's face appears above me, peering into the water. Their brow shoots up, and their mouth hangs open for a moment before letting out a squeaky scream.

Now that they've seen me, I can't let them go. *"I guess I get to eat you now."* I launch out of the water, using the edge of the tub to pull myself forward. They scream again as I tackle their legs.

"There's a fish person in the tub!" they cry, waving their arms like a trapped shorebird.

I try to drag them in with me, but my tail slips, its unresponsive length refusing to brace against the tub's edge. Gripping hard to their weird pants, I yank them toward me, but they toss their hands in the air, toppling backward.

"Stop that. You're making this very difficult." I haul myself out of the water, throwing my body on top of the human. They continue to wave their arms, their legs convulsing at random. Maybe they're in some kind of shock.

"There's a fish person out of the tub!"

"I'm not a fish!" I hiss in their face, catching their hands and pinning them down. Their throat vibrates as they shriek. If I don't kill them cleanly, they'll stain the floor red before I can drag them into the tub. I don't think Dejean will appreciate that.

"Dejean. Dejean!" The human screams, struggling against my aching arms. "Captain Dejean Gayle, you ass!"

"You're a friend of his?" I probably shouldn't eat them then. *What a terrible shame.* "You get off easy this time," I grumble, snapping at their face for show. But I can't just let them leave, not before Dejean has convinced them to keep me a secret. Maybe if I can find something to bind them with?

I glance through the junk scattered around the room. My grip fails as the human jerks their hands upward, one of their thumbs shorter than the other. They pull a tool from their hair and slam it into the side of my head. Pain spreads through my skull, my vision wavering. My heart skips a beat and I flinch, shying away, Kian's gruff laugh echoing in my ears.

But Kian is gone, and whether or not I can contain this human might determine whether she finds me again.

In my moment of weakness, the human knocks me off, flinging my torso onto the floor. I crush something small and pointy, and the partially healed sores on my elbows sting as they knock into the ground. The human almost stands, but one of Dejean's blankets trips them. They tumble onto the giant sponge pad.

My gills tremble as I growl, the chamber beneath them releasing. I could sing. I could sedate the human without attacking them. Stilling the tremble in my chest, I close my eyes, looking for the song within me.

But I can't feel it.

I love the ocean as much as I ever have, my desire to protect it unwavering. Yet the rejection I faced at the harbor taints my love, that one denial piercing deep into my heart until I think I might break open from within. Even with my gills open, the song won't come. I'm not worthy of it.

A blanket flies at me as the human kicks it off. I bat it to the side. I'll have to find another way to subdue them.

My tail lays crooked and unfeeling on the wood floor, but I shove myself forward on my hips and hands, ignoring the pain in my side from whichever of Dejean's treasures I crushed. I throw myself into them just as they rise to their knees, tossing us both off the big sponge. We knock over three of Dejean's long fish catchers, and land in a pile of spare window fabric beside the table.

"Don't eat me! I taste terrible," the human blubbers. "See, see here." They hold up their hand so close to my face that I flinch before my instincts take over and I snap my teeth at their stubby fingers. "I cut off a bit of my thumb once, and it fell into my rum, and I didn't know it was in there, you see, so I—" They make a funny noise in their throat, like they're gagging. "It was nasty. Really, really nasty, dammit. I promise, you won't like me. I'm not worth it."

"Do you know when to shut up?" I hiss at them. But their rambling, the tool in their hair, and their interest in the tub, not to mention their casual entrance into Dejean's house, all fall together. They—she's—that girl, Simone's fiancée, the one who couldn't keep a secret. *"Murielle?"* I ask, though her name sounds like a funny series of notes in my tongue, far from a proper replication.

"I—I don't talk fish. I mean, half the time I don't even talk human very well. Can you really expect me to know not-human languages too?" she sputters. "Though you know, I don't think people speak fish languages at all; isn't that like—"

"I am not a fish!" Stupid humans.

"Shit, sorry. You're mad, I know." She grimaces. "But please, don't eat me."

"I wasn't planning on eating you because you mean something to Dejean, but if you keep calling me a fish, I might change my mind," I growl, baring my teeth at the end.

She squeaks. The door clangs. Dejean shouts.

"Perle!"

I slide off the possibly-Murielle human, and roll onto Dejean's sponge, glaring at him. *"I was just keeping her from leaving. I wasn't going to eat her. Probably,"* I sign at him.

"Probably?" The fish in his transparent pouch bounce as he returns my last hand motion. "You can't just attack my family, Perle!"

"How was I supposed to know who she was? I didn't want her to go telling anyone else that I'm here," I reply in frustration, slowing my motions just enough that he can understand them. *"If Kian returns, she'll take me and kill you. I don't want that! I don't want that."* I repeat the last phrase, the words heavy on my heart. I don't want to see Kian again. And, strangely enough, I don't want her to hurt Dejean.

He sighs, walking through the room. "You were doing what you thought was best." Frowning, he nudges something with his toe. "That was one of my favorite models." The bits on the floor look like pieces of a tiny ship, which probably caused the bruise on my side.

"It's not my fault you leave your favorite things laying on the floor." I make a face. *"Or your back door unlocked."*

"That's fair, I suppose." He steps over the crushed ship, and his gaze focuses on me. A soft smile stretches over his face. "You don't belong on my bed."

"It's a nice sponge." I have to make up a sign for *sponge,*

but he seems to pick it up.

"Wow," Murielle says, breathless.

I'm amazed she managed to stay silent for so long.

"Dejean! Dejean, you have a siren in your bathtub. I made you a bathtub for a siren. A siren!" She laughs. Still tangled in fabric, she waves the tool she hit me with, her hair a mess.

Dejean kneels beside the sponge, setting the fish bag to the side. "The siren's name is Perle. They're a guest here." He opens his arms to me, and I let him help me back into the tub.

Though I haven't been out enough for the air to take effect, the water still feels wonderful.

"A guest! You have a siren as a guest." Murielle sits up, doing her weird bouncing thing again. Maybe she's still in shock. "No one's ever had a siren as a guest. I mean, no one I've heard of. And you're communicating with them, like properly communicating. That's—that's crazy." She pauses to glance at me. "Can they sing? They didn't sing at me."

"They couldn't sing when I first met them. Though . . ." Dejean's gaze lingers over my gills.

I shrug and look away, changing the topic. *"She's Simone's fiancée, right? And your . . . family?"*

"Adopted, nearly disinherited on multiple occasions."

"I thought she wasn't supposed to know about me?"

Dejean's cringe is all the answer I need. Removing his boots, he sits on his sponge. He pats the space beside him, and Murielle plops down, the hair piled on her head hanging lopsided.

"Yeah?"

"Murielle, you know I . . ." But he trails off, swallowing hard.

I release a snort. *"Threaten her already. If I eat her fingers, would that help?"*

Dejean shoots me a stiff glare, but Murielle speaks before he can reply.

"What did the siren say?"

[62]

"Perle wants to be sure you won't tell anyone they're staying here."

"Oh, yeah, that'd be a real bad idea. Everyone'll want them." She nods, then her eyes widened. "Oh—me? You're worried I might say something. That's fair. But I can keep a secret, you know. I think. I mean, I could just avoid people entirely for a while. Except I already agreed to fix Perceval's truck, and I have the parts I ordered for Ivonne, and I'm halfway through constructing a sexy bed for Dareil and Elita—that—that was supposed to be a secret too. Damn. You won't tell anyone?"

"I'm doomed." I sink backward, staring at the ceiling. Will Kian's ceiling look like this, or will she shove me back onto a ship?

The sound of Dejean's voice is perky, but his expression mirrors mine. "This is more important than Dareil and Elita's eccentric habits."

"You've got a siren in a tub next to your bed. That's a pretty eccentric habit."

I might not know much about human mating customs, but I can't suppress a snort.

The color drains out of Dejean's face. "I'm going to lock you in a closet and feed your fingers to Perle if you make too much noise."

"Please, can we?" I grin.

Murielle eyes my excitement warily. "Simone won't be real happy about that."

A strangled breath comes out of Dejean, his shoulders sinking. "You'll try your best not to speak of this, won't you?"

"Yeah, of course. I won't say a word. And I'll say as few words as I can about other things, just to be sure." She gives us a smile that I assume is meant to be reassuring. "You know I don't want to get you into any trouble." Waving her tool in the air, she adds, "But in return, you're going to finally marry Simone and I, properly, with a big wedding on the beach. And you're not gonna put up a fuss when we go honeymooning."

Dejean nods. "That's fair. But only after you've successfully kept Perle a secret."

Murielle's eyes narrow. She extends her mechanical tool toward Dejean, slow and purposeful. He shakes the end of it. I can't decide if this is a strange human custom, or if Murielle and Dejean are both just really strange humans.

Murielle hops up, bouncing along the rim of the tub to the water-pumping machine. "How's it holding up? I thought maybe it could use a once over, since I shoved it together from all those spare ends." Dropping down beside the humming box, she opens a side panel to reveal a strange array of turning cogs, with some other machinery farther in, beyond my view. She hums. "Looks alright, but I still think I should replace the third spoof with a number ten."

"Whatever you think is best. I have no idea how you got that thing pumping to begin with. My opinion would be redundant."

"All of your opinions are redundant," Murielle shoots back, closing the panel.

I laugh, the sound echoing like the wind through a series of sea caverns. *"She's not wrong."*

Murielle squats at the edge of the tub, looking me over. "What's the matter with your tail?"

Grabbing it, I pull it toward me, giving her a hiss as I bare my teeth. *"Nothing. It's just healing."* Like my arms and my gills did. It'll come back to me too.

"Perle says it's nothing, that it'll mend itself." Dejean doesn't sound convinced, and after a pause, he adds, "I don't know anything about a siren's recovery rates. It just doesn't seem . . ."

I hiss at him too.

He gives me a worried frown, and his signs wobble. "Can we look at it?"

Drawing further into the tub, I try to maneuver my tail away from him.

Dejean lifts his hands, his palms up. He's performed the motion enough that I finally understand what it means. Submission. Vulnerability. "I'm sorry. I won't force you."

"We won't hurt it, you know." Murielle says, joining him near the shallow end of the tub. "And hey! I ain't much good with people, but I've seen a few nasty ouches working on the machines. Maybe I could even help a little?"

Forcing my eyes to my tail, I try to draw it in closer. It remains stiff and lifeless. With hesitant fingers, I touch the area, feeling nothing from it even as my hand clearly brushes against the smooth, soft scales. I jerk my arm back. Maybe I do need help, though I don't know what these humans can offer.

Murielle's eyes widen as she watches me, her hair lopsided, and Dejean gives me his soft, open smile. They might not know anything about siren physiology, but they want to do what they can for me. At least, Dejean does. I'm not so sure about Murielle, but I suppose she can't be awful if Dejean and Simone put up with her.

Pulling myself back into the shallows, I prop my tail on my long sponge, using my arms to lift it when my hips won't give me enough rotation. Murielle leans over. A gleeful look consumes her face, but she sobers as I glare at her.

"May I?" She asks, hovering her hand over the water.

I would rather she didn't, but she can't hurt me when I already feel nothing. *"Fine,"* I snap, my hand motions brisker than normal. Dejean translates.

Watching Murielle slide her hand along my tail sends chills up my spine, but I don't pull away. Her fingers move higher, until the sensation finally appears. She presses gently, her hands calloused like Dejean's, but in different places. As she pulls her arm out of the tub, she makes a thoughtful noise.

"What is it?" Dejean asks.

"I have absolutely no idea. But 'not good' would be my general opinion." Murielle wipes her hand on her clothing.

"We should ask a proper physician. I could stop by the doc's place when I'm in town? She'd know what's up."

"No!" I pair the word with such obstinate hand motions that no human could misunderstand me, but Dejean echoes my feelings all the same.

"You can't tell anyone about Perle, not even Doc," he reminds her. "If we speak with a physician, I'll do it, outside of town, and it'll be Perle's choice."

"Right, right." She presses her hands against her cheeks. "But we should still do something."

"We will. I'm sure there're some books that'll help?"

Her face lights up. "Oh! I could find those! I won't even have to talk to anyone but the librarian."

Dejean grimaces. "Maybe stick with just books. No intelligent life."

"No talking to the librarian either," Murielle replies, slow and firm, as though she's trying to convince herself. "Got it." Standing, she twists her tight curls into something resembling a shell and shoves her tool back into it. "If you don't have anything else I gotta fix, I should be out."

"Check in on us tomorrow, as soon as you can," Dejean says. "And if you do accidentally tell someone, come immediately. We'll have to move Perle into the cove, at least."

The thought of touching the ocean again makes me recoil, an ache forming in my chest. If Dejean notices, he says nothing of it.

"Will do, weird bro." Murielle grins. She sprints out the back door, laughing as Dejean throws a pillow in her direction.

"I'm your only brother—you could be a little nicer!" He calls, grumbling under his breath. "She's the weird one anyway." He waits until she disappears around the front of the house before handing me a fish from the bag he discarded earlier. "Breakfast, a little late."

I accept the offering. Biting into it, I let the juices drip down my chin, a happy rumble in my chest. But my mind jumps back to my tail, laying unresponsive and crooked along the sponge.

Murielle and Dejean can't be right. It'll still heal . . . won't it?

"We'll figure out what to do with your tail." Dejean says softly. His weak smile turns to a full grin, sparkling in his eyes. "You know, it's good to see your gills reopened."

Whatever the sate of my tail, that look creates a soothing warmth in my chest, as though a ripple of morning light streams through me. It feels good to know someone else is happy for me. If I can hold onto this, maybe I can push through whatever comes of Murielle's library search.

I return his smile.

[5]

REFLECTIONS

Trust is a funny thing;
> *Half logic.*
> *Half nonsense.*

DEJEAN STICKS AROUND for most of the day, chatting with me about small things. He touches on the weather, his favorite being the warm winds from the east. I relate them to the glorious currents that run along the big island, far, far to the south. He shows me the little model ships in his collection, pointing out the features he loves best, and I tell him of the vessels I attacked in the past.

He digs out a big glass box and a machine like the one attached to my tub, only much smaller. After I ask enough questions, he finally teaches me how to set it up beside my tub, water and all. When he returns with my wiggling dinner, he brings three extra fish, putting them in the box. I tell him how my pod used to keep fish in a similar manner, locked in a cage made of rock and bone and braided seaweed.

Whenever Dejean's chores and fishing preoccupy him, I wait in worry of what Murielle might accidentally say about me, but he stays nearby once the sun sets and talks with me long into the night. I fall asleep happy, listening to the distant rush of the ocean out the windows and the gentle tune of Dejean's breathing. I hadn't realized how nice it was to have someone I trust nearby while I rest. It's almost like being in a pod again.

The contented feeling leaves me during my sleep. If

Dejean turns with nightmares, I don't hear them, for I have terrors of my own. Kian haunts me at every corner, threatening to take what little I've gained.

I pull out of the turmoil slowly. The sun peeks over the edge of the land, coating my tub in reds and golds. I startle as Dejean bolts upright with a cry, his blankets scattered around him. His stiff posture relaxes after a moment and he rubs his eyes, groaning.

"Did I wake you?" he asks, his signs sloppy.

"As if you could." I flick water at him.

Chuckling, he stretches his arms over his head. The back door bangs open, and we both jolt fully awake.

Murielle bursts in. "I got some books! And I read them too." She plants a small stack on the table.

"You read all those books." Dejean runs a hand through his messy hair, making the poof lay more evenly on his head.

"Well, more like I scanned most of them, and just read the important bits." Murielle opens one and plops down beside him. "See, here."

For a moment, Dejean seems to be looking and not seeing, but then his eyes focus and flicker across the page. He nods. Turning the book around, he presents an illustration of a human skeleton to me. "This is a spinal cord, inside your vertebral column." He traces the skeleton's backbone, from its skull down. "The nerves inside it transmit all your movements and sensations. This book says that if it's crushed or broken, it can't transmit to the lower parts of the body anymore. No more feeling, no more movement."

I stare at the drawing, and my whole body seems to drift. *"But . . . it can heal?"*

Dejean shakes his head, his expression grim. "Not the spinal cord, at least not in humans."

The world grows hazy around me, my arms as numb and lifeless as my tail. *"I'm not human,"* I plead with him in blurred signs.

"But you're not a fish either," he corrects me, his voice

pained. "If there was going to be a change, it should have already happened."

"I'm real sorry, Perle." Murielle sounds genuinely apologetic, but her words are like a distant echo.

It can't be true. My chest hurts, and I fling my hips, anger burning in my muscles. My tail smacks into the side of the tub, but I feel nothing. The air in my lungs seems to vanish, my torso trembling as my chest tightens. I drop into the water, begging it to soothe me.

The rumble of the pumping machine screams in my pounding ears, my gills flaring painfully. Dejean's hand brushes mine, and I yank away, curling up around my lifeless tail. I shake; shake until the darkness rushes in.

Gasping in water, I stretch my fingers back toward Dejean. I grab his hand, clinging to it. He lets me, though my long nails dig into his skin until I can smell his blood in the water. My vision continues to spin and flicker, but I latch onto the feeling of Dejean's fingers in mine. The awful panic wanes, turning to dread. Dejean draws me up, and I lift my head just enough to see him.

"This isn't the end." Somehow hearing the words I've been repeating in my head for days makes me doubt them more instead of less.

"Isn't it?" I snap, the emptiness inside me stretching until my words echo. I knew this would come. I tried not to admit it, but I knew.

Murielle catches my gaze with a smile. "It's not all bad news, you know. We make humans prosthetics, so maybe we can make you one? You can still use your hips and your arms, so you've got some viable muscles there. Maybe we can't get back your tail's motion, but we can try to mimic it," she says. "But I've got to know if that's okay with you first."

Her words meet my ears, but my mind spins them around a few times before they settle. It's too much; too much hope and fear, loss and longing. *I might swim again.* I won't heal, but I might swim. I want to curl up in a bed of sand beneath my reef back home and not think on any of it, or perhaps think on all of it for a very long time. But a ray of light still bursts through the emptiness. *This isn't the end.*

"Yes . . ." I sign the word sluggishly, adding a nod of my head so she understands. *"Yes, I want this,"* I repeat, stronger. *"If you think you can make something, then we might as well try it."*

Dejean translates, and Mur's face lights up. She reaches for a few books in the center of the stack. The others topple to the ground, but she ignores the mess, flipping one of them open and tucking a small pile of spare paper into it. "I'll draw up some schematics!"

As she moves to the table to start on her diagrams, I sink deeper into the water.

"Hey, Perle . . ." Dejean holds a little rag to the bleeding marks I made on his hand, his expression pinched in worry. But whatever he meant to say changes as it reaches his lips. "You know, I never asked whether you have a name you'd rather be called."

I blink, startled. *"No . . . no you may call me Perle."* The relief that washes over him, softening his features, fills me with a gentle warmth. *"Nicknames are never a problem, but there's a lot of meaning in who gives it and why,"* I explain. *"Sirens don't have birth names, just those we are given by others. A few simple colors are typically used for strangers or acquaintances—you got that right by chance. Between sirens in a pod though, often nicknames will change; become more personal."*

"What are yours?"

His question gives me pause. The sort of nicknames he's asking after are intimate, so much more so than I would ever dream of sharing with a human. But Dejean is not just any human.

"They're hard to translate." Like most personal nicknames, mine include all aspects of my kind's language, creating a label more complex and meaningful than any

human phrase or sign could portray. But I try anyway. *"As I child I was 'the one who goes after fish that's long gone.' A siren two pods ago gave me the name 'stingray,' because the sand there was so soft and fine that I would burrow into it. To other pods I have been 'first to the ship,' 'excites eels,' 'best when in the sun,' and 'attacks from beneath.' The siren who birthed me called me 'the one who is never full.' "*

Dejean chuckles, shaking his head. "A few of those make a lot of sense." A thoughtful smile lingers in his eyes. "Should I give you a new nickname then?"

"Only you can answer that."

He takes a moment to reply, looking at me intently. "I will, but not yet. I want to know you better." He adds a soft, "If you're all right with that?"

I shrug, but I can't stop my face from softening. *"I think it's a good decision."*

Bobbing his head, he looks as though he might rise, but then he pulls his hands through his cloud of coppery hair instead. "Perle? Are you . . ." His words trail into a small, awkward laugh. "Damn, I should have asked this ages ago, but, you don't happen to be girl or a boy, do you? That sounds like the wrong way to say it," he grumbles. "But man and woman is too human."

"It is too human, idiot." I snort, though I'm worried he might be going a bit insane. *"I'm not a boy or a girl. I'm a siren."*

"I know, I know. But, which pronouns do you like?" He must see my confusion, because he adds, "He pronouns or she pronouns?"

"I don't understand," I sign. *"What makes someone a he or a she?"*

A bit of color rushes through his face, his dark cheeks tinting red. "Well, many women can become pregnant, but then many women can't too, like Simone—she can't carry her kids, but she's still a woman . . . maybe I should just wait and have her explain instead."

I stare at him, trying to make sense of what he just mumbled. If anything, I feel as though I know less now. *"You humans have too many funny categories. I'm not pregnant right now. What else would you need to know?"*

"I . . . well I suppose that's one way to go about it." He nods, looking just as perplexed as I feel.

From his crude explanation and what I learned in my time on Kian's ship, I realize something odd. *"Do humans not change?"*

"Change?" He repeats my sign, his brow scrunching.

"Change." I can feel my own forehead tighten as I search for a proper explanation. *"Do you not switch your . . ."* We have no sign for anything near that word. I motion to the region in question, his covered in his clothes and hair, and mine sealed away by a slit of neatly overlapping scales.

"Oh." The redness in his cheeks spreads to his ears, but he manages to speak in an even tone. "No, not many of us, not naturally at least. There are a few rare incidents, but not as a whole species. We might switch pronouns, or alter our appearance, but most of us are stuck with what we have, at least until someone can develop better technology or medicine." He puts his thumbs into the pockets of his pants and then takes them out again, shifting awkwardly. "Does that change happen often with sirens?"

I shrug. *"Whenever it's needed. I became an adult as I am now, with the organs to give birth, but I've changed many times, whenever my pod does not have enough of what I'm not,"* I explain. *"Sirens only care whether one of us is currently pregnant. Pregnant sirens need protection, food, tending. Sirens who aren't pregnant don't require those things. The change doesn't make us feel any different about who we are, and other sirens don't think differently of us, so what use would your he and she be?"* I add the sign for *understand* at the end, my cheeks pinched in a question.

"Not . . . entirely. I think only certain humans can relate to that." He gives me a smile. "But I can respect it, even if I don't understand."

"That's all I want." I grin at him in return. *"I don't understand your funny he and she either."*

"Then it's good enough." He hums. "Humans have a pronoun that's not he or she, but implies neither. Humans who feel they're neither man nor woman often go by it. Can I continue using that for you?"

At least this, I can understand. I sign a quick, *"Yes."*

As I drop my hand, Murielle springs out of her seat. She flops on Dejean's sponge, slapping down a sheet of paper covered in notes and sketches. Most are too chaotic for me to make much sense of, but they seem to be variations on mechanical siren tails.

"So I'm thinking, a light-weight exoskeleton, yeah? If I build the right mechanisms in, you can control it with your hands, pulleys and levers and shit," she explains, tapping scribbles on the paper. "First though, I'm thinking we might need a brace of sorts, like a supported tube to help you move your whole tail with just your hips." Pausing, she looks up at me. "Won't be as good as what you're used to—none of it will—but it'll help. You'll be able to swim in the ocean again."

"Swim in the ocean." I don't know what to do but repeat the words.

"But it's no good if we can't get you into a nice big space to test it."

"What about the cove?" Dejean asks. "I still have that elevator you built me."

He must mean the machine with the neck he used to lower himself off the cliff.

Murielle nods, slow but enthusiastic. "We could work with that!" She shoots to her feet. "I know just the thing. You still have those parts lying in the back, from the thing-a-ma-joo?" She snatches up a stray pipe from under the table and waves it around. "Oh, this could work! This could work real well, mhmm." She continues talking to herself, moving through the house until she's a distant clatter.

Dejean stays by my side. "I know you feel differently about the ocean now." His words are soft, and he lets go of the little rag he's been holding to the claw marks I gave him: five red cuts. "If you aren't ready to go back to it—"

"I'm sorry," I cut him off, pointing to his hand.

The edges of his eyes lift in a weak smile. "I can't begin to imagine what you're going through. If I was in your place, I might do the same, or much worse. Just don't make a habit out of it, all right? I don't want too many scars from you." There's a light tease to his voice, and it settles something inside me.

I gaze out the window, watching the sea gleam in the morning sun. *"If I go back, it will be . . ."* I trail off. We don't have a sign for this.

"You're nervous," he guesses. He moves his hands in a new way, a jittery sort of motion, painting fear in the air.

I mimic it. *"Nervous, yes. But I want to go. I want my home back."*

"I understand." Rising, he glances toward the part of the house Murielle now echoes from. "You don't have to move any faster than you wish. But I think it's good, at least, to be moving in the first place."

With a faint sound of agreement, I slip further into the water once more, laying on my sponge. *"Go help Murielle."*

"You're sure? I can stay." He looks at me with such fierce dedication that a smile tugs at my lips.

"Go!" I shoo him off with a flick of water. *"I need time to think."*

"Alright, alright." He grins. "Call for me if you need anything."

"I will."

I mean that. However odd it is to trust this human, I can't stop myself. I glance at the distant ocean horizon, imagining the currents washing over me, a human contraption keeping me steady where my tail no longer can. If only I could return to trusting the ocean the way I do Dejean.

[6]

THE CLAMSHELL

The world comes alive,
    and I hold to every heartbeat.
    I live.

I FOLD MY arms over the edge of the tub, resting my chin against my hands. The windows hang open, a salty breeze blowing in, warm from the midday sun. I exercise my hips, shifting them back and forth as I watch the waves glisten in the distance.

At the edge of the cliff, Dejean and Murielle clang away at the elevator. It has doubled in size since this morning, becoming a monster of metal, ropes, cogs, and stacks, its long neck a noticeable mar on the horizon. Murielle wears another, baggier one-piece over her usual outfit, tools peeking out of her plethora of pockets. She sits on the neck of the machine, her legs wrapped precariously around it, and fiddles with something at its end.

Dejean kneels at the open side of the contraption's boxy area. He stares into it uncertainly, his tool raised but unmoving. His shirt is tied around his waist, and I can barely make out the bite I took from his shoulder, a scaly red-brown scab against his dark skin—a wound I won't inflict again.

Murielle sits up, lifting one of her tools into the air. "Pull the lever down!"

He does so and the machine's neck shudders. With a yelp, she topples off of it, catching herself by her ankles. She hangs from the metal with her bare feet crossed above her, swaying back and forth.

"Shit; other down direction!" She shouts, trying to hold her tools inside her pockets. One of them slips out, dropping through the air and vanishing behind the cliff ledge.

Shaking his head, Dejean fixes his error. "You mean the up direction?"

"If you wanna be all technical about it, yeah," Murielle grumbles. She pulls herself back on top of the neck, snapping her fingers in his direction. "The thing, Dejean. Hand me the thing."

Dejean goes through three tools before offering her the one she wants. Sighing, I drum my nails against the tub. After an entire morning like this, I'm amazed they've gotten as far as they have.

The breeze picks up, pricking along my shoulders. In the distance a massive swell crashes against the rocks guarding the cove. My heart leaps and falls with it, a shiver running through me. I don't want to be scared of the ocean. The water should be respected, for it's always restless, ever uncontrollable, but terror is for humans and birds and weaker sea creatures. My gills work perfectly once more; I won't drown. But the state of my tail frightens me. I barely make it across my tub without the handholds. How will I maneuver beneath the crashing waves, much less ride them?

I shiver again. I refuse to let my home dash me to pieces, but neither can I run from it. I have to trust that Dejean and Murielle know what they're doing. They wouldn't offer me a path to the ocean if they thought it would kill me.

Dejean waves to me as he passes my window, vanishing around the side of the house. He returns pushing a metal cage tied to a flat board with wheels. The whole thing is rounder and softer than most cages, a bit like a great clam, and large enough to comfortably hold my entire body. A huge claw with sturdy spools for the elevator's ropes attaches to the top of it, near its door.

That's what he plans to do. It pummels me like backwash.

Dejean wants to lower me into the cove in a giant, clam-shaped cage. I groan, dropping my head into my hands. I don't just have the sea to dread; now I have the sky to fear as well.

He walks to the house with a grin so wide that I want to bite him, but I only shoot a glare his way. As he comes through the back door, I jab my finger at the great clamshell structure.

"You expect me to ride in that?" I say, using the signs for, *you understand I go downward*, followed by a series of aggressive finger stabs toward the clamshell, which more or less mean *that damned thing*.

He wobbles between his feet, his hands making wordless babble in the direction of the ocean. "I . . . yes?" He doesn't sound too sure of himself, and his fingers waver as he signs. "If you don't want to do it, I understand. But the further we go from here, the more likely we'll be seen. I thought this would be best. It's a good cove, protected from the waves, out of view of any ships or fishing vessels. We've already tested the elevator with heavier objects. It's not dangerous."

Slumping my shoulders, I scowl at the clamshell cage. *"Fine. I'll do it,"* I concede, my hands more certain than my heart is. *"I don't like it though."*

Dejean's smile returns in full force. "Murielle is the best. You'll be safe in the . . . thing."

"Giant clamshell," I correct him. *"If I'm going to ride it, I get to name it."*

"Biting jaw? No. An animal? Shark? Some sort of dolphin?"

Rolling my eyes, I point to my own body, shining like a pearl in the morning light. I repeat the motion.

"Clam."

Again, I correct him.

"Very big clam? Giant clam!" He laughs, grinning from ear to ear. "I'm putting a pearl into a giant clam."

I stare at him, trying to prove my indifference, but I lose it after a moment, the corner of my lips twitching.

Dejean kneels down beside me. "So you're coming? Murielle's almost finished attaching everything. I'll have to carry you there, but it shouldn't be long before we can get you back into the water."

"I'm coming." Placing my palms on either side of the tub's edge, I lift my upper body out of the water, settling onto the floor. My tail lays crooked, unresponsive, but I shift my gaze away from it, focusing on Dejean. *"Carry me."*

He picks me up, one arm around my back and the other under my tail. With his chest bare, I can feel his skin, rougher than the scales that coat me, and far warmer. Pressing against him is like bathing in the sun, if the sun was coarse and a little sticky.

The clam hangs at the edge of the cliff, a series of ropes attaching it to the neck of the machine. Murielle opens the door on its top side and Dejean places me in. I recoil from the sea far below, my breath catching. The cove gleams with crystal waters and vibrant reefs, shielded from the brunt of the waves, just the sort of place a siren pod could take to. But from above, it spins dangerously. I feel far too small and too easily shattered. I seal my eyes closed.

"I'll be with you the entire way. I've done this a million times, Perle."

"This had better be worth it," I grumble, not bothering to move my hands.

The clamshell thuds and clicks, Dejean locking it closed. "Perle, look at me."

I peek at him with one eye.

Dejean points to a latch on the side of the clamshell. "This will open it. You can stay inside for as long as you'd like, but if you want to leave just pull it back toward you, all right?"

Nodding, I close my eyes again, gripping two of the clam's crisscrossed bars. The hard casing creates a barrier, a layer of protection from the outside. I don't want to leave it; not in the water, and especially not in the air.

"Murielle!" Dejean shouts. The clam rattles as he climbs on top of it, taking his place just above me.

The clamshell swings out from the cliff's edge. It careens in the air and I shriek, tightening my hold. *It'll be over soon. One way or another . . .*

"I'll lower it down now, but I've gotta run if I'm making it to that appointment before Arami's ship leaves!" Murielle shouts. "Levers on your end should work just fine to bring it back up." As she finishes speaking, a clunk sounds above me.

The clamshell lowers, slow but steady. I force myself to breathe. Dejean does this all the time. Dejean trusts Murielle. I trust Dejean. I *think* I trust Dejean.

The scent of the ocean grows as the rattle of the machine fades above me. Seabirds call and the waves rage in the distance, combined with the softer sound of lapping water from below. The sun beats down, but the cool breeze offers a refreshing caress, bringing a delightful brine with it. Something creaks far above. Dejean curses, his shifting rocking the clam. It drops.

The pit of my stomach rises like a surge of tiny fish. We crash into water. It hits me full force, as jarring as if I had jumped from a human's ship after an attack, but doing no real damage. The clamshell goes still, floating halfway beneath the surface.

The ocean surrounds me, turning my nerves alight. It's not like the water Dejean brings for my tub, though he tries his hardest to mimic it. Alive and wondrous, it beckons, calling the name it reserves for me alone—a name Dejean will never understand, will never be able to utter. My eyes still shut, I draw in the water, pushing it through my gills.

It stimulates and intoxicates and relaxes all at once. The water brushes against the clamshell. The soft waves are echoed by the sounds of sea life moving and communicating, low rumbles and high squeaks.

Slowly, I open my eyes. Below the thin bars stretches

golden sand. Vibrant reef surrounds it, growing on the rocky faces that spring up from the cove floor. Colorful fish dart between the corals, a lobster pulls into a cave, and a number of dark, spotted rays glide with slow but powerful fin strokes. Far along the reef, a small shark darts out of the sun, vanishing in the shadows of the cliffside.

Home. I relax against the bars and slip my hands through their gaps, feeling—just feeling—the motion of the water, the gentle rock back and forth. Dejean straddles the top of the shell, one leg on either side, his bare feet dipped in the ripples of the cove.

I am happy.

Opening my mouth wide, I form a hum deep in my throat. It grows into a proper song, great and vivid and beautiful, rolling out of me from a place I had feared I'd lost at the harbor. In some places it's melancholic, blissful in others, a dreamy melody that curls and caresses all it touches. The fish rise out of the reef to listen, dancing listlessly.

Dejean sinks against the shell. He draws one of his hands through the water, soaking the sleeve of the shirt he must have donned on our way down. With the ocean in his reach, he slips into a dazed, peaceful state, his conscious thought and rational logic gone. There seems to be no pain in it, merely satisfaction, his mind utterly and completely immersed in the song of the sea.

I continue to sing, the sounds rising from deep within. Another voice echoes it, richer and fuller. Through the shadows of the reef, a murky blue siren approaches, their scales like the water during a storm. Their gills tremble as they add to my melody. A mess of scars cuts up one side of their chest, but their tail beats powerfully, fins spread wide and taut.

A storm: that's what I think as I watch them. First from their color, but again from the way they move, unrelenting and chaotic, but worthy of awe. *Storm.*

Smiling, I stretch my fingers as far as the gaps in the

clamshell will allow. Storm gives me a quizzical look. Slowly, they return the motion, reaching out to me, their hand missing two fingers. Three tail lengths away, they pause. Their arm drops and their song wavers. Their eyes move to the top of my clam, hardening when they focus on Dejean.

Dejean. My voice cuts out, and I twist around to look at him. Storm moves faster, snapping through the water and launching themselves at Dejean. I shriek as they drag him into the cove.

His eyes barely open and his hands twitch with a pathetic sluggishness as he flounders. Storm drags him down, pinning him to the bottom of the sandy cove with ease. A cloud of bubbles bursts from Dejean's mouth as Storm clamps down on his shoulder in a solid bite. The water around Storm's mouth turns a sickening scarlet.

What have I done? My hands shake, my whole body as detached as my paralyzed tail. I voiced my presence to every siren in the area, not thinking of what it might mean for Dejean. Sirens protect their territory from land dwellers. Sirens kill humans who overstep their bounds. Sirens eat what they kill. Those facts are a part of me, but trusting a human has diminished them somehow.

Has led to this.

I open my mouth, to scream or shout or cry, but the ocean floods my lungs, choking me. Bolting upright, I breach the surface and cough the water out. My fingers quaver as I throw open the door in the top of the clamshell. The ocean, clear and deep and reckless, stretches out before me.

I stall. A million doubts spring forth at once, weighing me down, pinning me into the clam. I can't save him. I can't even swim. A stray wave, an odd current, and I'll be crushed, torn away. There are no handholds here, no lip of the tub to cling to.

Another cloud of blood rises around Storm's head, and Dejean's arms twitch, his face contorting in a way that tears my heart. I launch over the side of the clamshell and into the ocean.

My torso sinks through the water, but my tail catches on the door's latch. It sticks there, like a weight holding me back. Frantically, I shove myself forward, using the side of the clam to push off of. My tail slips, dragging along the lever. It frees suddenly and dumps me into the cove. I sink.

Storm glances up, hissing the sound for *mine.* I know what they mean: *my prey; back off.*

"*Not yours,*" I shriek, pumping my arms as I sink farther into the water. I propel myself toward the siren, one painfully slow stroke at a time.

Dejean is mine. My friend. The other part of my tiny, peculiar pod.

"*This is our territory,*" I hiss. Twisting my hips, I boost myself forward. I grab Storm by the neck, yanking them away from Dejean, and sink my teeth into the side of their head, grating against bone.

Storm makes a sound that could pierce skulls, that could attract the rest of their pod from any nearby reef. When that pod comes, they'll kick me out of their territory and finish off Dejean.

I cling harder to Storm's neck, cutting off the outlet for their gills. They kick their tail, thrashing and wheeling. My largest fin drags through the water, stirring up sand and knocking into rocks. Blood from three different sources fills my mouth. I glance at Dejean, making out his limp body, hovering just above the cove floor.

I have to get back to him.

Storm slams me into a ledge of the reef, and my back screams in pain. They grab at my hands, and I increase the pressure on their neck. My hold slips as their nails bite into my wrists.

I dig my fingers into their gills. Another scream bursts from them. Letting go, I shove them away, using their body to propel myself toward Dejean. I don't look back, but I can hear Storm swimming to the surface, probably supplementing their injured gills with air through their lungs.

Shoving myself forward like a lobster across the sand, I tackle Dejean's body. He floats, limp, his chest silent and his skin gray, his heartbeat a faint, tired echo. Fear pulses through me. Grabbing onto him, I burst toward the surface. The moment I shove off the cove floor, I immediately sink back down. I rock my hips, slamming my tail against the ground, and try again.

Nothing.

I choke on the ache in my chest, but I force the feeling out with a growl. I *will not let this be the end.* Dejean won't die here.

My tail does me no good, but if I can use my arms, maybe I can make it. I snatch the back of Dejean's shirt between my teeth. Boosting off the sand again, I shoot toward the surface, pumping my arms. The fear from the harbor hits me, the weight of my tail combined with Dejean's body dragging me down. But I'm stronger now, and sure of myself, sure of my goal. The ocean isn't against me today. I am against the ocean.

And I will win this battle.

I move my arms faster, shoving the water away. Snagging the rolls in the tide, I use them to my advantage. The surface nears, the sun bright overhead. My mouth slips around the fabric of Dejean's shirt. His body begins to drop.

Tackling into him, I bite into the back of his shirt once more. Blood fills my mouth. I ignore it, pumping toward the sunlight. Pain screams through my muscles, but they don't spasm. My fingers break the water first, an arm's length from the clamshell. Spinning my hips wildly, I lunge toward it. So close. I'm so close.

Catching the side, I pull myself nearer, wrapping my other arm around Dejean. I glance below me. Storm hides in the shadow of the reef, staring with wide eyes, the confused twist of their brows and the loose slump of their shoulder's a clear display of surrender. For today, they've backed down, but it won't matter if Dejean dies.

With one arm hooked through the side of the clamshell, I shove him onto it. My muscles clench up, but I grit my teeth, heaving my shoulder into his stomach once, twice, a third time, slowly edging him farther onto the top shell. He flops against it.

His body seizes. He coughs, water gushing out of his mouth, and his fingers clench. When he finishes hacking up the ocean from his chest, he breathes in great, hoarse gasps, trembling all over. At the center of his back a chunk of his shirt hangs loose where I grabbed it in my mouth, and the skin beneath it gleams red, oozing blood.

The metal bites into my fingers as I climb onto the clamshell beside him. I grit my teeth to keep the pain in, but I flinch at the sight of his left shoulder.

The chunk of flesh Storm took is three times as deep as the wound I made in his back. When he coughs once more, the pooled blood rushes down, revealing a glint of bone. He goes limp.

"*Dejean!*" I scream at him.

He doesn't move.

"*No!*" I hiss. "*I won't let you die on me.*"

I grab onto a little lever above my head, the one Murielle claimed would lift the clamshell. I yank at it. Nothing happens.

Cursing, I grip it with both hands. My finger slides over a notch in the side and it flies toward me. The clamshell shoots upward. I shriek, shoving the lever back the other way. The clam drops down, hitting the water again with a splash. Dejean's body jumps from the sudden descent, knocking against the metal. His eyes roll open for half a moment, but then they close just as quickly.

I pull the lever again, slower this time. The clamshell responds in turn, moving upward at a slow but steady pace. My certainty wavers the higher we rise. Dejean remains in place, but my tail slips back toward the sea. I cling to the clamshell with every ounce of strength I have left as the reef grows farther and farther away, and the neck of the machine pulling us up, ever nearer.

Dejean still breathes in ugly gasps, but his eyes flicker open, unfocused. He reaches a hand toward me and slips. I let go of the lever, locking it back into place just as the clamshell comes even with the edge of the cliff. Catching Dejean's wrist, I hold him steady. My arms tremble.

A gap stretches between the clamshell and the cliff's edge. My chest catches, frustration coursing through me. I release it in a muted screech. *I can do this. I have to do this.*

I don't know at what point I decided I would risk everything for this stupid human with his dorky smile and his sparkling eyes. But I did. And I will.

In slow, agonizing movements, I reposition myself on the edge of the clamshell and draw Dejean's shoulders into my lap. His blood slips down my tail, dropping off the tip of my fin and vanishing into the cove below. My head spins.

Leaning backward, then forwards, I rock the clamshell, building speed with every motion. Each swing brings us closer to the edge of the cliff, but it throws me off balance. I slip, clinging to Dejean.

The upward stroke brings us back toward the land. Shoving off the clamshell, I fling us both toward the cliff. We hit the ground hard, barely clearing the edge. Dejean rolls. I slide backwards, my largest fin still hanging over the ledge, dragging me down. Dejean's eyes focus, blearily. He grabs my hand. My wrist slips, but he tightens his hold, pulling me back up. Curling toward him, I clutch his forearms in return.

My vision swims, but my fin lurches toward me. I tumble into Dejean. His eyes slip closed once more, a fresh spring of blood welling in the wound on his shoulder.

In the shadow of the elevator's machine hides the long wooden plank Dejean used to wheel out the clam. I pull it over and roll Dejean onto it, not bothering to be gentle. If he lives through this, I won't let him complain about a few bruises. The world sways around me as I climb on top of him, but I ignore it, using my arms to pull us toward the house.

My arms wobble, my muscles numb, and my tail might be dragging along the dirt for all I know. I refuse to think about that. I keep moving forward. The back door of Dejean's house nears, but darkness clouds around it. I have to shake my head, drawing in burning mouthfuls of air to keep myself conscious.

As I pull open the door and wheel us inside, I take one quick look behind us. A trail of blood marks our wake. Not Dejean's blood, but *mine*, thick red liquid seeping out of a gash in the side of my tail. My head lightens in a haze of lethargic panic.

"Perle." Somehow, Dejean's weak voice breaks through my wooziness. He points to a short piece of furniture beside the door, with six little handles in its side. "There's a box . . . top drawer. Long tubes. Green."

He's talking.

I reach for the furniture, but the world turns dark. Tipping my head down, I force my hand into the nearest drawer even though the movement feels like a dream. My fingers brush a little box with no lid. I pull it out and hand it to Dejean.

He doesn't sit up, but he takes a little thing that looks like a funny pistol from it and loads in a green tube. He places it clumsily to his shoulder and squeezes. Green gel shoots out, filling up the gap Storm made in his muscles until it overflows, clinging to the surrounding area. It turns cloudy. A red tint pools beneath it and then the bleeding stops.

Removing the used tube, Dejean fits in a new one and offers it to me. I take the thing, swallowing hard. Sticking it against the long, nasty looking gash in my tail, I pull the trigger. I can't feel the gel anymore than I can the cut, but it fills the gash and spills out. I turn back to Dejean, but he lays limp once more, his breathing shallow. A brown tablet the size of my nail sits in his palm, his fingers curled around it. A second one sits in his open mouth, deteriorating on his tongue. I take a chance and steal the one from his hand, swallowing it. It tastes like metal and dirt and sea grass.

My whole body protests as I force him off the wheeled plank to check his back. The stiff cut gleams with nasty brown clumps, but it no longer bleeds. With only one more tube of the strange green gel, I decide to leave the clotted wound alone.

"Please be okay," I whisper, quiet and mournful. With the last of my energy, I drag myself to my tub. I dump my torso in, drawing water through my mouth and against my gills.

The world dims, and this time I don't fight it.

[7]

TROUGH WATER

What do I want more:
> *Safety or the sea?*
> *Or the ability to choose both at once?*

THE WORLD COMES back in pieces. Water caresses my head as the pumping machine hums. My muscles burn like they've been taken out and fried and then put back in place, charred and useless. My hip aches where the edge of the tub presses against it, my tail lying crooked off the side of my sponge.

I force my eyes open, but the world takes a moment to appear. Starlight from a moonless sky filters through the windows. A light breeze rustles the fabric hanging over them. Stretching my arm out of the tub, I press my wet palm to Dejean's chest. He doesn't stir, but his skin is his usual temperature, warm as wet beach sand in the sun, and his torso rises and falls with a slight wheeze.

Breathing a sigh of relief, I sink my sore body onto my sponge. My eyes slip closed, and I open them again to proper sunlight. It coats the sills of the windows, the sun itself high overhead. My stiff muscles all but refuse to move, painful even at rest. The spinning of my head fades, darkness no longer threatening to consume my vision.

Sitting fully upright in the tub, I lean toward Dejean. I can't hear his breath any longer, but his chest rises and falls in a steady rhythm. An even, rosy gold brightens his face, his dark skin vibrant once more. The gel on his shoulder arcs down in the middle, but no blood coats it. I leave him to sleep.

My stomach makes an unhappy noise and I steal the last fish from the small tank Dejean set up yesterday. It's not the same surge of hunting and killing as cornering fish in the reef or whipping through schools in the clear ocean, but pinning its scaly body to the bottom of the tank is all I can manage, and it smells just as fresh as if I caught it straight from the sea. It wiggles when I bite down.

As I eat, I watch the ocean. The cliff blocks all but the bleary edge of the reef and the line of rocks that protect its waters, giving way to deep murky blue as it stretches toward the horizon. Grumbling to myself, I toss the fish's leftovers out the open back door. I meander along the tub using as little effort as possible. Pulling my torso out of the water, I snatch up one of Dejean's funny spyglass tubes.

I lift it to my eye, like the sailors do when looking for something far away. The scene inside blurs and spins awkwardly, colored like the back wall. I nearly drop the spyglass. Aiming it out the window, I try again. This time, I can make out the individual waves knocking against the rocks along the reef's edge, and the outline of a turtle moving through them. *Perfect.*

I search for the silhouettes of sirens. In the sea, just beyond the reef, a dolphin pod plays in the waves, lingering for a while before moving on. A large whale breaches in the distance, and a while later it releases a spout from its blow hole, farther to the north. Sharks pop in and out of the shadows of the rocks as they hunt, growing few and farther beneath as the sun rises into the sky. Not a single siren appears.

Storm must not have a pod after all. Maybe they were wandering, looking for a new territory to join. If they were alone, they had likely been scared off, either by my attack or the oddity of the situation. No siren wants to be caught trespassing on a claimed territory without permission, especially not a loner.

A groan startles me. I twist toward Dejean. His eyelashes flutter, his brow knitting together as he finally squints my way. He makes another low, pained noise.

"You look like you were eaten and regurgitated."

He closes his eyes again, his expression pained. "I caught none of that," he says, his voice strained and weak. "If it's not important, give me a moment."

With a sigh, I set the spyglass off to the side and move closer to him, settling against the edge of the tub. I watch him breathe, his face shifting slowly, as though thoughts crash like turbulent waves in his head. His salty hair lies in a lopsided mess. Bored of his need to rest, I brush a couple of the curls away from his forehead.

I refuse to worry. Annoyance, confusion, irritation: these things are all better than the sharp pains careening through my bones when I consider the pain he must be facing. The fourth time I rearrange his hair, he looks up at me, his eyes almost clear. The lines around them soften and the corners of his lips quirk.

"You saved my life."

"I saved us both." I adopt simple signs so he need not focus hard, *I* and then *take* followed by *same*, using the motion to imply the both of us. He must understand my implication, because he smiles wider.

"You could have left me in the water, but you came in anyway," he objects. Dipping his head, he adds a soft, "Thank you."

"You thought I'd let another siren eat my prey, in my territory?" I tease.

He closes his eyes through the end of my sentence, but he finds my arm with the hand opposite his wounded shoulder and pats it gently. "It looked like you just belittled me for something."

"For almost dying on me!" My face surely reveals more than my voice, and I'm glad his eyes remain closed. I never

imagined a human's life would matter to me, but seeing him awake and happy makes my heart leap and my sore muscles loosen.

The shadows shift as the sun slips farther in the sky. Finally, Dejean moans and sits up. He holds his head in his hands and I give his arm the same little pat he gave me. A gruff laugh leaves him.

He wobbles as he stands, slumping back onto the floor. Instead of rising, he creeps across the ground, favoring the arm where Storm bit his shoulder. He gathers a box of supplies from the little drawers and a couple stacks of containers behind the table. Settling on his sponge, he pats the space next to him. "Can you make it here?"

I answer by placing a bit of absorbent fabric there and settling down at his side. I point to the box. *"What's that?"*

"Dressing, for wounds. The gel isn't a cure; it'll go bad soon." He cringes. "It's also expensive. I've only got one left at this point."

In that case, I'm glad I didn't put the last shot of gel on his back wound.

He reaches for my tail, but I shake my head. Leaning behind him, I tug at his shirt. He relents and offers me a little knife before turning. I cut the fabric away, and he grimaces when the edges of it tug on his back wound. The rough, lumpy crust turns my stomach. I put that scab there. If I hadn't grabbed him so harshly, hadn't needed to rely on my arms to swim, hadn't let my song rise with him near, then there would be no wound in the first place.

I clean and bandage it, following the motions I saw Kian do on occasion. I try not to think of her while I work; of what might happen to us if she catches Dejean weak and injured. Because of me.

I secure a piece of fluffy sponge to his back by wrapping a long bandage around his torso. He must feel my hands shake because when I reach past him to put the leftover bandage back into the supply box, he catches my fingers.

"This isn't your fault you know. None of it is." He gives my hand a squeeze.

He's wrong though. *"My song . . ."*

"I love your song," he says, shifting until he can look me in the eyes. "It's the most beautiful thing I've ever heard. I want to lie on the water and listen to it a thousand times over," he says, soft and genuine. He tries to hold both of my hands at once, but the motion pulls at the muscle Storm bit into. A flash of pain crosses his face, and he drops his arm. "But next time let's check for other sirens first. I don't have many shoulders to spare."

I try to laugh, but the tightness of his expression and the delicate way he hangs his arm rip into me as viciously as Storm's teeth. I motion to the chunk taken out of him. It hollows out the muscle that connects his shoulder to his arm.

He glances at it, swallowing hard. "We'll deal with it after we look at your tail."

An objection rises in my throat, but then I remember the trail of blood that followed me to the house. Though I don't feel any pain from my wound, I suppose it still needs to be cared for. As lifeless as my tail is right now, I don't want to lose it entirely.

The cut runs deep and jagged, from the base of my big fin toward my hip for the length of my forearm. The goop of green coating recedes along the corners, revealing swollen, angry flesh. Whatever pierced my tail caught the side of my fin as well, slashing through the spaces between the rays of bone. Strips of the once solid membrane lay awkwardly, curling at the edges.

My head floats, and I turn away from the sight, focusing on Dejean's hands. He works with only one, preparing the supplies with his injured arm hanging loose at his side. As he starts on my tail, I move my gaze to the sea.

"Is there normally a pod in this area?" I ask as he begins to wrap the wound.

"Hmm?" He glances up, and I repeat my signs. "Oh, once. I think it was a good number of years back, before I bought the house. A terrible hurricane brought part of the cliff down, wiping most of them out. There hasn't been a single pod in the waters on this side of the island since, from here to the smaller isle just north."

It's not strange for a territory to go unclaimed. With few of us spread over such a vast ocean, we keep away from human ports as much as we can. Our songs are powerful, but the humans are creative. They find ways to kill us without ever being present.

"I saw no sirens in the cove while you slept." I sign slowly, and he pauses to watch. *"The one who bit you must have left."* If not, they should have been flaunting their presence, daring me to return for another fight.

"That's good." He sounds monotone, but his face betrays his relief.

I quirk my brow. *"You're scared of us."*

"I'm scared of most things that can eat me." He flashes me a grin, tying off the bandage. "But not you."

"I'm plenty fearsome," I object with a hiss, baring my teeth to prove my point. *"And I can still sing."*

He laughs, his eyes sparkling. "You're adorable." He signs for the first time since waking, all his motions done with one hand. Pain mars his expression, and he gives it up for spoken words. "And plenty frightening to other people, I'm sure."

He checks over the shredded half of my fin as I grumble, crossing my arms and glaring at him.

"What should I do with this?" He motions to my fin. "They're clean cuts, miraculously."

My experience in this holds no value. When something similar happened to another of my kind, our pod rejected them without question. My chest warms. Dejean knows I can do little to benefit him, but he helps me anyway, asking nothing in return. He's a strange pod-mate, but I'm grateful.

"Leave it," I tell him. *"We should deal with your shoulder."*

He groans.

"I let you fix my tail."

"You couldn't feel me fixing your tail."

"You're a pirate, aren't you? I see the other scars."

"They're not like this one," Dejean replies, weakly.

That leaves a painful knot in my stomach. The handful of scars on his limbs and torso are all simple raised lines, pulling together two strips of flesh. This wound is like a hole in the side his body, a bone visible near one edge. It covers the area a little lower than where I bit him back at the harbor. Most of the half-healed imprint from my teeth is ripped clean out. That Dejean stays conscious despite it amazes me.

My mind hops back to the moments before I first passed out. *"What were those brown pills for?"*

"They help your blood regenerate," he says. "They're high grade, from a large island quite a bit to the south. When I was third mate, we took a merchant carrying them, and I filched as many as I could get away with. They've saved Simone's life more than once."

"And now they've saved ours," I mutter without signs. I might slip a couple into Murielle's pocket, in case of a freak accident. With her tools all tucked into her hair, it seems likely.

"Your shoulder," I remind Dejean, pointing at it.

He gives me a pathetic look, his lower lip jutted forward and his brow scrunched. A low, whimpering noise leaves him, but the approaching sound of blasting steam and crinkling metal cuts him off. We both go silent. Dejean grips the edges of the sponge and pulls his feet under him to stand. I grab onto his wrist, signing, *"Don't."*

I want him here, where I can defend him if I must.

Somewhere beyond the front door, the machine rumbles to a stop. A figure marches into view of the side windows, a dark cloak billowing dramatically around them. Very dramatically. Almost too dramatically.

Dejean's eyes go wide and then he laughs, a soft, contained noise, squeaking in his throat. Not until the intruder shoves through the door do I understand. A dark, fluffy mess of hair springs to life as Murielle throws back her dark hood, grinning.

Dejean suppresses his laughter enough to say, "Isn't that from one of the trunks in my attic?"

"Maybe." Murielle makes an overly suspicious face, her lips pursed downward as she avoids Dejean's gaze.

"The embroidery around the clasp is the same design."

"A common pattern seen in lots of cloaks found in suspicious old trunks next to piles of cogs. I mean, sure it was locked, but you shouldn't keep the keys so close by." Murielle swings her arms, setting a swell through the fabric. "And it's for a good cause! If no one can see who I am, then they can't ask me about any particular sirens hiding in any particular tubs, or the genius of those upgrades I made to the elevator, or why you . . ." She trails off, her eyes settling on Dejean's shoulder. "Why do you have a huge hole in your shoulder?" Then, louder: "Why the hell do you have that big, huge hole in your shoulder? Damn, Dejean, you should be at the doc's!"

"Perle was just going to patch it—"

"Oh no, no, no. You don't get your siren to patch up messes like that—no offense Perle," she pauses, glancing at me with a smile before her face contorts back into a frantic rage. "For this, you need a fellow who knows their shit!"

"But . . ." Dejean looks faint.

"She's right," I add. *"I'm the worst person to look at it. Most sirens will leave you for dead over a wound like this."* Besides, I know nothing about humans except which of their organs tastes best. I want him to heal properly.

Dejean drops his head into a hand, avoiding us both. Grabbing his wrist, Murielle yanks him up. He looks faint and sways, but she wraps an arm around his waist, letting him lean on her shoulder.

"Come on, you idiot," she grumbles, walking him toward the door.

When she glances back at me, I sign to her, though I know she can't interpret it.

"Take care of him."

She must understand my intention, because she smiles at me. "I'll bring him back, good as new. Or . . . better than this. Best as any good doc can get him."

I shift myself into the tub. My body remains tense long after Murielle's machine pulls away, and I barely relax into a fatigued, wavering sleep. The sun sets during one of my restless naps, leaving the house cloaked in darkness. No one comes up the drive, not to bang on the front door and not to bring Dejean back. Having him so far away feels painful, and I don't know whether I miss him because he's gone or because I'm simply worried.

These humans seem more compassionate than sirens, but if the doctor thinks his shoulder isn't worth saving, will they cast him out? They won't. They can't. Dejean doesn't think any less of me for the state of my tail; the doctor can't turn him away for having a chunk of muscle missing, right?

I would've left him. The thought springs on me like the mouth of an angry eel from a dark, rocky pit. Before the loss of life in my tail, it would've seemed the natural course to take. Now, the idea makes me shudder. I can't imagine letting Dejean go over something so trivial as an injury, no matter how terrible.

When the machine finally rumbles back up to the front of the house, I go limp with relief. Murielle helps Dejean inside, rambling all the while. Layers of fabric cover his shoulder, the gap of the wound no longer visible. His dark face holds little color, but he smiles at me as he collapses onto his sponge.

"I live," he moans, covering his eyes with a hand.

"That's good. I like you alive," I say, signing my words out

of habit as he drifts quickly to sleep.

Murielle spreads a thin blanket over him. "He'll be alright." She grins weakly, but sadness clouds her relief. "He might never be able to lift his upper arm in an outward sort of direction, which would be a bugger on him if he weren't captain, but he'll live."

Might never again. A rush of emotion clenches at my heart, like a subtle acceptance of my tail all over again, but this time it's an ache instead of an oozing wound. *Dejean won't be the same.*

But the inability to do all that you once could isn't the same as uselessness. It's a change, a painful one, but still just a change. Nothing less, nothing more. Dejean won't be fine, but he's here. As long as he lives, I can accept him as he is.

I give Murielle a smile. *"Thank you."*

"I . . . I dunno what that means." She looks embarrassed, and shrugs her shoulders. She lays her great cloak on a chair, and the numerous buttons on her one-piece outfit rattle. "I've gotta get Dejean to teach me this weird hand language you've made. I like it. Pictures are always better than words, if you ask me."

I huff. *"You think you can join our pod that easily, do you?"*

Murielle stares at me. "What's that mean? Twirling? Lot's of fish? A wash machine?"

"You're terrible at this," I grumble. *Fish, hungry,* I motion, ignoring the signs Dejean and I have settled on, in favor of gestures I think she'll understand.

"You want food?"

"Yes!" My stomach agrees with me in a series of gurgles.

"I haven't been fishing in years and years . . ." Murielle glances out the window. "It's kinda dark now."

I point aggressively in the direction I assume the kitchen to be.

Mumbling things under her breath, she follows my instruction. She returns with a bowl of seafood in one arm and a stack of giant, fluffy sponges Dejean once called pillows in the other. Dumping the pillow sponges on the ground beside the tub, she hands me the plate. I slurp down a few tiny squids that only smell partially foul and gnaw at the insides of a set of crab legs. Murielle settles on the pillows, stealing an unused blanket off Dejean's sponge.

"You're staying?" I ask. When she gives me a quizzical look in return, I ignore her, slipping onto my sponge. I let my head float on the water as I stare at the ceiling. Shadows hide the uneven white paneling.

"I was worried too." Murielle speaks in a soft, delicate tone, nothing like the loud, brash, self-assured person I've seen so far. "He's not really my brother, not in blood, but I love him like it, you know?"

I lift my head out of the water, settling against the edge of the tub to watch her curl up in her heap of pillows.

"His mom offered me a spot at their table, whenever I wanted it. It was nice to have a place to go where someone thought I was worth a shit."

"Pods are good," I whisper, tucking my elbows under my head. Humans seem to put much faith in the pod they form with their parents. *"Was his father there too?"*

Murielle could not possibly understand the question, but she nods to herself, as though swimming through a memory. "After my parents died, Dejean's mom taught me to work the machines same as she did. Said she needed someone to pass the knowledge to, seeing how Dejean just wanted to fish and sail." She snorts and tucks her pillow under her head, looking at Dejean's sleeping form. "He's only ever thought a thing was worth building if it's got rigging and masts."

I try to imagine them as gangly, young humans, Dejean fishing off some city harbor and Murielle learning which of the odd tools she stuffed in her hair did what.

"He left for the seas a bit after that," she continues. "But he came back when his mom passed. Moved with me to this little isle, to get away from the old house and the crazy pace of the big island life." A soft hum rumbled in her throat, a smile on her lips. "I met Simone after a merchant vessel dumped her here with half its crew. Dejean never faltered when I asked him to vouch for her to his captain." She glances at me. "But he needs more than just me and Simone, so it's a good thing you're here now too."

"I can see that." The words spill out easily with no one to understand them but myself. *"I didn't think I'd ever have someone I could trust the way I trust Dejean. Sirens aren't the best at compassion. I survived because I was tough and could contribute to the pod, because I was always ready to let go of anyone who would slow me down . . ."*

A deep snore cuts me off, and I glance at Murielle to find her eyes closed and her mouth hanging open.

"You're a terrible listener," I grumble, but I can't keep the smirk off my face. It's nice having a group to call my own. Even if it's a group made up of humans.

I drift to sleep to Murielle's rhythmic snoring and the subtle churn of the water machine, relaxed and happy.

The next seven nights are much the same; Dejean and I asleep on our sponges, and Murielle crashed on her ever-growing pile of pillows. Dejean offers her a proper sponge, but she refuses, just as she refuses to leave. She claims she prefers Dejean's house to her own, because he keeps a higher number of junk piles. From what I know of them both, I figure Murielle's home is made entirely *from* junk.

Dejean rarely minds her presence. They quibble and fuss without any real irritation, in a way I assume is typical of human siblings. Would I have had such a relationship if sirens stayed with their birth parents as humans do?

Dejean's shoulder wound begins to mend, the healing quickened by whatever the doctor gives him on his daily visits. By the end of the week though, it's clear he'll have limited range in his arm for the rest of his life. The more he tells me not to worry over him, the more determined I grow to never let it happen again. The next time someone—siren or human—threatens Dejean, I'll be ready to defend him.

As this promise deepens, my agitation grows. Doom hangs over our peaceful healing process, with Kian out there somewhere, hunting me down. The longer Dejean and I linger here, the more likely she'll find us. We need to flee. But running to sea with half-mended injuries carries a danger we would prefer not to face.

As Dejean's wounds knit, so do mine. The beginning of a mangled scar forms from the gash in my tail, but the strips of my fin refuse to bind back together. They hang awkwardly, drifting through the water with haunting fluidity. But when Murielle asks if she can build me something to compensate for the aesthetic loss, I turn her down.

I look at my tail differently now. Even if I couldn't stop Storm from biting the chunk out of Dejean's shoulder, I still pulled him to the clamshell and up into the house. I don't desire a dead tail any more than a life of tubs and tank food, but this could still be a good life—once we're free from Kian. I can still be happy. I can still protect my pod, so we can go on laughing and living. I have a good thing here, just as rich and wonderful as the life I had before, only a little different.

Sometimes a little different isn't bad.

Sometimes a little different isn't bad. I repeat those words to myself as Murielle crashes through a heaping mound of clutter Dejean just piled in the archway to the front room. Junk and collectibles clatter as they spill across the floor and I pin my palms to my ears.

"Mur!" Dejean snaps, his head shooting up from where he sketches at the table. When he sees her, his face softens. She holds a giant tubular thing in her arms, composed of fabric and what must be a lightweight metal of some kind, forming a structure of plates and poles around the cloth.

Grinning from ear to ear, Murielle sets the strange object in front of me. I lift myself out of the tub to sit on the edge, glancing it over. It's about the width of my tail, and a bit longer.

"This is it?" I keep to simple signs with her, choosing ones we went through during the recent evenings.

"A brace!" Murielle beams. "It's just the first part of the set I'm building, but I can't get the rest done 'til I know this one fits."

"Right."

The brace scares me just as much as it excites. Dejean must see the fear, because he hurries over to help me lift my tail out of the water, giving my shoulder an encouraging pat. Together, we fit the brace to my body.

The gray fabric clings to my tail, secure without much rubbing. It covers from the base of my large end fin all the way up past my hips, with openings for the smaller fins along my side. Silvery poles give it structure but still allow for some bending, with plates covered in a layer of sponge providing added support. A bit of fabric crosses over my back and chest too, preventing slippage.

I twist, trying to get a feel for it. It sits bulky and cumbersome, but weight little overall. Hesitant, I give my hips a rock. My tail moves as one, awkward and unnatural, but with far less effort on my part. I look up at Murielle. *"Good enough?"*

She squeals. "It's perfect!"

"You did good, Mur," Dejean says, slapping her on the back so hard her pinned hair topples over, spilling a small, leftover pipe onto the ground.

"Now we've gotta test it out."

"I'm not getting in the clamshell while wearing this. I won't make it out again." I buck my hips again for emphasis, my entire tail bobbing up and down stiffly.

Nodding, Dejean grabs his sketch paper. "I was thinking of adjusting the elevator like this. No top, with handholds and a sloped entry. Perle shouldn't have any problems."

Murielle hops up and down. "Wonderful!"

His gaze shifts to me, his brow lifting. He hands me the illustration. "If you think you're ready to go back out there?"

I look the image over without truly seeing it. Running from Kian is one thing, but the ocean is my home. I will not fear it.

Returning the paper, I give him a solemn nod. *"This is our territory, as long as we're here. I will swim in that cove, and the sea beyond it—whatever it takes."*

[8]

RIPTIDE

The current rips a pod apart; tenacious, devastating.
> *If I fight it, will we come together?*
> *Or will it only break us further?*

THE RECONSTRUCTED CLAMSHELL sways as it lowers. I grip the sides, my heart pounding with each motion. With the top half gone, the sky looms above me. I lay on a long, flat board at the bottom, far too exposed. At least this time I don't have a dying Dejean riding beside me. He sits on the catamaran floating in the middle of the cove, dumping an anchor over its side.

It's a small boat compared to most, relying on sails and a rudder instead of a steam machine. Its too-long hollow hulls are shaped like funny porpoises, with a set of crossbars connecting them, finely woven netting stretching between. One tall mast springs from the middle, both its sails drawn in so as not to catch the soft breeze coming off the ocean.

Dejean says we'll keep to the cove until I feel comfortable. If I'm honest, it's a relief to move slowly, to adjust at a speed that's good for my body. It's also annoying that he feels the need to coddle me so, but I don't put up a fuss. In human terms, I think it means that he cares.

The clamshell shakes as it plunges into the water, nearly throwing me off. I clench my hands along the metal and glare up at Murielle. I can't see her expression, but she waves both her arms in such a way that I'm afraid she may fall in my stead.

From the boat, a rope flies toward me with a hiss, slapping against the water near the clamshell.

"Grab it!" Dejean shouts.

I take a deep breath. I can do this. I pulled Dejean up from the bottom of the cove. Swimming down to the end of a lifeline is nothing in comparison.

I dive for it. My tail thumps against the side of the clamshell, but the brace keeps it from twisting about. Pulling water through my gills, I use my arms to swim toward the rope. It sinks, and I snatch it just as it hits the sandy bottom. I wrap it around my forearm a few times and grip it firmly, drawing comfort from its firm connection to the boat.

Twisting onto my back, I settle against the sand. It welcomes me, both soft and tough all at once. I close my eyes and let the wash of the water consume me. The song rises in my chest. I focus on pushing it away, though doing so hurts something deep in my soul, like the creeping sting of a jellyfish. But for Dejean and Murielle's sake, I'll refrain.

I want to explore.

Keeping a tight hold on the rope, I push off the sand. My tail floats behind me. With the brace to support it, the lifeless limb no longer weighs me down with the same helpless drag. The sharp twisting of my hips offers some forward momentum. I quicken the motion, laughing at the water that rushes over me.

The reef comes in fast. I swing to stop myself, but my tail doesn't turn like it should. Stretching out my hands, I catch some of my weight as I slam into the rocky ledge. Coral splinters under the impact, and I cringe, shaking small shards off my palms. I guess even a little speed does me no good if I can't slow down.

I'll have to find a way to navigate without the aid of my fins . . .

Still clutching the rope, I swim through a bit of the reef. Colorful fish flee my presence, along with a fever of rays and three decent-sized squids. Even the few nearby sharks give me a wide berth. The energy it takes to bring one down doesn't make them profitable prey for a single siren, but they know to fear large pods. I fit my fingers into a sea anemone for the joy of it. It curls tightly, the sting it uses to paralyze small fish more sticky than numbing to something my size.

Motion from the cliff catches my attention, and I glance over my shoulder to find Murielle swimming toward me, completely submerged. She wears a pair of loose, checkered shorts that go all the way to her underarms, clinging there. Her red hair poofs around her. Though ridiculously unpractical, the curls look beautiful, lit by the glow of the sun and flowing in gentle waves as she moves.

Dejean says something from the boat, but his words dissolve into muttered chaos beneath the surface. I can only make out his feet, his weird, stubby toes trailing through the water. He leans forward. Through his rippled image comes a look of sheer longing.

But it's best for him on the boat. My body heals in the salt, and his in the air. As Murielle dives down to me though, her grin consuming her face, I miss him like a gentle throb in my chest. I turn away from the catamaran.

Together, Murielle and I swim through the reef. I show her little sea jewels: fancy shells and pretty corals, the clams most likely to hold pearls, and sea creatures slow enough—or unafraid enough—for me to catch. She still only knows simple signs, but the treasures of the ocean speak for themselves.

The sun has shifted somewhat by the time we head back to the boat. I pull my lagging body up using the rope, Murielle pausing for me to catch up every so often. My muscles ache, but I can't remove the smile from my face.

"You two enjoy yourselves down there?" Dejean asks.

I loop my arms over one of the long, upside-down dolphin hulls, giving him the smuggest look I can muster.

He glares at me in return. "I bet sirens taste like swordfish." He stabs a fork teasingly in my direction.

"I'm not a fish," I correct him, for the millionth time.

Leaning forward, he pokes his utensil at me again. "Maybe you'll taste *better* than fish then?"

I snatch the fork out of his grasp with my mouth and slip back under the water, coming up beneath the netting section to jab it at him from below. He yelps the first time it sticks him, but he topples backward against the net, his chest trembling with laughter. Murielle joins him. She watches Dejean, her eyes wide and her lips curled in a soft, wistful way, as though she sees something new and beautiful there.

Moving back to the side of the catamaran, I toss Dejean's fork at him. Murielle catches it and uses it to wrap up her hair, despite Dejean's objections.

She snorts. "What'd you even need a damn fork for? Didn't you get us sandwiches or something?"

"Yes, but there's a jar of pomegranate seeds, too," he whines, still eyeing the fork.

"All fruit's finger food!" Murielle snatches her sandwich out of Dejean's hands, sticking the better part of it into her mouth in one go.

I look at him expectantly.

"Get in," he motions me over. "I'll throw out a line."

"But—"

"I'm not letting you swim with fishhooks in the water." There's no room in his voice for protest.

I want to flick my tail defiantly, but I manage only a swivel of my hips. The urge to catch my own food gets the better of me, though. I doubt I can manage anything edible, but I won't know unless I try. I slip back into the water, pausing long enough to sign Dejean a quick, *"You can throw out that line when I get back."*

Binding the end of the rope around my waist, I let myself sink. Just before hitting the sand, I turn to the end of the cove Murielle and I didn't touch, swimming toward it in the lagging, lopsided way the brace allows. I try to be stealthy, but wiggling through the bright sunlight in my bulky contraption makes me more obvious than a single ship on a flat sea.

I creep along the lip of the reef, pulling myself forward by grabbing outcroppings of rock. A few fish dart above me, far too fast to be worth my effort. I lower myself down, glancing into the caverns running like broken tunnels through the rock. Maybe I can find a lobster hiding somewhere.

At the fourth large arch, something moves in the shadows. I slip my shoulders in, glancing down a side tunnel. Light streams through openings in the reef, creating a patchy network of green shade and golden beams. A murky blue siren tail flickers in and out of the light.

Storm. I creep a little farther through the arch, baring my teeth at them. Storm returns the look with a hiss.

My instincts all scream to attack. Storm isn't one of my pod. They shouldn't be here. They were already warned once.

And they hurt Dejean.

But I remember what I had been when Dejean found me, how easily he could have kept me a prisoner, or stuck a blade through my heart. He showed me compassion. Perhaps this siren, with their scars and missing fingers, needs the same offer of grace.

"What are you doing here?" Like the signs I developed with Dejean, our language portrays the underlying concept instead of the exact words. *"This is my territory. If you won't join my pod, you must leave."*

Storm flicks their tail, but their eyes drop to the sand beneath them. *"I have no one,"* they say softly. *"This is a good place."* They hesitate then, returning their gaze to mine. *"You took my prey . . . though you did not eat it?"*

"The humans aren't prey," I retort. *"They're my pod-mates."*

Shock puckers Storm's face, and they curl their upper lip. *"You are crazy!"* They hiss. *"Humans are not meant for the ocean. We give them room to sail between the islands, and they disrespect it! They have no honor for territory. They kill us whenever they can."* Their fins flare, gills pulsing in time. *"We should kill them first."*

Everything they say is true, to an extent. But Storm doesn't know my humans—my wonderful, terrible, devoted humans.

"They're not all the same. These ones are good. They've helped me. They would help you, too." I glance at my palm, curling and uncurling my fingers. Determined, I offer my hand to Storm. *"We could protect you."*

They stare at my hand like an octopus grows out of it, but a look of hope passes over their face. Slowly, the softer expression fades, harsh lines pooling around their eyes. *"The humans have always done their best to kill us. The moment they learned to ignore our songs, they began slaughtering our kind in droves and taking us from the sea to be sold like fish."* Storm creeps closer to me, coming out of the shadows. The scars across their chest glow as reflected light from an upturned shell bounces off the mangled scales. *"Those humans you protect will hurt you too, just like the others."*

"You don't know them!" I snarl. *"They aren't like the ones who hunt us."* The twinkle that lights up Dejean's eyes when he sees me happy proves that.

"They took you out of the ocean! They made you dependent on them." Storm launches forward with aggression this time, anger pinched across their face.

I scoot out of the tunnel, clinging to the rock face to steady myself. My heart pounds and the end of the rope I bound to my waist wavers. There's truth to what Storm says. I'm a siren—a siren living in a tub.

They take my silence as a sign to continue. *"You eat their food and let them fit you with pipes and cloth."* They burst out of the tunnel, holding onto the sides of the rock, same as I do, their fins flared. *"You do not act like a siren. You act like the human's pet."*

Anger rushes through me. *"I'm not!"* I growl, a deep noise of defiance that quivers my chest. But doubts creep in.

Without Dejean hunting for me, I can't eat. Without Murielle's brace, I couldn't even swim in the slow floundering way that I do now.

With a shudder, I shake those thoughts away. I've saved Dejean as often as he's saved me. Maybe I depend on him for some things, but I repay him in the ways that I can. We're valuable to each other, like pod-mates should be.

I open my mouth to tell Storm so, but their eyes flash toward the double hulls of Dejean's catamaran.

"Come back to the ocean," they demand. *"You belong to the sea, not to them."*

"They're my pod. This is my home." A slight tremble rises in my bones. I bare my teeth. *"If you won't accept that, then you must leave."*

Storm's gaze flickers between me and the boat. Their face hardens, and the remaining nub of one of their lost fingers twitches. *"Even if you do not realize what the humans have done to you, I refuse to abandon you with them!"* they snarl. In a gust, they swim toward the catamaran. Toward Dejean and Murielle.

Something flashes upon Storm's face as they move, the same burst of emotion I feel when I think of Kian; an agonizing mixture of hatred and terror. It stalls me for a moment, but I force down the rising memories and launch myself off the side of the rock.

"You will not hurt them!" Ramming into Storm's tail, I wrap my arms around the powerful limb, digging my nails in deep.

Storm screeches with pure frustration. They slam their tail back and forth, but I grip harder, clutching onto one of their small side fins. We careen, a swirling mass of iridescence and darkness. My world spins one way, then the other, the sand and the reef and the sky alternating in chaotic pulses as water whips through my gills. The lifeline connecting my waist to the boat runs through it, encircling us as we roll.

You will not hurt them. I pound the words through my head, my anger building with each pulse. Using our momentum, I release Storm's tail and fling myself onto their shoulders.

They spear their elbow into my ribs, shoving me away, but the rope wraps around us both like some kind of terrible trap, tangling us together. It burns against my scales, tightening as Storm thrashes, shudders racking through them. They grab the untangled section of rope, yanking themselves toward the catamaran. A coil connecting our tails drags me forward.

I refuse to let go of their shoulders. *"You will not hurt my humans!"* They think they can help me by taking away my humans, but they know nothing of my life. They know nothing of me.

Yanking myself up Storm's back, I clamp my teeth into their arm, in the same place they bit Dejean. I bite down until my teeth meet bone. Sharp, briny siren blood clouds my vision, distorting the slowly nearing form of the boat's underside.

That's for Dejean.

Storm shrieks. They buck and wither, spiraling us through the water. I grip them with shaking arms as they thrash, rolling us under the boat's shadow. They slam me into the side of the nearest hull.

My head knocks against wood, pain shooting through my skull, down my neck, and into my shoulders. I hold in my cry, but a lump clings to the base of my throat, rage and pain and terror all churning together. I bite harder.

Again, Storm slams me into the hull. Once, twice, a third time. I will not let them go. My vision wavers, black dots filling in from the sides. Panic rattles in my chest, seizing my gills. *I will not . . .*

My grip around Storm's waist loosens.

Out the corner of my eye, a brown blur sweeps through the water in the shape of an oar. It slams into Storm, knocking the back of their head. Storm screeches. Their flesh disappears beneath my teeth, leaving a cloud of red as they drop downward. The ropes coiled around us loosen, floating through the water like an endless, deadly eel.

Storm darts out of the mess, but a coil catches their tail as they swim under the catamaran. It yanks the end of the rope I bound around my waist. I snarl in pain, grabbing the side of the boat. If they tow me away from it, away from Dejean and Murielle, if they leave me somewhere far along the reef, I will never make it back in time to protect my humans. My hands cramp up, burning as I dig my fingers into the wood. I grit my teeth. I can't let go.

Large, calloused hands grasp my wrists, Dejean's face a swirling blur in the air above. He pulls me toward him, but the rope around my waist continues to tighten. My chest catches as terror sweeps through me, and I can't tell if the agony comes from my fear or the feeling of tearing in two.

I'm being ripped apart. But I can't leave them. I gather my pain and scream.

Suddenly another blur slides through the water, this one with a cloud of red hair. Murielle swims past me, a knife in her mouth. She grabs the rope connecting me to Storm and saws. After three quick cuts, it snaps.

The poles on my brace grate against the ship's hull as Dejean yanks me onto the boat. I collapse, gasping in air until it fills my lungs, spasms racking my core. Panic rushes through me.

"Murielle!" I rush the sign for her name, nearly scraping into my head fins as I make an illustration of the tools in her hair. *"Where is she? Get her on the boat!"*

A round, wet mass flops onto the catamaran at my side, grinning. "Thought you could get rid of me that easily, huh?"

My body goes numb, then limp, and then I burn from the inside out. *"You idiot!"*

"That was dangerous!" Dejean shoots her a glare, but his relief seeps through in the drop of his shoulders and the scrunch of his lower lip.

I mirror him. The faintest murmur of a body shooting out of the sea attracts my attention. Droplets of water sprinkle onto the gentle waves, and a flash of storm-colored scales glimmers in the sun, heading straight for Dejean.

I throw myself into Storm's path, knocking into them before they can reach Dejean. We tumble across the netting, matching snarls, a layer of blood and water slick between us. I try to get a firm bite, but I can't hold onto Storm for long enough. Their teeth rake across my arm, losing their grip before they can dig in. We hit the edge of the netting. Drawing on all my strength, I shove Storm over the side of the boat, grabbing hold of the netting's edge to keep from falling in after them. They vanish below the surface.

Dejean shouts something, but I can't focus on his words. My heart pounds. My chest heaves. I made a mistake.

I should never have let Storm go.

The beginnings of their song rises through me in a terrible rhythm Dejean and Murielle can't yet detect. Rolling toward Dejean, I grab a hold of his arms.

"Storm will sing. We have to leave!"

But it's already too late. Murielle stares at the waves with the same look she gives the mechanical gizmos scattered around Dejean's house, her eyes wide and alight. I let go of Dejean to snatch her wrists, pulling her away from the edge of the boat.

The song rises around us, an eerie but beautiful melody, spinning a tale of love and of death. I feel the rage of emotions as strongly as Storm does. The wounds they've faced from the human's traps. The betrayal from their pod. The longing to be loved, and the ever-present knowledge that the sea will be there, no matter what befalls them.

From somewhere deep inside me, I ache for Storm. But that pain turns to fury at the crooked smile that lights up Dejean's face as he tries to stand, his gaze on the sea. I must stop this.

Shoving Murielle beneath me, I lunge at Dejean. I yank him back as Murielle struggles to get out from under me. I can't hold them both. But somehow, I have to. I have to keep them away from the water. I have to force Storm to either leave or to climb back on the boat.

My arms tremble as I fight to hold down both my pod-mates. A scream burns itself into my throat, rattling my lungs. My strength will fail. Storm can sing for as long as they wish, as long as it takes for my arms to give out, for my scales to fry in the sun, for Dejean or Murielle to break from my grasp.

I have to make a choice.

A harsh whimper escapes me as I let go of Murielle. Dejean already lost part of his shoulder to Storm. His half-healed state will put him in danger in the water, even without the presence of a siren.

I pull Dejean against my chest. It takes every muscle in my body to toss us toward the catamaran's mast. We roll once and smack into it. I grab the length of excess rope coiled at its base and loop it around Dejean, tying it off as quickly as I can. He struggles, shouting words I ignore, his panic and frustration clear in his voice.

They mean little, but they hurt all the same, his pain digging into me like rows of needle-sharp teeth. But I've done my part. In the daze of the song, he can't figure out how I tied him. Each time he strains against the rope, it tightens the knot.

Grabbing the edge of the boat, I heave myself into the water. Murielle swims in slow, sluggish strokes. Soft and enthralling, Storm sings her deeper. They move around her, circling like a shark, watching her every move. Light ripples off them both, sparkling in the slow stream of bubbles Murielle releases from her mouth.

I rock my hips and pump my arms, propelling myself forward frantically, but I manage little better than a fast drift. Any moment, Storm will notice me and go in for the kill.

Any moment.

But their fixation with Murielle never wavers. Lines wrinkle their brow, their eyes narrowed. Their shoulders tighten, each motion guarded, but they tip their head.

Murielle giggles, the last of her air leaving her mouth. She reaches for Storm, her fingers spread wide.

A fearful shudder runs through them, and their demeanor changes. Their aggression renews in bared teeth and hunched shoulders, their song turning to a bitter, vengeful requiem. As I reach Storm, they lunge toward Murielle. We collide.

With a shriek, I knock them to the side. Their teeth barely scrape the base of Murielle's neck, but they cling to her, dragging her down toward the reef. She doesn't protest, though her chest trembles as if forcing herself not to breath the water with every conscious thought.

I will not let her die. Not by Storm and not by the sea.

Using Murielle as leverage, I shove into Storm with all my weight, slamming them against the rock. They shriek, their eyes rolling once. Their remaining fingers find my gills, digging into the flaps. Pain floods my head and my mind goes numb.

Simple thoughts echo through the agony. I can't do this much longer. I can't fight Storm into submission. One option remains. One chance, and I have to take it.

Baring my teeth, I ignore the pain and the darkness threatening to consume my vision, and lunge for Storm's throat. They don't block me. I hit my mark and I tear.

Storm's song dies, and blood fills my mouth as their fingers fall away. I pull back, prepared to attack again, but it's done. Storm touches the base of their neck, hollow shock on their face. They tremble for a moment, then go limp.

My heart pounds inside my chest, aching in a way I've never felt before, could never imagine feeling. I don't want to look at Storm's body, but my gaze holds there, stuck. I can feel every bit of myself, from my shaky arms and tight brow to my tongue, which curls with the taste of Storm's blood sticking there like a brand.

What have I done?

Murielle floats through the corner of my vision, and I finally yank my eyes away from Storm. She's still conscious, but each kick of her feet is a little weaker as she flounders in the water.

I launch myself off the rock. Grabbing Murielle's wrist, I slip under her, lugging her along on my back. The rope attached to the catamaran still hangs in the water, drifting along the sand. It takes me a series of forceful surges to reach it. Climbing to the boat is easy from there, even with Murielle slung over my shoulder.

We break the surface. I shove Murielle against the edge of the nearest hull. She gasps, spitting out water, and clings there, her feet slowly kicking again. I pull myself onto the catamaran and drag Murielle up after me. She collapses onto the net.

"Murielle? Perle!" Dejean's shouts penetrate my mind. It sounds as though he's been yelling our names for an eon, his voice rough and quivering. He tears at the rope that binds him to the mast with red fingers. It falls away and he rushes to our sides, dropping to his knees. "What happened? Are you hurt?"

"Little, tiny bit woozy, I think," Murielle mumbles. "Just gotta lay here." She must be alright, because she sprawls out overdramatically, moaning like she's dying.

"Perle?" He looks at me anxiously.

"*I . . .*" The weight of what I did descends like a tidal wave. I killed another siren. The knowledge shakes through me, rattling my core. We are cruel and demanding, and we leave our own to die, but we do not kill them ourselves.

Especially not for a human.

Dejean reaches out to me, his palm up like an offering. The same motion I used with Storm. I breathe in and take his hand, squeezing it. I killed a siren—a good siren—a siren who tried to keep me safe in the only way they knew how. I killed them for this human and for the moaning mass beside him.

Again, I breathe. I should not have ended Storm's life, but I chose to save my pod. I can't regret that they lived. *I can't.*

A lump grows in my throat, and I pull myself against Dejean, curling into his broad chest. Stiffening, he hovers his unrestricted arm around my shoulder. Slowly, he relaxes. He wraps me up, pulling me close. His solid form radiates warmth, and I can feel every rise and fall of his torso as he breathes, every beat of his heart.

My chest trembles, tightening when I try to draw in air. There's something wrong with it, as though I'm drowning in the sky instead of the sea. Humans release their emotions through their eyes in a stream of salty liquid. I long for that now, to be free of the aching in my chest.

Dejean rocks me back and forth, like the gentle churn of the ocean, the boat bobbing beneath us. I don't want to let him go, not now, not ever. I need the reminder that he's alive, that he's here, that he's with me.

Reaching out a hesitant hand, I find Murielle's bare foot. She twitches her toes under my fingers, snorting. But then she sits up. She takes my hand in hers and presses her lips to it.

"You're a damn pearl, you are," she teases.

Dejean makes a disgruntled sound. "Aren't you engaged to my first mate?"

"I can flirt with pretty sirens if I want to!" she protests. "Perle doesn't mind, do you Perle?"

A bubble of joy floats through my misery. *"Never,"* I say, but I sign the motion for *idiot* instead.

A chuckle rolls out of Dejean, shaking his chest as he holds me tighter. "You've been rejected, Mur." His breath warms my forehead, and I glance up to see him smiling; a weak smile, but a smile all the same.

The lighthearted exchange takes away some of the pain.

But it can't take back what I did to Storm. Their body still floats out there, drifting against the rocks. By now the sharks may have found it, and if not them, then the little fishes or the crabs. I look at my hands, resting my head against Dejean's chest. I ignore the reef, and the body lying within. The ache in my heart already hurts enough.

I am to blame for this. But the actions of others led to it, the pain humans inflict on sirens and the terror sirens instill in humans in return. The worst of these offenders is Kian. Storm's suffering was one small polyp in a much bigger coral, to which Kian has added more trauma and death than any other.

I curl my lips, a soft hiss rising in the back of my throat. Running from her might save me, might save Dejean as well. But as long as Kian lives, the wounds she inflicts will grow, taking more sirens and humans down in the process.

Dejean runs a hand over my head, the quirk of his lips vanishing into worry. "What is it?"

"I want to kill Kian." I sit up far enough to sign properly, glaring at the line of the horizon. *"I will taste her blood."*

"Kian?" Dejean repeats the sign, an angry fist tapped against the eyebrow.

"Captain Kian?" Murielle asks. "She's the one who's got the fancy song-blocking instruments, yeah? S'been catching sirens and selling them—or their hides." Her ears go pink, and she dips her head.

I poke her cheek, silently telling her I don't mind talking about it. *"I was the first she captured, or one of the first, at least. I was trapped with her until Dejean found me."*

Murielle watches my signing for words she knows, but Dejean translates anyway.

"I . . . didn't know," she says. "I'm so sorry." Then her eyes narrow and she whacks Dejean in the side of his better arm. "Why didn't you tell me it was Captain Kian's *Oyster* you sailed into port!"

With a muffled whimper, Dejean tries to shove Murielle

without letting go of me. "It wasn't important for you to know! The more people who found out the *Oyster* had been in harbor here, the more likely someone would trace me and Perle back to this island."

Murielle grumbles something under her breath, making a face at him.

I interrupt her. *"Kian's a monster. As long as she has the means, she'll murder or capture all my kind. It was hard enough for us to deal with traps and poisons. With Kian hunting us, the sirens won't keep to their rules or territories for much longer. If Storm's any indication, there will be worse conflict to come, and death with it."*

Both my humans are silent, somber.

Murielle speaks first. "Then we've gotta catch this Kian and get rid of whatever she's got that's blocking the siren songs. Set everything back the way it was."

Dejean sighs, dropping his chin onto the top of my head. "It's not that simple. If she or anyone else on her crew knows how to recreate those blockers, destroying them won't do us any good. We'll have to kill Kian too, and the first mate she escaped with, possibly any others she's gathered since. It'll be dangerous and difficult."

"I have to do this." I lean away from Dejean, forcing him to meet my gaze. *"I have to protect my kind. They've been hurt enough already."*

"Then we'll help you." Dejean pats my head. "We are your pod, after all." He grins, his eye sparkling.

"My pod." I nod, returning his smile. After a moment of hesitation, I wrap my arms around his waist. Water soaks the front of his shirt from when he first held me, but it'll dry soon, my body with it. *"I can't comfortably stay in the air much longer."*

"Do you want to swim more?" He asks it softly, as though he already knows the answer, but wants to be polite.

"No. I'll go back to the tub." I don't want to see Storm's body again, at least not yet. The cove is my home now, just

as much as any place my pod resides, but I can't bear to swim in it with the reminder of what I did still drifting on its waves.

Murielle stands. "You both get up to the house. I'll follow in a bit."

She doesn't explain why she's staying, but there's no need. I can see it in her gaze.

"Put them out to sea. The land isn't a resting place for a siren."

"Figured that out myself, matter of fact. You sirens do love your sea." She smiles at me, her half-dried hair a mess of tangled coils sticking up at all angles. "Not that loving the sea's bad or anything," she adds before launching herself off the boat. She curls into a ball in the air, creating a splash that washes over Dejean and I.

I breathe a little easier as I slide off Dejean's lap and let him move the ship closer to our elevator.

These humans make a good, loyal pod. I won't let anything happen to them, no matter the cost. But I won't stand by while my own kind are hurt, either. I will swim this cove in peace for as long as I wish, and open our pod to all who need the sanctuary, siren or human.

And no one will stop me, least of all Kian.

[9]

MOMENTUM

I was changed.
    Therefore,
    I change.

DEJEAN CARRIES ME toward the house, holding most of my weight on his unrestricted arm. The brace lifts my tail off the ground, though the shredded half of my limp fin hovers a finger's length above the grass. The low sun casts harsh shadows off the building. Dejean's comforting warmth stings my drying body. I can't wait to sink into the tub.

I unlock the back door while Dejean supports me. Orange light shines through the water from the windows along the far wall, turning the metal beneath a brilliant gold and sparkling off the bits of dust that float in the air above. It lacks the majesty of the cove, but in its own way, it's beautiful.

It gives me pause.

I want my human pod to have a place in the cove. But they've made this stretch of land their home, and they granted me a piece of it even before I considered them my family. A smile tugs at my lips, and I lean my head against Dejean's chest, the pain of what I did to Storm drifting a little further away.

Dejean steps through the door, somehow managing to close it behind him using only his bare foot.

I snort a humorous noise through my nose.

"Did you say something?" He lifts a brow, looking

suspicious.

"I was laughing at your toes."

He huffs, tossing me into the air just enough to unsettle me.

I grab his good shoulder with a yelp and glare at him. *"They're weird! Little, stubby, wrong-shaped fingers. They—"*

Something crashes in the next room over, and I squeak as Dejean nearly drops me in surprise. He regains his hold, his fingers tighter than before.

"What was that?" I sign, making no sound.

He shrugs, his brow scrunching.

The floorboards squeak as someone walks across the room. My fear fades as Simone appears in the hallway, her blotched flounder-like skin unmistakable. Her usual cascading cape of blood-colored fabric swirls around her ankles, the matching colored feather in her wide-brimmed hat bobbing. She carries two large pieces of a broken vase, similar to the ones Murielle stores her tools in.

Dejean releases a long breath, his eyes lifting to the ceiling. "You and Mur must stop doing this! I have a doorbell and a front porch for a reason." He sets me down beside the tub.

"I have your spare key," she states, her tone unconcerned.

Dipping my hands into the water, I splash it over my face, letting it soak through my scales. It makes me yearn to dive in, but I don't want to deal with removing the brace in the confines of the metal tub. I set about unlacing the complex ties near my waist. Dejean and Simone talk as I work.

"When did you get back?"

Simone sets the broken vase onto the table, turning her nose at the mess. "An hour ago. The ships are still well away from the harbor. I came in on a dinghy, with Chauncey and Ynez. They're still in town." She moves forward, her gaze sweeping over the tub and settling on me. "I see you kept the siren."

I pause from my unlacing and hiss at her.

She tips her head, whisking off her hat. "It's a pleasure to see you again."

I can't tell if she means it, but she plops the hat on my head, and I decide the oddness of it is far more interesting than her feelings toward me. Why anyone would want a weight on their skull blocking part of their vision, I can't fathom. I take the thing off and spin it between my hands. The feather dances like a dolphin in play. Grinning, I set it back on my head and return to the brace.

Simone chuckles, then shifts her attention to Dejean. "What's with the arm? You're carrying it funny."

"You noticed," he grumbles.

"Yes," she says, matter-of-fact. "Show me."

He groans but does as she asks, unbuttoning his shirt with his unrestricted arm and tossing it to the side. "I have to change the dressing soon anyway." A large white sponge still sits on the wound, held there by long, white strips. The first few days, blood soaked through, but now it looks pristine on the outside, save for some wrinkling around the edges.

I unbuckle the poles on the sides of my brace and slip it off as Dejean removes his dressings. A dip remains in his shoulder, but the quickly forming scar tissue covers some of it. The speed he heals isn't natural for humans. It's their science that makes it happen, though Dejean assures me the knotted, off-colored scar tissue would not be any different had he let his body take its good old time. I can't decide whether I believe him.

It's an ugly thing that sprouts between the peak of his shoulder and the beginning of his arm, a mar against his freckled skin. The scarring bothers me little compared to the knowledge that Dejean won't ever lift his arm in certain ways. Because of my oversight.

Because I sang in his presence.

"Something took a good bite out of you," Simone mutters, examining the wound.

"A siren; last week."

Simone's eyes flash toward me, but Dejean shakes his head before I can respond.

"Not Perle. A dark blue loner, in the cove," he says. "Perle saved me."

"I don't know whether to thank them or scold them. If you weren't here, I'd have two fine vessels to my name." Her face remains expressionless, but a teasing edge clings to her words. "What happened to this other siren?"

Dejean glances at me.

"I killed them." It hurts to say, but it won't stop being true just because I deny it.

I sink into the water as Dejean translates. Simone nods, but her words are cut short by Murielle racing at her through the back door, a blur of brown in a red and blue swimming sack.

Murielle tackles Simone, throwing her arms around the taller woman. Simone spins her once and sets her down, burying her face in Murielle's hair. When she lifts her head, her expression is alight with something distant and happy. Murielle laughs.

"Elle!" Simone snaps, her eyes traveling over the scrapes Storm left on Murielle's chest.

"It's nothing. It'll clean up easy, don't you worry none," Murielle replies, grinning. She plops down on the table and it wobbles, rattling a pile of odd metal bits she stacked there yesterday. Batting her eyelashes, she shoves the medical kit in Simone's direction.

Simone's expression turns deadpan, but she takes the box and begins to clean the small cuts. "You should put a few stitches here," she says.

"Bleeding's already stopped. Why the hell would I want to prevent cool scars? No damn fun in that."

A huff leaves Simone's lips, but she says nothing further.

"Ask her about Kian," I sign to Dejean, poking my finger extra hard in Simone's direction.

"What's the status on Captain Kian?" As he speaks, he

leans in and takes a few supplies out of her box to tend to his shoulder.

"Not great. You still have that stack of maps in the front room, I take it?"

Dejean nods. "Of course."

"I imagine they won't be relocated unless Murielle uses them as fuel for one of her crazy machines," I grumble.

Only Dejean notices my hands move, but he chuckles and replies with signs I interpret as, "You aren't wrong."

He pulls tube the doctor gave him, now almost empty, out of the little drawer where he keeps the blood rejuvenators and squeezes the rest of its contents onto the scarring. From the changes I see in each daily redressing, the end of the medication means he should be healed soon. Healed, but not returned to the way he once was.

There's a difference between those two things. I know that now more than ever.

I still wish beyond all else that Dejean could go back to what he had before. Physical change is a hard current to ride. No greater than most others, but still hard to be sure.

Simone breaks up my thoughts by spreading out a large map on the floor in front of me, kneeling beside it. Murielle lounges over her fiancée's back, playing with her hair, and Dejean sits across from them.

"As far I can gather, Kian took the dinghy she escaped with and made it to this port here—" She points out the island nearest to the spot where Dejean first attacked Kian's *Oyster.* "She gathered a crew and a new vessel, offering payment in the form of knowledge about her song blockers, and then returned to the place where you left your ship."

Dejean's brow shoots up.

Simone waves her fingers at him. "Would I be here if I lost the *Tsunami*?" She sounds offended. "Kian arrived hours too late, but she's been tracking us since. I hid our route as best I could, working up through the northern lanes and around Soleil Isle." She draws it out on the map, and I track the area based on the little I know of the route. "We've lost her for the moment, but if the ships stay here, she will catch up."

Squatting beside the map, Murielle glares at it. "What does Kian want that she'd go to all this trouble over? She has those blockers, and she can make back the gold she lost right quick with them, yeah? Why give a week's chase when you could spend the time catching sirens?"

"Me." Even Simone knows that sign. *"She wants me."*

"You're certain?" she asks.

"Kian is possessive, aggressive, vengeful," I hiss. *"The way she interacted with her crew—with me . . . She must be furious Dejean stole me from her grasp."* In some places I use signs that aren't the word I want and in others I make them up, but it will have to do.

A mixture of confusion and worry crosses Dejean's face, but he shakes his head and translates. "Kian's controlling and violent even with her own people. Perle doesn't doubt that she'll come for them."

Simone nods once. "Then we'll have to be ready."

"Agreed." I glare at the map, the wide expanse of the ocean stretching in all directions, far beyond what this single paper shows. *"You said Kian offered knowledge of her blockers as payment for her new ship and crew? Are there others now creating the same instruments?"*

Dejean translates.

"No. From what I've heard, she's only promised it, not delivered," Simone replies. "She seems to have plans to mass produce them herself when she grows tired of hunting. My guess is, she'll delay handing over the information as long as she can, or else dispose of those she promised it to."

Dejean taps his chin, his gaze distant. "Does Kian have the blockers with her now?"

"If she didn't, my kind would have long since killed her," I answer in Simone's place.

With a nod, Dejean relays the information to Simone. Their expressions sink into thoughtful creases, tinged with worry.

Murielle stares at me, unblinking. "So," she says, her voice unusually soft, but extremely intent, "how do you plan on killing Captain Kian?"

Simone's brow shoots up. "You want to fight Kian?"

"*We* want to fight Kian," Dejean corrects her.

A shiver runs through me at the thought of what this means, for them, for me. Going up against Kian will be a dangerous undertaking. The hole in Dejean's shoulders might seem like a scratch compared to our state after the battle. If something happens to Murielle or Dejean because of this . . .

I swallow down a sticky mess in my throat. They are my pod. I can't tell them not to stand by me, not when I mean to stand by them through whatever trials come. Besides, I don't think I can do this alone.

"We shouldn't wait for her here. We'll need a place to regroup if we fail." I sign with slow motions, giving Murielle enough time to decipher what she can, and Dejean a chance to translate to Simone.

"Will the other side of the island be far enough?" Simone asks, her gaze on the map. She continues without waiting for my answer. "Fighting Kian headlong on the water won't be optimal. We had luck and surprise on our side last time, but if we want to guarantee those again, we'll have to make our own. There's a massive rocky outcropping just here . . ." she points to a spot of ocean off the southern coast.

"Luciole Rock." Dejean hums. "We can send Chauncey with the *Tsunami* around the far side of it. He should have no problem hiding the ship long enough for us to use the *Oyster*, and Perle, to attract Kian's attention and lead her around to it from the north. Once Kian follows us past the outcropping, Chauncey will come up behind her, cutting her off."

"It sounds like it might work." I nod as I sign, so Simone understands. *"What's my part in this? Kian is my . . ."* My

what? *My flash of panic in the dark.* I combine two signs Dejean already knows, shoving them together to create something new. *"Kian is my sleep-fear. I need to be a part of killing her."*

Dejean looks thoughtful. "We'll figure out something as we plan further. You'll be a part of this, I promise."

"I'll need to finish Perle's prosthetic," Murielle says. "Won't be any guide ropes out there this time."

Nodding, Simone rolls up the map and taps the end against her palm. "How many days do you need?"

"How many we got?"

"Four. Maybe five, but I would place my bet on four."

"Then I'll whip this shit together in two." A grin fills Murielle's face, and she springs to her feet. Pulling her curls up, she shoves a stray tool and a pair of pencils into the cloud of red. Not a moment after, she vanishes into the other end of the house and a metallic racket starts up.

With a sigh, Simone stands too, carrying the map toward its place in the front room. She glances back at me. "I'm glad he kept you."

The hints of pride in her tone make me smile long after she leaves the room.

Dejean leans backward, crossing his unrestricted arm behind his head. "Are you nervous?"

"Nervous?"

"About facing Kian."

"I suppose." A light tingle in my stomach confirms it. *"I'm not afraid to fight her,"* I conclude. *"But when I do fight her, there's a chance she might capture me a second time. I don't think I could survive that. Those first few days . . ."*

Dejean's brow tightens, a look of sorrow weighing down his eyes. He opens his mouth, but closes it again without speaking.

Sinking deeper into the water, I lean against the edge of the tub. *"It was our second ship that week. It didn't look like anything special, just another pirate vessel."* The words spill forth on their own, signs following out of habit. *"I was the first on board, as always. The net came out of nowhere, metal, warm in the sun."* The searing, terrifying sting of it first pinning me to the deck still crawls across my scales. *"I called a warning to my pod, and they fled."*

Dejean sits up. "They left you with her?"

"I told them to. It's our way, to let our pod-mates go down with honor. I don't blame them for it. I would've done the same, back then."

Again, his mouth hangs open. I take his hand, tracing the lines of his palm. He relaxes under my touch. His rough skin calms me, too, the little dark spots distracting from darker thoughts.

"What are they from?" I ask, pointing to a large speckle.

His brow lifts and his lips quirk. "They're freckles, made by the sun."

"Humans are weird."

A laugh rolls out of him. "I guess we are, yes. But so are sirens!" He leans over, running his fingers over the short rays on my head. "What's this supposed to be? Hair? A fin?"

"Watch what you're calling hair!" I snap, but a grin scrunches my cheeks and I flick water at him as I finish signing.

His next tease is buried under a crash of metal from the room over. He shakes his head.

"You might as well go help her."

"Yes, fine." He chuckles again, rising to his feet, and a moment later he leaves my sight.

I miss him already.

The noise continues all through the evening and part of the night, pausing only when I shriek loud enough to get Murielle's attention. It takes a grumpy lecture from her fiancée and quite a lot of glaring on my part, but she finally stops her work and shuts off the lights long enough for us to sleep. When she finishes the prosthetic midmorning the next day, she complains that it took too long and it's our fault, but she's bubbly and excited as she helps me into it.

It's an odd thing, and I'm not sure what I think of it. Murielle shaped it like a fin, made from the same soft fabric and lightweight metal-like material she used for the framework of the brace. It holds my dead and mangled fin within it, and if I pull strings in the upper parts of my brace, the fake appendage opens and closes as mine would.

But it's not *my* fin.

It's a dull machine meant to replace it, and I can't look at it and see anything but harsh ridges and unnatural shapes. It makes me yearn for my old tail; makes me feel emptier instead of fuller. But more than wanting my own fin to work and function as it once did, I want to function in the body I have now, without trying to change myself into an imitation of what I was before. If I change something, I want it to be the ocean, not me.

But I don't know how to do that yet. So I smile as I let Murielle help me into it. The elevator terrifies me a little less this time, but I sit at the edge of the clamshell long after it hits the water, staring into the cove.

No trace of Storm remains. Wherever they lie now, only the crabs know. But my memories of them linger, a dark, taunting mass upon my heart.

Dejean plops down on the edge of the clamshell. He scoots closer, wrapping an arm around my shoulders. His unrestricted arm. I lean into him, sighing.

"You can take your time, you know." He speaks the words softly, his voice nearly lost in the gentle rush of the water as it hits the cliff. He doesn't use his other hand to sign, as he would have before Storm's bite. Once all this is over, we should adjust our hand motions for the loss of his arm.

"We have two days still," he continues, "And if you need longer, you can have it. I know after all Kian's done to you, you want to help us confront her, but we'll take her down either way. Because it's important to you, we'll see it through." He smiles, his eyes resting on the horizon. "Just by creating this life for yourself and embracing it, you're already winning against Kian in the most important battle."

My words fail me, the warm ache in my chest too incredible to describe. Instead, I rest my head onto his chest and close my eyes, signing him a single motion. *"Thank you."*

For a long while, we let the gentle lapping of the waves and the distant calls of seabirds fill our pleasant silence. When I finally open my eyes, my gaze rests on a long, tubular case attached to the side of the clamshell.

"What's in that?"

Dejean smiles, his eyes twinkling. "Spears," he says, opening the case and pulling out a long pole. Attached to one end is a springy band, and the other splits off into two sharp points. "We're going fishing."

I snatch the strange hunting device away from him, my hands shaking from excitement. *"Why didn't you mention this earlier!"*

"You seemed caught up in the moment," he says, drawing another spear out. He holds it awkwardly, barely lifting his restricted arm. "It's not powerful enough to bring down the really large fish, and you'll still have to get close, but it should give you the extra distance you need to catch things."

I reposition mine in my hands. The whole thing is flexible but sturdy and longer than my tail and half my torso combined. *"How do you use it?"*

"Hold it in one hand. With the other, pull the band toward the spear tip and aim. When you let go, the tension in the band will propel the spear forward."

"Easy enough," I mutter. Most of the humans' contraptions seem pointlessly complex to me, but I like this one. I grin at Dejean, baring pointed teeth. *"I'm going to murder some fish."*

"Bloodthirsty siren." He shakes his head, but his expression fills with admiration.

Giving him one last smile, I slip into the water. I let the air leave my lungs in a burst of bubbles, the weight of my body and the prosthetic combined drawing me toward the sand. Holding the spear close, I reposition myself, giving a tentative beat of my hips. The new fin propels me forward. The moment I try to turn, it catches the water, dragging me off my course.

I hiss to myself, pulling one of the strings in my brace to adjust its shape. I feel the shift from the way it interacts with the water, pulling here, pushing there. Fixing my gaze on the reef, I try again.

This time it manages to turn the way I wish, but each new movement requires a thought process I'm not used to. It's a foreign way of swimming, mechanical, everything done in stages.

I hate it.

Sneaking up on fish is hard enough when I only have to concentrate on the motions of the water and the sight of my prey, but the tail distracts me even more. It takes three tries to get near enough, and the first shot I launch bounces fruitlessly off the sand a hand's length to the side. Grumbling, I realign myself and creep toward a spotty, brown grouper hovering along the edge of the rocks.

I draw the band forward and release it. The spear flies from my grasp, piercing through the grouper, and the fish streaks off, flapping about in shock. I surge forward. Recapturing it, I yank it off the spear and bite down. Its juices flood my mouth and I moan, letting the taste linger.

The grouper stops moving as I take another slow mouthful, savoring my kill. Colorful fish dart through the coral, and a pair of turtles swim in the distance. A whale's song rings out from somewhere far beyond the rocks, where the ocean floor sinks away to darkness. At the clamshell elevator, Dejean kicks his bare feet slowly in the water.

The song rises in my chest, trembling through me like a swell of joy. I push it back down. For Dejean's sake, I can be happy in silence.

I toss away the fish's remains, the larger bones sinking to

the reef floor to be picked on by crabs. My stomach feels pleasantly full, but after waiting for me all this time, Dejean deserves a part of the catch as well. Besides, I want to hunt something else.

Moving along the edge of the reef, I peer into the rocks, glancing through crevices and tunnels. Uselessly small fish dart away. A sandy-colored octopus stares at me, and I pat its head. It recoils, flashing to a dusty red.

"It's all right, I won't make you leave." I laugh, moving on.

The next few clefts give me little more than odd, wispy white coral. Holding my spear with one hand, I brush aside some dense wisps covering a crack that runs up the side of the rock and stick my head through. A massive spotted eel darts toward me, its great spiky teeth bared.

Yanking my head out of the hole, I plant the end of the spear against a firm part of the rock, shoving off it with my arm strength. The force of the push arcs me through the water as the eel shoots out the gap where my head just was.

It latches its jaws around empty water. Looking dazed, it twists until it finds me. I wave at it. It seems content knowing that I'm not trying to take its hiding place and retreats sluggishly back inside.

Shaking my head, I turn my attention to my spear. I shift it between my hands. It drags in the water a bit much, but the way I shoved off the rock with it gives me an idea. Letting my fin prosthetic go slack, I fit the spear into the side of the reef and propel myself upward. It bends, then launches me forward.

I aim for the clamshell. Holding the band in my mouth, I swim with my arms and hips, using the spear's added momentum to carry me along. I come up beside Dejean. Setting down the spear, I loop one arm through the side of the clam and grin at him.

"I see you're enjoying yourself." Longing seeps through his voice, his gaze drifting back to the reef.

I poke his limited arm. *"In a few days you'll be hunting*

behind me."

"You've been using that spear for half an hour. You can't possibly be more skilled with it than I."

I pull back my lips, hissing playfully. *"Don't question someone whose teeth are sharper than your own."*

"It wasn't a question," he says, a smirk lighting up his face. "It was a statement."

Growling, I splash him, aiming for his unrestricted arm.

He laughs, lifting one hand, palm facing me. "You win, you win." It's a humorous gesture, but it makes my heart sink, his other arm hanging awkwardly at his side.

"We both win this time." I pull myself onto the clamshell beside him.

"I don't think it works quite like that."

"It's how you do it in a pod. We all win or we all lose. It's . . ." I falter, the concept itself within my grasp, but the exact words still floating about in the farthest reaches of my mind. *"It's the reason sirens reject anyone they feel no longer fits into their original pod,"* I explain. *"We don't like to broaden our way of living. If one of us can't survive under the established rules, we try to change that siren, or we make them leave. But we could just as easily be changing the rules instead."*

One of Dejean's hands drifts over mine, resting there as he watches the waves crash along the edge of the reef. Finally, he signs, one-handed, "Our pod is going to be different."

"Our pod already is," I reply. And someday there will be more of the same, because I'll help build them. I pick up the spear I fished with and flip in it my hands. The rocks mangled its tip, perhaps beyond use.

I know what I want Murielle to build next. Not something to change me, but something to change the ocean I move through.

Leaning over Dejean, I shove the spear into his case with the other. *"Bring us up!"*

[10]

LANDSLIDE

In the darkness we flee,
    to each other's breath.
    To the steady beat of faithful company.
    To peace.

AN ALL-CONSUMING QUIET stretches through the dark house. Only Dejean's gentle breathing echoes in the halls, and even that trembles, blending into the woodwork. In two days, we will leave the comfort I've grown to associate with this home and move back onto the *Oyster*. The day after that, we face Kian. The thought sends a tremble down my spine, angry and fearful. I push it away. Tonight, it's still peaceful. I want to savor this time.

I let myself drift into sleep, thinking of Dejean and Murielle, and even Simone; of the many happy ways our lives could progress with the threat of my old captor gone. But my mind slips back to Kian sometime in the twilight hours. She crashes through my dreams like a vengeful current, impenetrable and untouchable.

She is the power behind a storm, suffocating and lashing, her fist against my jaw and her fingers around my gills. I thrash and scream, but my actions do nothing, and my voice catches like a hapless fish within her grasp. She is the darkness of the abyss, the sense that there's no up or down, no way to escape. No matter how far I flee or which direction I move, I hit the seafloor, and a swarm of white-eyed sea crabs rises up, agonizingly tearing away my flesh.

Worst of all, Kian is a captain in a gilded cabin with a floor made of siren skins and a desk of human skulls. The tub gleams its usual harsh copper, but for once I can feel the weight that holds down my tail, searing heat and then bitter cold. No water sloshes around me, only blood. My heart beats like a drum in my ears, a steady pounding that makes my bones tremble. Drops of scarlet fall into the tub. I look up to find Dejean hanging above me. His head lolls, his eyes dead as glass, but his heart still beats in his chest. It pumps between his ribs, mangled muscle hanging off the bone, dripping scarlet tears onto my face.

I burst awake, shaking all over. My chest tightens painfully and the back of my eyes sting. Just a dream. I try to find peace in the thought, but the terror of the nightmare refuses to leave, the lies it spun too ingrained to forget.

A soft noise from beyond the tub startles me upright. Dejean lays on his sponge an arm's length away. He turns fitfully, his breath coming in gasps.

"Dejean?" I whistle my version of his name. When he doesn't wake to my voice, I reach out a hand. But I think better of it. I don't want him to wake in fear, as I had, with his heart fluttering and the sense of a monster lurking, always just behind him. If I can change his thoughts, turn them to something soft and beautiful, the nightmare will fade.

I shift, dropping my chin in my hands. My gaze falls to the bandages peeking through his sweat-soaked shirt and my stomach turns. I shake my head, releasing a little tremble down my spine. I can calm him—if I find the right tune. There's nothing here to hurt Dejean but his thoughts. This time, my song will help instead of harm. I have to believe that.

Closing my eyes, I begin with a hum, a deep soothing sound that reminds me of the peaceful ocean at night, the quiet turning of the tide as sleepy fish drift in their homes. From there, I build into a soft melody: the light glinting through the surface of the water, the warmth of a shallow lagoon, the gentle beat of the ray's fins.

Dejean's movements slow and his breathing evens out. He settles onto his side, facing the tub. His fingers creep toward me until they dangle off the sponge. Laying my head in the crook of my arm, I take his hand in mine, holding it gently as I sing. His slumbering expression softens in the starlight.

A layer of sleep descends upon me, the song and Dejean's presence settling my nerves. I drift off. My dreams flit around me like a distant fog, neither good nor bad, always too far off to make proper sense. I wake with my fingers still touching Dejean's, and leave them there until he comes to.

His eyelashes flutter and a smile brightens his face as he meets my gaze. He looks more alive than I've ever seen him, his brown skin vibrant, his freckles like constellations of dark stars. The copper in his hair gleams almost gold, his curls springing in every direction.

"You slept well?" I ask.

He leans back, stretching his unrestricted arm over his head. "I had a very nice dream." His eyes sparkle as he sits up. "You were in it."

"I was?"

He answers by scooping up my hand once more and pressing his lips gently to the joints of my fingers.

It's a strange human custom, and I'm not sure what it means, but it warms me inside. *"What was that?"*

"Part of the dream," he says.

I decide I like this dream of his.

All through the morning meal, I think about that warmth in my chest, and the brightness of Dejean's smile. My heart swells with pride to know I helped him, if only in a small way.

Murielle and Simone seem affected as well. Murielle nearly bounces out of her funny one-piece as she slaps goopy, pink jelly onto a piece of nut bread. Simone's lips create their usual firm line, but they quirk up on occasion, and she kisses Murielle on the lips or cheek every time her fiancée passes.

Those little kisses tell me something about the one Dejean gave my hand.

The happy morning ends when Dejean dons a pair of slim, water-worthy boots. He glances at me. "I'm taking the catamaran around to the harbor so we can load it on the *Tsunami;* give you something comfortable to ride on while we're waiting at Luciole rock." His cheeks pinch in the siren expression of a question. "You'll be okay here?"

"Murielle's still working on my new aids. She'll take me down to the cove to practice with them when she's done."

As I finish signing, Simone looks up from the pile of Dejean's junk she's attempting to sort through. "There's a storm coming. You might want to hold off on the sailing for now."

Dejean shakes his head, opening the back door. A gush of salty breeze rustles his tight curls as he stares out to sea. "It shouldn't be in until late afternoon. But I would like a ride back here from the harbor, if you don't mind? Biking dirt roads uphill in the rain is hard enough with two working arms . . ."

"I'll pick you up from the general store. Mur was shouting something about turtle-back wiring earlier. I can pick it up for her while I'm there."

I click to catch their attention, waiting for Dejean to look at me before signing. *"Murielle already left. It's the last piece she needs for my aids."*

Dejean translates. He lifts his brow at Simone. "Tavern then?"

"Only if you're buying a round."

A robust chuckle muddles his reply, his laughter turning to a lighthearted whistle as he treks out the door.

I lounge against the edge of the tub, tugging on the little piece of fabric Murielle left my new aids on. Carefully, I pick one of them up. It just fits in my palm, the round metal casing enclosing a stone that glows a soft blue—a rare, newly discovered power source from the south. Murielle explained its workings in rambling, nonsensical details, but the information I did gather meant more than enough. The glowing stones are an important treasure of hers, unique and powerful, and she's given them to me. I'm eternally grateful for that.

She also mentioned they would become unstable if I connected the turtle-wiring wrong, and to avoid doing that unless I plan to detonate them. I'm not sure whether to be grateful or afraid. I'm also not sure why Murielle thinks I would ever want to blow up something so rare.

The front door rattles, jarring me out of my thoughts. I set the aid back with its partner as Murielle bursts into the room, her red curls a mess around her dark face. She looks grave.

"I—I fucked up, dammit." The words fall from her mouth like a cascade of water, impossible to divert. "I'm sorry, I'm so sorry, I didn't mean to, I just—I said shit and one thing led to another, and I'm so damn proud of these new aids, and I'm so proud of you, Perle, and I—I—"

"You what?!" But I already know.

"I mentioned you . . . mentioned a siren."

Everything inside me closes in an instant, numb and empty. I drop deeper into the tub.

"I was just—I was at the store and it . . . it all came out." Her face goes slack with fear. She cusses under her breath, spinning once, then again, shoving her hands into her hair. One of her tools falls out, clattering to the ground.

I snatch it with a shaking hand and chuck it at her. It sails over her head, but she looks at me, wide-eyed.

"I'm sorry. I fucked up. I thought I could—"

"How many heard?" I sign over her sputtering.

"I don't know. Elita and Florent and Adeline and the doc, and the Bisset family, and . . ." She swallows. "In a town like this? By now . . . everyone." She shoves her fingers back into her hair. "Oh, fuck. *Fuck.* I'm sorry. I didn't mean it, I didn't."

My heart races, panic burning through my veins. I distract myself by looking for something new to throw at Murielle. Perhaps I could launch myself at her instead? Simone charges into the room before I can decide. She takes her fiancée's hands, muttering something low and soft in a human language I don't recognize.

The breath they share makes my chest ache for the same. Trembling, Murielle collapses into her arms and sobs. Simone brushes her messy curls away from her face and straightens her back up, tenderly cupping the side of her head.

"We'll fix this, Mur. Together."

A space the size of an ocean seems to strand me. Murielle and Simone are my pod—my family—yet a hole gapes in my side where Dejean should be, and I look for him instinctively. A painful whimper rises when my brain finally connects to my heart. He's on the catamaran, sailing peacefully toward the harbor. And I'm here. Without him.

Simone glances my way, and her lips twitch, her brow furrowing in worry. Or pity. She pats Murielle's shoulder. "We can't stay here," she mumbles. "You bought those turtle-wires, right? Go put them in Perle's aids. We might need them soon."

Murielle nods blearily. "I left the bag in the car . . ."

Simone takes my aids and hands them to Murielle. "Then go work on them there. I'll bring out Perle." As Murielle sprints to the front door, Simone kneels at my side. "Is that all right? We can lower you into the cove, or bring you to a beach near the *Tsunami*, but we must leave before the town comes looking for you."

"*Leave . . .*" I whisper the word, my whole body speaking it in a distraught inhale. I don't want to leave Dejean's home— my home. A biting question forces its way out, "*Can we return afterward?*"

Simone only looks at me, lost. "I don't know what you're saying, Perle. I need a straight yes or no."

Closing my eyes, I let the pulse of the water pump drown out my fear. If the humans can't tell I was here, if we convince them Murielle's eccentric babbling was just that—worthless babble—maybe I can be safe in this tub after everything blows over. Drawing a deep breath of my human's wonderful, salty air, I point between us and then toward the front door. *"We should go to the Tsunami."*

Simone nods. She reaches for me, but I pull away, holding up one finger. I snatch up the stock of live fish from my little snack tank, careful not to injure them with my nails. One by one, I drop them into the tub. *Now it's a fish tank.*

A soft look tugs at the corners of Simone's face. I climb into her arms, relaxing against her broad chest. She feels stronger than Dejean, somehow, but she radiates far less warmth. A chilling gust blows over me as we leave the house, drawing pinpricks along my skin.

Simone's grip tightens for half a moment. She quickly relaxes, rubbing a soothing hand up and down my back. "We won't let anything happen to you."

I believe her. Human and all.

She sets me on a blanket in the back of the machine. Murielle sits in the main compartment, working steadily on the wiring in my aids. Her face pinches, but she's more relaxed than before, her hands steady and her focus unwavering. Simone rushes back inside the house, returning with my brace and a few sopping wet pillow-sponges. She piles them all in with me before covering the back of the machine with a long, slick piece of fabric.

The machine roars to life and we pull forward. I shove my tail into my brace and then cling to the sponges, burying my face in them as the metal beneath me jolts and shifts. Time slows to single bumps in the road and the sporadic thumping of blood in my ears. Then Murielle curses.

"Have they seen us?" She asks, her words met by a rumble up ahead.

"I don't know," Simone replies, almost too low for me to hear. "I'll turn off once I pass them."

The rumble grows and we lurch by it. It fades, then returns, just behind us.

"Shit." Murielle's voice rattles. "They're pursuing us now."

"We'll have to turn off anyway. If we stay on the main road with two trucks on our tail, anyone else heading this way will follow suit."

I hold my sponges tighter as the machine swings left suddenly, heading toward the coast. A bit of the fabric above me peels back, revealing thick foliage. The plants fade away and a human's house flashes past before the view clears to a graying sky that stretches for eternity.

Simone stops the machine and it goes silent. I still myself, trying to release my tense, battered muscles in a slow breath. Behind us, the other two machine roar to a halt. They shut off as well. Simone gets out, her boots crunching against small rocks as she walks toward our stalkers.

"What seems to be the problem here?" she says, low and demanding.

"We just want to see what's in the back of that truck," an equally deep-voiced human answers her, their machine's door slamming closed.

A human with a high inflection echoes their companion. "Shouldn't be a problem for you, should it?"

Another door opens, followed by nearing footsteps. "Now, now, we don't need to be causing any trouble, fellas."

I recognize his voice the moment he finishes speaking.

"Chauncey?" Simone's confusion strains her tone. She must be motioning him over, because he breaks into a jog. "Who are these folks?" she whispers.

"They're here off a small merchant vessel," he replies softly. "Kian offered a reward for some ghostly siren she claims she had on the *Oyster*. But I told them it was nothing. Captain Gayle didn't find any sirens . . . did he?"

"Hey!" The squeaky human calls. "What's that you're

muttering about?"

"We just want to see what you've got in your truck bed, then we'll be on our way," their companion adds.

Their menacing footsteps draw nearer, the jarring clunks of their shoes grating into my ears. I clench my fingers, piercing holes in my wet sponge. The truck shifts as Murielle gets out, her wild hair visible through the crack in the fabric covering. Her nearness calms some of the squalls in my chest. I'm not alone. Whatever these humans want with me, Murielle and Simone won't let them do it.

"Hey, now—" Simone's words are cut off by scuffling, gravel flung from the soles of shoes as someone stumbles. "Stand down!"

"You're not getting rid of us!" the deep-voiced one snaps, too close for comfort.

"Murielle," Simone calls over them, "Get Perle to the water!"

My heart seems to shoot me upward as Murielle rips off the fabric covering. I scramble into her arms, lopsided, clinging to her shoulders. She drags me over the edge of the truck, and my tail smacks into the ground with such force I grimace on instinct.

"Shit. Sorry, sorry!" She doesn't bother to pick it up, jogging away from the truck in a hazardous gate that makes me cling to her all the harder.

She runs along a gravel path toward a small, rocky cliff a good distance off. Behind us, the two humans—a lanky person in a small square hat and their much larger companion whose only visible hair grows out of their chin—see me and shout. They sprint toward Murielle and I, but Simone drags a sword from the main compartment of the truck. She cuts them off with ease.

The chin-haired human bellows with their deep voice and draws their own sword. Just behind Simone, Chauncey twitches in place, his gaze flicking between me and the stalkers. His expression shifts as the lanky one draws a small pistol from inside a pocket.

"That's my gun, you leach!" He shoves into them, forcing down their weapon.

They wrestle, their motions punctuated by the clashing of Simone and the chin-haired human's blades. Simone moves on the balls of her feet, shifting and launching and retracting quickly, staying out of her larger opponent's reach. They snarl as her sword nicks through their shoulder, blood seeping from the wound. Steadying themselves, they attack with renewed ferocity.

"We just want the damn fish," They bellow, slamming their sword down with such force that it seems Simone's might break. "We'll split the profits with you!"

"I'm not a fish!" I shout at them. Murielle and Simone know I'm not a treasure to be bought and sold. They don't waver in protecting me, even for a moment.

A rush of salty wind off the ocean prickles along my scalp, tossing my head fins and pulling up what little moisture remained on my scales. I glance at the cliff. Nearer now, it looks nothing like the dizzying elevation of the one near our house, but it's still a precarious trip to the water lapping at sporadic, jutting ledges below. A catamaran glides along the coast, moving away from us. *Dejean.* He's not far. *If I can call to him . . .*

But I lose the thought as a pistol fires. We're almost halfway to the cliff, but Murielle stops short, her grip on my waist barely keeping me from hurdling from her arms as she turns to check on Simone.

The chin-haired human still engages Simone in a violent dance of blades. Chauncey scrambles backward on the ground though, clutching his bloody shoulder as smoke drifts off the pistol in the lanky human's hands. He takes one look at Simone and her opponent and bolts for his machine. It roars to life and speeds down the road. The lanky human turns their gun on Simone.

My muscles tense, my whole body aching to fling itself to

Simone's aid. Last week I would've suppressed the impulse, but every pod-mate is worth more than my life, even the human who only joined us recently. I knock myself from Murielle's arms, shrieking in a way that needs no words. *"Go to her!"*

Dropping my new aids beside me, she flies at her fiancée. She hollers as she runs, launching tools at the lanky human with uncanny precision. "Get the hell away from my girl, ya bastards!"

The lanky human points their pistol at Murielle. She squeaks, changing course for her machine. They fire, and my heart stops with the same quavering beat that slows Simone's sword strokes. Murielle ducks behind the machine and the rear little wall splinters, a hole blast into it. I release a breath. Simone's attack resumes.

Murielle slips halfway into the machine's main compartment, grabbing something off the ground.

I glance at the ocean. Dejean's boat grows farther away, a much larger ship sailing across the edge of the horizon, perhaps toward the harbor. My hands curl around the small rocks on either side of me as I open my mouth to shout for him. But the catamaran is too far away, too far for the roar of machines or the blast of pistols to catch his attention. I need something stronger, louder, farther reaching . . .

Closing my eyes, I pull up my emotions from the last day: writhing anger, quaking fear, the pulse of pain behind my eyes and the weight upon my shoulders, and lastly, a soft, overflowing rush of joy. Pouring it all into one long, ear splitting vocal, I scream three consecutive notes.

All four humans stumble, the lanky one fumbling with their pistol. Dejean bolts to his feet, his catamaran swaying as he turns it, heading back toward me. My head feels light and my throat sore at the end of my deafening shriek, but my soul soars.

My relief fades as the humans regain their footing.

The lanky stalker raises their gun at Murielle once more.

She ducks their fire and her piled mess of curls quiver, a few strands breaking off. Three bullets: one for Chauncey, one for the machine, and one for Murielle's hair.

That's all the pistols hold.

The lanky human curses and begins reloading, fumbling over the supplies, their squeaky words met with clashes of metal as their companion and Simone continue to fight.

"Mur!" Simone shouts, the strong sweep of her sword growing frantic.

Murielle dashes out from her cover, dragging forth a long rope of wires. It connects somewhere within the machine's main compartment, but she unwinds a spooled loop in her arms to give it more length, taking care not to touch the end of it. She rushes at the lanky human just as they lift their gun. My hands tighten around the rocks once more, another scream building in my chest.

Before I can release it, a crack splits the air, followed by a sickening zap that makes my scales crawl and my chest seize. Murielle stumbles backward as her rope vibrates against the lanky human's chest. Sparks rush over the human like a swirl of lightening, their hair standing on edge. They collapse, motionless, the faint smell of the cooked meats the humans love so much hanging on the air.

Dropping the lightning rope, Murielle clutches at her leg. Blood pools through the fabric on her thigh, thick and red. "Shit." As she plops onto the ground, her machine's front metal hull sparks and erupts into an engulfing blaze of fire.

The cry that bursts from my chest leaves me in a whimpered rush of worry and stress, but it's nothing compared to the sound of horror Simone makes, the violent howl rising out of her like the ragged crash of storm-blown waves on a rocky cleft. She shoves the chin-haired human's blade to the side with the edge of her own and charges for her fiancée. Grabbing Murielle by the undersides of her arms, she pulls her away from the raging flame, ignoring—or forgetting—the armed enemy at her back.

I ache to rush to them, or to sing their enemy into a stupor, but my lifeless tail does me no good on land, and my melody will drive them all to the water. I do the one thing I can. Picking up the largest rock at my side, I chuck it at the human. It hits them on the shoulder, bouncing off and ricocheting toward Murielle's fire-cloaked machine.

They turn, their grip on their sword going lax as they focus on me, alone and stranded.

"I'm the one you want!" I throw another rock, then a third. *"All this excitement is making me hungry,"* I jabber to keep their attention, but my stomach grumbles at me as though to confirm. *"I bet you have a delicious, juicy heart."* If only I could reach it.

As they near, they tower higher and higher, a boulder-sized human with anger pulsing through their face. Tucking my aids into my brace, I scramble away from them, pulling myself across the ground by my arms. As I near the edge of the cliff, the gravel slides beneath my grip, refusing my hold.

The ocean's salty tang, the call of seabirds, and the crash of waves all flood my senses, but the edge of the cliff lays three impossible body lengths away. Simone still sits with Murielle near the blazing machine, much farther off than the approaching human. Farther from the pull of the ocean.

Its draw will be weakened for them—perhaps just weak enough.

The instant the thought hits me, I release the fear and longing welling inside, pooling it into a low, mournful melody. Mere paces away, the human slows. They shake their head, refocusing their gaze, and press forward. My voice cuts in and out, obeying the tremble that runs through my spine.

The human blinks, their gaze flickering to the ocean. But their eyes return to mine.

They loom over me, off-kilter. Tossing their sword to the side, they reach for me with a giant fist. A flash of panic snaps my voice, my gills sealing closed as I cover my face, Kian's voice in my head, laughing. She sits in a new boat with a new crew, hopefully days away, yet her past actions incapacitate me.

But her punch doesn't come.

Rough hands latch around my shoulders instead, yanking me up. I shriek, writhing in the human's grasp, and my gills open again, releasing a pounding vibration. The human shudders and stumbles forward. The ground knocks the song from my chest once more, and I roll, gravel and rock digging into me. I come to a stop an arm's width from the cliff, my fingers hanging out over the disjointed edge.

The human slams against me, pinning me down with a smothering weight of sweat and skin, fabric and hair. Kian crashes through my thoughts, suffocating me faster than any weight ever could. Her hands curl around my neck, her nails in my scalp, her heel on my ribs. She's everywhere and nowhere, her pain all-encompassing but her body too far for me to catch. I wither.

But this human smells different, stinking of oils and muck instead of salt and spice. They aren't Kian. Kian isn't here. Kian doesn't have me. Not yet.

Not ever.

I sink my teeth into the nearest piece of the human I can reach, finding the edge of their collarbone. Clothing fills my mouth, then flesh and blood. I grip harder. They howl, their hold giving way as they jerk to one side. Toward the cliff.

The edge crumbles, dropping us both down its rough side. Jagged rocks rise up to meet us, but the human hits them first, landing with a harsh thud over the uneven surface. Their neck snaps back. I smack into them and roll again, dropping to the water below.

It rushes over me, gently cradling, a ripple of bubbles fluttering in my wake. I pump my arms, rocking my hips with all my might. Not until I leave the immediate draw of the waves do I breach the surface. The terrifying rush of the fight sinks out of me, leaving my mind free to worry.

"Murielle!" I shout, swimming farther away from the cliff

in an effort to see above it.

Simone walks into my view, half supporting, half carrying her fiancée with one arm. A piece of fabric wraps around Murielle's leg, stained in blood, but she grins.

She waves her free hand at me. "I live!" She shouts down. "I got a piece of metal lodged in me. I'll be half-machine in no time!"

"What do we do now?" I sign it in a rush, struggling to keep my body afloat without the constant strokes of my arms.

Murielle talks with Simone in tones too soft to hear from the distance.

Repositioning her hold on Murielle, Simone lifts her voice. "Trying to drag you back up this cliff will be more work than it's worth. Can you make it to Dejean?"

I glance over my shoulder, finding him a few minutes' swim away, and approaching at a quick pace. Nodding to Simone, I point at them both questioningly.

"Mur's leg doesn't look bad, but I need to take her back to the house to clean it up. We can check on things while we're there, and then meet you at the *Tsunami*," she says. "Her truck isn't going anywhere fast, but we can take the sailors'. . ." Her gaze drifts to the body of the chin-haired human on the ledge near the water. "They won't be needing it any longer."

I nod again, signing a quick goodbye to them both. Simone stops me.

"Hey, Perle," she says. "You both be careful. At this point, it's better to be seen loading onto the *Tsunami* than to be too cautious and get caught out in the storm."

The dark, billowing clouds in the distance look ominous for certain, but the thought of humans forcing me off this island for good sends a tremor down my spine no gale ever could. If it comes time to choose between safety for the moment and a home for a lifetime, I would rather take the risk. But I smile at Simone for her thoughtfulness, then shoo her off with a wave.

As Murielle calls her farewell, I slip below the surface and head for the catamaran.

[11]

WRAITHS

The ocean is not sentimental.

> *It moves ever forward: current and wave and undertow.*
> *But it still meets itself in the backwash.*

SPARKLING WATER WHIPS by beneath the netting, the wind coming in strong and bitter, carrying an ominous scent with it. Though blue sky still lingers above, a dense cloud layer builds on three sides. I stare out along the horizon. Not a ship in sight—the approaching vessel I saw must be docked at the harbor by now, happy to wait out the storm.

Dejean shifts, his eyes darting along the coast. When I told him what had brought Simone, Murielle, and I away from the house, and all that happened since, he began tapping two of his fingers erratically. The sound echoes in my ears like a crab trying to chew me up from the inside.

I lean over the edge of the boat, skimming my hand along the tiny waves. The clear water gives me a good view of the ocean floor and the rocky slabs upon the sand. They're farther below us than the reef in the cove, with schools of bigger fish swimming along them.

"Dejean?" It takes a loud hiss to get his attention.

He jumps, losing his grip on the steering plank at the end of the boat. "Yes?" His finger tapping stops, but the tired circles beneath his eyes deepen in worry.

I hesitate, then sign the words, *"Why do you turn in the night?"*

For a moment it seems as though he might not answer, his gaze crossing the line of the horizon. Then he gives me a weak smile. "My dreams bring me to things . . . things I wish I could forget." His quiet voice makes my heart ache. "But it's long in the past. I've dealt with most of it, slowly, with Murielle's help. It's just the last bit that clings; the ghosts in my dreams, and the little voice that tells me not to reach out to others. That I'm not—I don't know. Not worth their time. Or that they're not worth mine. It goes both ways, depending on the day."

"I am worth it? Your time, I mean."

"You're a fish—you're *not* a fish," he corrects himself, "But you're not human either. Honestly, I didn't know what a siren was like when I found you. You could have been a beast or a god, and I hadn't a clue." A hint of pink fills his cheeks. "But then it turned out that you were wonderful and clever, different enough from humans that the voice in my head didn't care about you, but similar enough that I could understand the way you thought and acted; that I could see where the difference came from, when we'd talked about it enough." He pauses, swallowing. "And . . . and I knew you had been through something similar to myself, and the pain that came with it."

"You were hurt before, like I was?" I want to know who dared touch my Dejean without his permission, so I can rip their throat out. But I force the feelings down. Humans prefer quiet, tender nudging, not the fierce bloodthirsty drive I possess. At least, humans like Dejean.

"It's not a nice tale."

I give him a deadpan look. *"I've torn out more human hearts than I can count, and one siren's throat. We're going to kill the pirate who kept me captive for months. My tale isn't nice either."* I pause for a moment and duck my head. *"But if you aren't comfortable talking about it, I won't push you."*

A chuckle rises out of him, bouncing his shoulders. "I would tell you anything, Perle." He breathes out, his chest rising and falling heavily. "It's not worth the details, I'm afraid; they're dull and painful, mostly." His gaze drifts to the sea before us, but his focus is gone, his eyes seeing something else. "I joined a merchant crew as soon as I finished school, but we were taken over on our first run. They weren't the sort of pirates I manage—not even quite like Kian's, though the foulness in Kian's crew is similar. They murdered most of the sailors, slower than anyone should die, especially not the honest people of that vessel. The captain, though—he liked me. He decided to keep me, like Kian kept you. But some humans they . . . do nasty things to humans they think are pretty, or those they want to show dominion over. From me, he wanted both."

Dejean must see the horror in my face, the bitterness and anger rising up with it, because he continues quickly.

"He's dead now, though not by my hand. A freak attack by another pirate vessel. The other captain shot him through the heart. She took me on as part of her crew, asked no questions. Even after my mother died, and I went home for a while, she still let me join her again; made me third, second, and then first mate. She lives up north now, retired to a mansion on the beach, with her gray hairs and her grandchildren. The *Tsunami* was originally a part of her fleet."

My heart aches for him, for what he's gone through, and my fingers twitch, wanting desperately to do something, to make it all better. But instead I say the first thing that pops into my head. *"How am I supposed to eat this monster if he's dead? I can't eat bones."*

Dejean stares at me. Then he blinks. A boisterous laugh pours out of him, until he's all but bent over against the catamaran's steering mechanism. "Bones are a bit tough, aren't they?"

"If anyone else hurts you, I'll eat them instead." I'm very serious about this, and I want him to realize it. *"Bones and all."*

"I know." He brushes moisture out of his eyes. "I lo—" He cuts himself short, switching back to his original words, "I know. Thank you, Perle. It would be an honor to have my enemies eaten by someone like you."

I smile at him, my teeth bared, fierce but not harsh. Never harsh with him. I want to be thoughtful with Dejean, the way he is with me. I want to tell him things, truthful things, and be told the same in return, even when it hurts in the moment. I don't want him to feel that voice in his head when he looks at me. The secrets he shares with me are safe.

"Perle?" He interrupts my thoughts. "I think I know what I want to call you."

A little wave of excitement rushes through me. I nod.

"It's still Perle. But I have a reason now." He takes a deep breath. "You're a pearl because of your iridescence, yes, but you're also a pearl for other reasons. You're like the sand that you love so much, but when your oyster trapped you, you took the sorrow it tried to instill in you, and you survived it. You're stronger than any sand."

My chest warms at his words, and I give him a little grin. *"It took you that long to figure out the obvious?"*

He smirks in return. "Well, that and pirates want to keep you near."

"Pirates are all idiots." I dip my fingers into the water, pooling it into my palm, and flick it his direction.

He laughs, ducking out of the way, his dark eyes alight.

"I . . . have a name for you too," I admit.

His face lights up all the more. "Let's see it then."

I tap just beneath my eye, and then open and close both my hands, imagining the twinkle of the stars. *"It's for the joy that shines in your eyes; the light you've kept despite everything you've been through. It's intoxicating, in the best of ways."* If I'm a pearl, then a few of my luminous coats certainly came from him, from his incessant kindness and overwhelming compassion, from the warmth that spreads through me whenever his eyes sparkle—the way they're alight right now. *"But don't think I won't use the idiot version when I think you deserve it!"* I add, twirling our old sign for his name.

Every line of his face softens in a look so bright and tender my very bones melt within me.

"Sparkling eyes," he whispers his nickname. "Sparkling eyes and the pearl."

His words are met with a storm rumble too faint for human ears. Gathering my thoughts to more pressing matters, I glance at the clouds gathering above us.

"I should practice with my new aids before the waters grow choppy," I sign.

He slows the boat but follows my gaze to the approaching storm. "I don't think we should stop. If the storm comes in before we return to the harbor, we'll have to pull onto the nearest beach and wait it out." The unbroken line of rocky cliffs along the coast ahead of us speak for his worry.

I nod. *"I'll be quick. If they work you can keep sailing at full speed and I'll swim alongside."*

Holding one of Murielle's inventions in each of my hands, I slip off the boat and sink into the water. Beneath the touch of the wind, the waters hang eerily quiet, the minor currents shifting uneasily. I drop to the sea floor, releasing the air from my chest in a stream of tiny bubbles. My attention moves to my new aids. I'll call them tides . . . if they work.

They're small enough to fit comfortably in my spindly hands, round metal spheres with pieces of flexible fabric to wrap around my knuckles like gloves. The metal isn't quite so light as whatever makes up my brace and fin, but it gleams the same gray color. A series of little buttons trace along the sides of the spheres, a perfect fit for my finger's natural reach.

Flipping my hand over, I check the inside of the tide. The small glowing bit in the center pulses the vibrant blue that means it's running. I know little of how it works, but the core's rare power draws in energy and channels it to a concise burst of power—something not even Murielle's machines can mimic.

I turn my palms down and press the middle-most button. A pulse surges out of it, shooting me upward. It comes in a wild flood, and it takes skill to aim the tides, pushing myself in the right direction. I swivel my hips to help guide, still rocking them rhythmically.

I race past the catamaran, smirking at Dejean. The water rushing at me in full force brings a giddy laugh to my lips. But more importantly, I turn with precision, shoving the ocean away and launching myself smoothly in the direction I wish to go. When I near the rocks, the energy from my tides stirs the sea grass, and when I come close to the surface, their surges shoot into the air, throwing off my movement.

I swoop through a wide canyon and release another sharp burst, swerving to avoid a skeletal mess of metal and rope lodged between a tight passage. The bones of a long-dead siren lay across the sand within it, metal spines jutting through their vacant rib cage. With a shudder, I keep moving.

By the time I'm far ahead of Dejean, the power the tides spit out fades to a mellow ripple, not enough to propel me. I turn them over and check their core. It gleams a dim blue-gray, like a polished pebble in the sun. My heart sinks, but as I watch, the glow slowly returns. Relief floods through me. Slipping them off my hands, I attach them to a strap on my brace.

I flip over, my back to the sand, and work on the motion of my hips, waiting for the catamaran to catch up. Without the aid of my arms, I manage no more than a slow drift. I can accept that—for now.

From down here the approaching storm looks distant, the water not yet turbulent. But I sense it in my bones, a sharp tingle at the back of my neck. I watch the bottom of Dejean's approaching catamaran, checking on my tides in increasing intervals. They shine with nearly their original color, which should mean they're almost ready for another use. I hope.

When I turn my attention back to the surface of water, my blood goes cold. The catamaran skims the water just above me, but a series of small boats sail toward him from farther down the coast, dinghies and little fishing vessels and some other tiny ship I can't identify, their hulls piercing the surface. Dejean slows the catamaran, and I swim for it, using a few surges from the tides to help me along. Coming up on the far side, away from the approaching ships, I hide my body with the hull and peek out.

Humans occupy all five boats. A few of them wear proper clothing, dresses or breeches with strips of fabric around their waists and forearms, but the others flaunt the fabric humans like to swim in, small baggy outfits composed of fancy patterns. Many of them hold weapons: spears and tridents and nets. The unpleasant tang of the human's happy-liquid carries on the breeze.

It's a hunting party. But the question is, what do they intend to catch?

A properly dressed human with a head of black curls waves Dejean down. "My good sir!"

"Chivalry at its finest, aye Renaud!" Another calls, their bottle sloshing as they stagger against a shorter human with a spear and a swimming outfit, slurring out, "He's a mess, that one."

The Renaud human pays them no mind. He swings his arm in the air once more as his friends bring their single-sail dinghy up beside Dejean's catamaran. "Dear sir, mind helping us out?"

"Renaud Savatier?" Dejean's voice sounds light, but it holds an edge. "Don't you live on the opposite side of the island?" He stands in the center of the netting area, leaning against the top of his oar, his posture relaxed. He holds his restricted arm in such a way that it almost looks natural.

"Do I know you?" Renaud's brow scrunches and the human at his side smacks him in the arm, to which he grumbles a slurred, "Jaquelin!"

"He's the captain of that big ship come to harbor a few nights back. Dejean Gayle," Jaquelin says, so soft I can barely hear it. She tucks her brown hair behind an ear glinting with the ring of a woman and flashes a brilliant smile at Dejean, white against skin the beige of the sand on the sea floor. "It's a pleasure to meet you."

My insides crawl like a million tiny crabs are scampering over them. She carries a blade the size of my torso with arm muscles so toned that I can't help envisioning all the giant chunks she could cut out of her prey.

Dejean tips his head to her. "The pleasure is mine. What are you folks doing out here? That storm's coming in quick."

"We're hunting an oversized fish," Jaquelin says. "Sturdy gray-blue one. Someone got close half a week back. Said the thing's got scars already, fingers missing too."

The air refuses to fill me, leaving my chest aching and my head light. *Storm.* I did their work for them. I feel sick over the thought, but something else pulls at my attention. They mean to kill a siren, with swords and spears and nets. Only Kian pursues my kind like that.

"Hunting a siren?" Dejean parrots my thoughts with a laugh, but bitterness seeps into his words, and his bare toes curl against the net. "How do you plan to attack a siren up close like this? Being in immediate range of their song is a death sentence."

Renaud's sloppy grin stretches itself, and he answers in Jaquelin's place. "That's the mystery now, isn't it!" He drops his voice, as though there's someone he wants to conceal the information from, despite Dejean being the only human not in his group. "You heard of the great Captain Kian, picking off sirens like anchovies? Don't spread it around, but we got a load of her little mechanical doohickeys, on loan you see. Storm or not, we're gonna use them to get that fish off our coastline."

I grate my nails into the hull of the boat, closing my eyes

until my anger settles enough to think straight. They have Kian's blockers. Here, at the edge of my territory, hunting sirens with the very devices I want most to destroy. If only Kian had come with them.

I scan the faces on the boats, though I know I won't spot her. She's loud and brash and would have knocked Renaud down for speaking without her say. But my eyes catch on a different familiar face, one I've seen many times haunting the space just behind Kian. Kian's first mate, Theirn, leans against the mast of the farthest boat, most of his many braids covered by a large brown hat. His full lips form a firm line, his eyes narrowed. They lock onto me.

Ducking my head behind the hull, I hold absolutely still. No one would look for a siren resting casually behind a human's boat. But then, Theirn knows me, and he knows more of sirens than the others.

For a long moment an uneasy silence stretches out. It's not Kian's first mate who breaks it.

"What're ya lookin' at?" One of the humans on a boat near Theirn's speaks the slurred words.

Don't tell them, please. Let me be. Theirn never hurt me the way Kian did; his hands were lighter, his gaze distant. He showed hints of pity in the only way he knew, coupled with cowardice, hesitation, and small doses of something almost near to compassion.

The other humans all shift about. I can feel their eyes scanning the hull until a few of them mumble, "Something's there, see the shadow?"

"Ay, Thirm? Theon? What'cher name?" One of them shouts, banging the edge of their spear against their boat's deck. "You know these fish, yeah? You see one or not?"

Theirn finally speaks, his soft voice somehow carrying as though riding on the strong wind. "Yes. I see one."

The humans' steps turn to scrambling, mimicking the rattle in my chest. I lurch under the surface. Dejean transfers his weight between his feet, the netting sinking and rising beneath him. Pulling myself under the boat, I poke my head out of the water, just beneath him. *Maybe they won't see me. Maybe they'll move on . . .*

The tight knitting hides Dejean's face, but his toes curl. He yelps and catches his balance as the catamaran rocks, and the bottoms of Jaquelin's boots appear on the netting. She charges across the boat to look over the other side. I tuck my tail in as best I can, but the brace keeps it stiff, and my shredded fin trails behind me.

"Ha! I see it. A little light to be the one we're looking for," she says in a frenzy. "It's beneath the boat now."

"It must be a part of the darker one's pod," Renaud replies. "If we catch it, we might lure the other out."

More humans speak after him, but my ears ring, their words a meaningless echo. They want to capture me. They will pull me out of the water, like Kian did, strangle me, then roast me. Nightmares flash through my mind, with Kian's face haunting in the background, but I know these are real, memories I've taken and recycled time and time again. I can still feel the pain of them, the burning of the sun, the rough wood of the deck and the biting stale air, the pinch of the cuffs around my wrists and the heel of Kian's boot in my sides.

I won't go back to that.

I drop further into the water, fighting the instinct to swim out from under the boat, as far and as fast as I can go. I can't risk that. Even with my tides fully charged, I can't swim much faster than a human, nor the mechanical weapons they're are so fond of. Then there's Dejean. Can I leave him? What would humans do to their own kind if they know he's been helping a siren?

Above me, Dejean protests, but Jaquelin cuts him off.

"Throw the snag and circle the boats around! I want a diver with a readied spear at every edge. If it escapes the wrap, we'll cut it down," she shouts to her friends, before turning to Dejean, "Stay back from the edges. If it starts singing, we'll keep you from jumping in."

As she finishes speaking, a hefty wave crashes along the underside of the catamaran. It pushes up through the netting to hit Dejean's feet. As it continues forward, it shoves me into a crooked roll. The shadow of the boat vanishes, leaving me exposed in the water. A dozen eyes turn, just as many weapons following. My blood goes cold. I bare my teeth.

I sink into the water, but the shimmer of something below catches my gaze. Four of the hunting party's boats hold the corners of a massive fishing net, sunk deep into the water. They sail around the catamaran, pulling the net beneath me. Panic strikes like a bolt of lightning as the frayed edges of my fin brush against it. It rises up. Without a second thought, I throw myself at the end of the catamaran. Grabbing the edge of the hull, I pull onto it, choking on air as I fail to open my chest cavity the first time I breath in.

The boat rocks, and I whip my head up. Jaquelin rushes at me, hand on the hilt of her weapon. Tackling her from behind, Dejean forces her out of the way and shoves past. He moves between us, struggling to catch his balance as another wave crashes against the side of the catamaran.

"This—this siren is mine." His words sound louder than a gale. "They are mine, and you will not touch them," he repeats, firmer this time, his stance stiff. The hand on his lowered arm tightens into a fist. "Leave."

I don't know what else to do, not with the nets or the weapons or the threat hanging over us, not with my arms trembling against the hull as I hold myself there, my tail still in the water. So I do the only thing I can. I coo at him, a soft sound I hope he finds encouraging. *"I love you."*

His shoulders rise and fall and the tension drains from them, replaced by solid determination.

"A pet?" Jaquelin makes the human equivalent of a hiss as she speaks, voice deep and anger in her eyes.

Renaud staggers toward the edge of his boat, a drink in one hand and a spear in the other. "You're one of the ones

Kian gave a live fish to? Lucky bastard." He laughs, as though he cracked a joke. "How did you get it to stay? Thought a monster like that couldn't be broken."

"They shouldn't be," Jaquelin snaps, but she seems curious beneath the ferocity. "Did you really . . . train it?"

A shudder runs through me, my mind jumping to Kian, terror and anger surfacing with it. I am Dejean's pod-mate, not his pet. Sirens are to be feared or loved, never trained. But Dejean knows as much, and that is enough for me. I want us to come out of this alive.

"Lie." I whisper, my fingers aching to form the sign I know he can't see. *"Tell her anything. Make her go away."*

But Dejean seems to grow taller, his head rising and his curls bouncing in the wind. "Their name is Perle," he says, his voice deep and strong. "They're my friend, not my pet." Without turning, he points his finger in my direction. "You will treat them as they deserve, with respect and compassion."

I want to scold him, to tell him how stupid he is, how these cruel humans will never understand, but I want to crush him in one of Murielle's giant hugs just as much, to show him what his support means to me.

"A friend?" Renaud sounds confused, his voice echoed by a few others.

But Jaquelin's louder voice wins out, and the angrier companions take her side. "This is ludicrous. You're a traitor to your own kind, choosing the side of a monster like that, treating it like it's human." She lifts her voice over the shouts of the other hunters. "Take the siren!"

"Dejean!" The net drags me backward by my tail, yanking me away from the boat. I cling to its sides, barely keeping myself there. Something in my brace snaps, relieving a bit of the pressure, but it builds up again just as quickly. My chest tightens. Dejean turns, and I find his eyes, begging him to answer. I don't know what to do. I can't go with them. I'd rather die first.

He bursts toward me. A glass bottle flings through the air and knocks onto the side of his head, spilling sharply scented happy-liquid out as it shatters. He stumbles forward, collapsing onto one knee as a human—perhaps the one who threw the bottle—laughs wildly. Jaquelin draws her sword without faltering and places it against the side of Dejean's neck. He stays still. The look on his face breaks my heart, all the terror and vulnerability I feel inside painted across his features.

A trickle of blood wells along the side of his neck, but I flinch in his stead. My grip on the hull slips, and I dig my fingers in, shrieking at everything at once.

"Tell it to let go," Jaquelin demands.

He says nothing. His eyes never leave me as he lifts his hands, running them through a few familiar signs, one arm never quite raising as it should, "I am happy to have known you."

"*No!*" I scream at him, my chest tight and my head aching. The sound echoes through my ears. I let go.

As the netting drags me away from Dejean, the sound in my throat turns to a song, a high bitter screech that builds out of my chest, composed of a few brilliant notes. Half the humans sink to their knees, looking faint. Dejean is among those, his eyes glazed over.

Jaquelin is not.

She appears as fierce and resolved as before. Her blade doesn't waver, though Dejean's blood pools at its tip. A tiny device inside her ear begins to glow, making itself visible. *Kian's blockers.*

Jaquelin stares me down as the net caught around my fin rips me backward into the waiting hands of her companions. My tail is wrenched out of the water, along the edge of one of the hunter's boats, pulling the rest of me with it. A wave surges over my head for a moment, and when I come back up, one of the humans shouts in dismay, another three calling back in alarm. I twist my head in time to see the outline of a huge swell as it hits the farthest boat out. It washes over the small dinghy, tipping it on its side. Then it slams into me.

I choke, forcing the water out of my chest and through my gills instead. Whipping my tail around, I ride the wave forward. I twist as it lets me go and rip the netting off my fins, snatching my tides free of the brace. *Dejean.* Where is Dejean?

Bursting forward with my tides, I look for him in the mess. Two of the boats bob, upside down. The dazed, off-kilter humans still struggle in the water as others attempt to right the boats. Another wave hits them, and I brace myself. It spins me once and lets me go.

I can't find Dejean anywhere. The moment I lift my head out of the water, a clap of thunder booms in the distance, followed by a familiar sound: the strong echo of a song I know all too well.

Sirens are coming.

[12]

STORM SONG

A song speaks louder than words.
It's a moment come alive: a contradiction.
Love and pain. Joy and melancholy. Peace and terror.

THE SONG CUTS through me, piercing and bitter. It's not our usual love song, not the beautiful melody of adoration and protection. This song haunts with cries of agony that tear the listener from within, a call for the sea to consume and destroy for its lover's sake. This song carries no blessing, only tragedy.

I shove my head through the surface, using my tides to stay afloat as I search for Dejean. I find him sprawled across the catamaran's netting. He lies there lifelessly, the wind and waves throwing the boat about. My heart clenches into a knot, leaping and falling as he moves. He picks himself up, only to pitch toward the water, toward the call of the approaching sirens.

I shoot a burst of power from my tides. Catching one of the catamaran's hulls, I pull myself onto it and roll over, crashing against Dejean. I wrap my arms around his waist. He shoves me backward as another wave nearly tips the boat. Arms shaking, I grab onto his feet, my grip loosened by the tides on my palms. Dejean kicks me off.

The siren's song reaches a peak. They burst into the ring of boats, flashes of fin and scale. There's more than I have fingers to count, a group larger than any single pod I have ever seen. Some streak through the water, ripping into the submerged humans, the puffs of red churned away by the force of the shifting waves. Others leap through the air, catching those who remain on the boats and dragging them into the sea.

Jaquelin climbs into the dinghy nearest our catamaran. Her sword gone, she clutches a spear, the blocker in her ear shining as it protects her from the song. A deep red siren launches at her. She thrusts the spear into their chest, twisting so that Red drops into the boat with her. Red shrieks a blood-curdling sound that makes me yearn to help. But I ignore the feeling, grabbing one of Dejean's ankles with both hands.

Another siren comes to the call, this one black as the abyss. They leap up behind Jaquelin and grab hold of her shoulders, tackling her over the edge. She vanishes into the water, a deep strip of flesh torn from her neck.

Never again will she threaten Dejean, but the sirens streaming around me will rip him apart without a second thought. I shudder, tightening my hold on his ankle. A wave pounds into us, tossing me backward. My grip slides, the rushing sea peeling between my scales and his skin. *No.*

Laying on his stomach, Dejean uses the backwash of the water to scoot himself closer to the catamaran's edge until his shoulders hang over. I flounder, reaching for him, but I find no hold on the wet boat. He prepares to shove off.

I can't reach him in time.

The sea seems to toss slower as that realization sets over me. My body doesn't know how to respond, how to feel. How can I lose him? How can I watch them tear him apart?

I refuse.

Drops of water fall in a lopsided torrent, and the world bursts back to life. I try the only option I have left. I sing.

I sing to Dejean with everything I have in me. My tune harmonizes with the other sirens' vicious elegy, but it rises above theirs, soft and sweet and inviting. It harbors everything I feel for Dejean, and everything I've seen of the ocean through his eyes. I sing for him and for the sea: I sing of the love I hold for my home and the way he worked to meet me here, in this dangerous, turbulent, wonderful ocean.

For a terrifying moment he does nothing. Then he pulls away from the edge. Turning, he sits up, his eyes on me. His focus drifts, bleary, a hint of confusion crossing his features. But he moves toward me. When I sang to him last night a beautiful, soft look had crossed his features. How different this is, glazed and muddled, the twinkle gone from his eyes. But he comes. He comes to me, drifting into my arms as though he belongs there. I shove my tides onto my brace and hold him close, clutching the side of one hull as waves toss the boat. My voice remains strong and unwavering until the songs of the other sirens die down.

All other sound dies into the beating rain and the crashing water, bringing us ever closer to shore, and beneath that, the soft cry of mourning. The black siren lays over the side of the nearby dinghy, Red's head against their chest. Red's eyes still flicker with life, but the wound Jaquelin left them with is visible even against their scarlet chest.

Corpses floated around us, churning in the water, chunks taken from them, more bodies likely scattered beneath the waves or dashed against the rocks. Dejean is the only human left alive. Among the destruction, the ship Kian's first mate manned has vanished. The rain blocks the horizon on all sides. It could be lost beyond my vision or smashed into an offshore rock and drowned into the water, but I suspect he fled in time.

"Leave them!" A murky brown siren comes up beside Abyss and Red. *"They'll not last long. We must move."*

Abyss only glares at Murk, shielding Red's neck in a protective motion. Though younger and smaller than Murk, Abyss growls with determination, refusing to let Red go.

I want to help them, to do something for Red, but I don't know how to heal like a human doctor, and I don't have any of Dejean's green goop or blood-building pills. At this point,

I'm not sure if they would save Red anyway. I tighten my hold on Dejean, burying my chin into his wet hair. He shifts. His hands find mine as he comes out of his tranced state, but he stays silent.

"Fine. We will leave you too," Murk hisses, turning away. They pause, chin in the water. Their eyes flash toward me. No sound leaves them as a series of emotions crosses their face; first fear, then confusion, and finally anger. They call the other sirens with a long drawl of wordless vocals.

Heads pop up in the chaotic waves around us, the same string of expressions churning through the mismatched pod. Even Abyss stares at Dejean and I, a spark of hatred flaring in their dark eyes.

"What is this?" A familiar looking teal siren with black markings hisses. It takes me a moment to place them as the one who tried to help me escape Dejean back when I was still on Kian's ship. *"You are not yet from among us."* They say it in fewer words than the human language would use, a simple phrase of greeting to establish my lack of connection with their odd group while still offering me a chance to join them. *"If you are eating the human, do it quickly."*

If only they would leave it at that and sink back into the water without caring if I follow through. I haven't accepted their offer to join them, and this is not their territory to set the rules of. They should leave me be.

But these sirens have been hurt. For this many of them to appear in one group, hunting humans without any notion of territory or honor, they must have been driven from their homes by force. Only one person has the power to do that. For all they know, Dejean is part of Kian's hunting party. The hunting party they sought out and hunted in return.

But how can I fight them if I could barely handle Storm? The lifeless weight of my tail tugs me whichever way the catamaran tips. The cry Red makes breaks my heart, the painful, wilted noise of someone dying. Even if I could fight them—if I could kill them like I killed Storm—would I want to?

I wrap my arms tighter around Dejean, giving him a coo so soft that the crashing of the storm nearly drowns it out. *I won't let them have you.* I can't keep that promise, but it's a nicer saying than the alternative: *If they kill you, I will die at your side.*

The sirens bob underwater as another wave rolls over us, but Murk's eyes never leave me. *"What do you have on your tail?"*

"A human contraption?" Another siren asks, echoes of the same thought mimicked among the rest. A few move forward, teeth bared, as others drift back, fear trembling through them.

What do I say? What will they accept? There's no good lie here. If I claim Dejean as my friend, they'll see me as a traitor, and if he's anything else, they'll kill him.

"It is human made," I say finally, my voice quavering once. *"Without it, I can't swim."* I don't give them time to respond, their contempt urging me on. *"This human is my pod-mate. They're not like the ones who are hunting us. They have saved my life and would help me however they can. They are good; a friend of the sea."*

It's the same reasoning I tried to use with Storm. It won't work. I can see it in their faces, just like before; a moment of contemplation, then denial. I have to find some other way to convince them. Something. There must be something.

The nearest siren bursts forward, grabbing hold of the edge of the boat with a hiss.

I flinch away, drawing Dejean closer and shrieking at them in return. Dejean tenses in my arms. I can almost feel him thinking. If he would only turn and sign to me, I would know what was going through his mind. But he doesn't.

He pulls away. "You know of the human pirate Kian?"

That halts the sirens. Teal narrows their eyes. They don't seem to understand Dejean's language like I do, but they know that word.

"Kian," Teal hisses. "Kian hunted us until our pods were decimated. They drove us from our homes. What does the human know of that monster?"

Dejean looks at me, and I translate for him in as few signs as I can manage. He looks at Teal, holding their gaze with determination. "I am going to help Perle kill Kian."

Kill, and then, Kian. They understood nothing but those two words. The concepts echo through the pod, building into a storm of their own.

"This human is like the others; they say they are hunting us for the monster, Kian!" Murk shouts, teeth bared. They lunge forward.

Like a flash, Teal stops them, snapping over the noise of the sirens and the churning of the wind and sea. "Humans are evil, not stupid. They would know better than to say that which will seal their death." Teal's gaze flashes toward me, the pounding rain blurring the suspicion puckering their face.

"The human is coming with me to kill Kian," I translate, staring Teal down. "We'll stop Kian's hunt and destroy the instruments they use." I tinge my language with anger, a sharpness and vehemence in my sound and a curt drive to my motions. "If you stop me and this human—if you kill them—you'll be helping the monster escape."

Murk barks a laugh. "They're a human! Humans kill each other without a thought," they snap. "They're using you! They'll take the instruments and use them just as Kian has."

A response boils in the back of my mouth, but one glance at Dejean stops me. His gaze fixes on the red siren dying in the nearby boat.

"I have to help them." The rush of the wave that hits us as he speaks nearly drowns out his voice. But the signs he pairs with his words ring in my mind. The moment my fury fades, I feel the same.

"There's nothing we can do," I confess, though the knowledge hurts.

He narrows his eyes. "Maybe there is."

"*What—*"

Dejean cuts me off. "Have them bring the dinghy over, as close as they can."

I glance between the sirens and the quickly approaching shoreline, rocks spiking out of the water along the cliff's edge. What can Dejean do for a dying siren with so little time and no options? But that's not my question to answer. My job is making the others listen.

Lifting my voice, I ignore Teal and Murk and focus my attention on Abyss. *"My human would like to help your Red. Will you allow that?"* Every curve of my being and fluctuation in my tone speaks for me, a plead and a resolution all at once.

Abyss's stance immediately shifts, protective arms tightening around the bleeding siren. *"They'll hurt Red."* With the rush of the sea blurring their face, I can't tell if it's a statement or a question.

"Red's already dying," I counter. *"What do you have to lose?"*

The empty, broken look that slips onto Abyss's face is hard to meet, but I have my answer loud and clear.

"I want the human's help," Abyss says. The sound of their voice dies as Murk shrieks a shrill noise, lunging at the boat. Teal tackles them into a wave before they can reach it, and they both vanish below the surface.

"Bring the boat closer!" I snarl at the nearest siren. They cower under the water, but a sandy brown and a gray move toward the dinghy. With Abyss's help, they drag it against the catamaran's side. Dejean leaps over, dropping to his knees beside Red. He receives nothing more than a weak hiss as the siren glares at him, their face pained.

"The box, near the mast." Dejean doesn't look toward me to see if I'm moving. Carefully, he begins extracting the spear from Red's chest, earning himself another hiss. "It's okay, we're going to fix this, lie back." His tone takes the soft, musical flow he's heard from me. Red responds to it, some of the tension easing out of them.

Rolling myself across the netting, I grab the box and yank at it. My hands slip as it stays firmly fastened to the mast. Scowling, I throw it open instead. *All right, Dejean, what am I looking for here?* I dig through a rolled-up sheet of something silver and shove a few bottles of water to the side before finding it: the gun with the gel Dejean used to seal our wounds closed last week.

Snatching it, I roll to the dinghy with Dejean and Red. I glance toward the shoreline and my hands grow clammy. I can make out the ridges in the sides of the rocks, swells of turbulent water crashing off them into plumes of white foam. Another few waves and we'll be crushed as well.

I shove myself into the dinghy, shouting at Abyss, Sandy, and Gray, *"Keep us away from the shore!"*

They grab hold of the sides of the little boat. Detaching it from the catamaran's side, they push it back toward the open sea. For each tail-length they manage to drive us forward, a rolling wave takes us back just as far. Water sloshes inside the boat, and more fills it with each swell.

I shove the gel shooter into Dejean's hands. Behind me, wood snaps and metal scrapes as the catamaran hits the rocks, Dejean's precious boat shattering into splinters. I force myself to breathe in air, my head going light.

"I don't know if this will be enough, but it's your best shot," Dejean says, preparing the gel gun. "I can't do any more until the storm blows over." He holds the instrument in place.

Then a massive swell hits. Bigger than the others, it crashes over the entire length of the boat. The dinghy tips in the water, submerging. I grab a hold of the planks, trapping Red's tail under my body so we don't lose them to the churning sea. Abyss and Sandy brush against me, ramming the boat back to the surface and righting it as best they can.

Red still lays in the bottom, slumped in far too much

water for a boat of this size. They hold their hands over their face, trembling fiercely. Dejean is gone.

My heart rises into my throat, pulsing there with the scorching of the midday sun. I have to find him. If he's hurt, if he crashes into the rock, if he passes out beneath the surface . . .

I turn to leap from the boat, but my hand brushes over a little cylinder caught between the fabric and tubing of my brace. The gel gun. I glance at Red, their eyes wide and their body shaking. They won't survive. Every instinct tells me so. But I can't ask my own kind not to give up on our injured if I won't do the same.

Tightening my grip on the gel gun, I press it to their stomach wound and squeeze the trigger. Green goop fills the oozing gap. I don't know how long it will take to solidify, but we have no time to spare. As another wave rushes toward us, I grab Red and throw us both into the sea. I dive downward, avoiding the worst of the swirling water.

Abyss appears beside us in an instant.

I give them Red. *"Hide where you can. If you survive this, stay in the coastal waters. I'll find you."*

The currents still pound us, and a rock approaches steadily. I spiral out of the way, snatching my tides off my brace and putting them on. Manipulating a fin prosthetic would be impossible in a storm like this. Even with my tides, I can't begin to fight the waves. I have to make do the best I can.

By the time I steady myself, Abyss and Red have vanished in the clouded storm waters. I spin, searching for any sign of Dejean. Nothing.

"Dejean!" I scream his name, though I know he doesn't have the vocal capacity to reply below the surface. The strength of my body and the power of my tides feels weak against the coursing of the water. He must be worse off, with no knowledge of these currents and no way to breath them in. *One smack against the rocks . . .*

I can't think about that. I have to find him, wherever he is. Stealing the rush of the waves, I let them throw me toward the shoreline, riding their chaotic energy with minimal success. Unable to fight the water, Dejean would be somewhere ahead. Near the cliff; near the rocks. Just near them, not dashed against. After all we've survived, he can't leave me, silent and alone.

"Dejean!" My voice catches, coming out as a wail. *"Dejean, where are you?"*

I almost pass him, his shadow melting into the blurred line of the reef. With a yelp, I shove my tides up to my wrists and grab the underwater rock, pulling against it to stop from being carried away. If Dejean were a siren, his position would have been favorable, his body wedged into a cleft in the reef. But he's not. He needs air.

I reach him through the gloom to find his eyes closed, his lips bunched. Two jagged rocks lock his arm in place. I grab a hold of it, and his face twists, his eyes opening a sliver.

"I'm here," I sign. A wave hits as I drop my hands, throwing me toward the cliffs. Snarling, I fight for another hold on the rock. The rough surface scrapes my palms, a bit of hard coral driving into my hand as I find a grip. Ignoring the pain, I yank myself back toward Dejean.

"Go," he signs. It's a simple motion and he makes it with just his hand, shielded from the yanking of the current by the lips of the crevice, "Go, Perle." It's not a command. It's a plea, soft and gentle.

He wants me to save myself.

"To think I'd ever leave you behind." I grab his arm once more. Working my fingers around the outside, I shift bits of the rock away. I clasp his hand in mine, pulling against the current. The rock digs into his shoulder and he winces, but his arm comes free. His body lifts out of the reef cleft.

The water rushes him away, and I follow, refusing to let go for even a moment. We surge toward the cliffs. I pull Dejean against me. The rocky wall approaches out of the gloom, but one darker gash cuts through it from reef to sky. Wrapping my arms around Dejean, I shoot a pulse from my tides, angling us toward it.

Jagged rocks race past us as we enter a gash in the side of the cliff. The current fades into a sloshing pressure, and the water turns to a foamy brown. A faint light shines somewhere above. I drag Dejean toward it, applying power from my tides. We break the surface of the water, coming up in a small cave.

Dejean gasps in a breath, his chest heaving. He pushes me back into the water to reach for more air. I let him, giving him as much lift as I can until he paddles with me toward a rock ledge sticking into the pool. I pull myself onto it and drag him up after.

My whole body feels raw and shaky, my muscles trembling. The tunnel we came through rises like a tall, tight archway. Foam and water course through it, reaching the center of the little cavern. The low ceiling blocks out most of the rain, but a few open patches reveal a dark sky, the evening sun annihilated by angry, black clouds.

Dejean lifts his unrestricted arm, examining a vibrant red scrape that covers much of his skin.

"You all right?" I ask him, brushing a strand of his wet hair out of his face.

"Yeah. It's not deep enough to bleed properly, though it burns like it's on fire."

"Let me check your shoulder."

He makes a face. Not giving him a choice, I work the buttons of his shirt open and pull off the bandage beneath. A mess of scar tissue covers the old wound, the wrong color for his skin, shiny and warped. But it's still in one piece.

"How does it feel?"

"Tight. Useless. Wrong." He cringes, drawing in a sharp breath. "But none of that's unusual. I don't think anything's been pulled."

"Be careful." I glare at him to be sure he catches the

command in my signs, then help him back into his damp shirt.

"I will," he says.

A lapse of speech follows, but there's no silence here. The rain beats down above us, and waves crash into the cave before pulling back out only for their foam to shoot at us once more, coating my face in a briny mist. What are Abyss and Red doing? Perhaps, like us, they found a calm place to wait out the storm. The alternative makes my chest ache. There's been enough loss already in these recent weeks.

Slowly, Dejean stands, working his way toward the gap in the ceiling. He climbs over a few wet stones to reach it, and I hold the air in my lungs every time he takes a step. For a long while, he looks out. The wind blows rain into his face, his copper curls dark and limp from the water.

I make a harsh noise to get his attention. *"What do you see?"*

"The ocean." He plops down on the rock, his feet dangling near my shoulder. His toes are funny as ever, but I suppose they have their use when it comes to climbing. "There's a bit of cliff above us still," he adds after a moment. "I can climb it, if I go slowly, but there's no way I can carry you at the same time."

"We're not leaving," I demand. *"We're safe here."* Safe from the sea, from the sirens, from the humans. Here in this cave, no one can hurt Dejean.

"My ship is out there," he speaks gently, leaning down to brush his hand over my head. "With my crew . . . with Murielle and Simone."

"They know how to wait out a storm, don't they?" I retort, though I like his touch, and I tip my head up to nuzzle his fingers while I sign. *"They're in the harbor. You can't help them more than that."*

"That hunting party had Kian's blockers."

"So?" It hits me slowly, like a storm coming in, the incessant brewing breaking over what little peace I have left. I

[176]

turn, looking up at Dejean. *"She's here. On the island."* In the harbor, with the *Oyster* and the *Tsunami*. With Murielle and Simone. With the rest of our pod.

"I have to know they're safe," he says. "And if Kian hasn't appeared yet, I have to warn them. The storm might persuade her to leave us alone for now, but she might also decide it's good cover for a surprise attack. She doesn't know Murielle, but it won't be hard for her to connect us if she talks with anyone in town, and she's well aware that Simone is my first mate."

"Go." Nothing I can say will convince him to stay, no matter how much I want to remain at his side. Forcing him to sit here and worry with me is wrong. *"Find Murielle and Simone. I'll meet you at the house when I can."*

I hope he adds to my ambiguous words: *When the storm lets up. When it's safe.* I have no intention of waiting that long, but I won't let him know that.

He smiles, the corners of his eyes tightening. "Thank you." His shoulders loosen and he pulls himself to his feet once more. Standing there, with the rain against his back and his face in shadow, he looks down at me. He opens his mouth again, as though he means to say something. Instead, he presses his lips together. Making a quick sign—a soft, fluid one I've never seen before—he turns away.

My heart warms, filling my chest with a ripple of pride. But as his foot vanishes through the hole in the ceiling, a chill descends over me. I slip into the water.

[13]

SEA MONSTERS

Fear is a trench—it leaves two options:
  To swim toward the light,
  Or to sink into the darkness.

I LET LOOSE a burst of energy from my tides just as a large wave recedes from the cave. The turbulent water rushes over me. I shoot out of the tunnel. Another crashing swell sends me into a sprawl, and I use my tides once more to distance myself from the rocks. Their glow weakens, their blast turning to a shaky sputter. I should drop deeper and use the reef for cover. But I can't leave without knowing Dejean will be safe.

Surfacing between the swells, I search for his figure. I almost miss him against the muddled, dark brown rock, his body tiny amid the lofty cliffside. The rain beats down on him, blurring his slow movements. His restricted arm hangs at his side as he hoists himself crookedly upward. He skids, and my heart jumps painfully. But he keeps moving, slowly nearing the top of the cliff.

An outcropping crumbles beneath his hand and he slips. He slams into the ledge. The pouring rain and the crashing waves mute my cry, but I feel the knock of his head against the rock like a pounding through my skull.

"Get up!" The plea escapes me in a whisper, drowned by the water rushing into my back. It tosses me into a spiral. I fight to get out of its hold, pumping my arms and flinging my hips back and forth, panic driving out all logic. I need to see

Dejean. I need to know he's all right.

The current throws me downward, and I fling my tail harder. A jolt runs through me as it knocks against the reef. The wave rolls by, but I stay in place, one of the brace's poles locked against a notch in the rock.

I push at the mass of metal and fabric, my muscles numb and clumsy. Another wave cracks over me, spinning the world as it flings my body about. I need to see Dejean.

Frantically, I shove the pole until it pops free. The water carries me away, back toward the surface. I release the last bit of energy from my tides, breaking from the torrent and breaching the surface.

Dejean still lays on the rock. Slowly, painstakingly, he shoves himself onto his elbows and stands. He wavers, all but collapsing again, and grabs the cliff face. With sluggish, terrible movements, he starts climbing. Five more waves come before he makes it to the top. He wavers at the edge of the cliff, then stumbles forward like he's a fresh sailor taking to the deck for the first time. I can't tear my eyes away until he disappears from view.

He's alive. He's not well, but he's alive. *I must get to him.* Dejean will come to the house as soon as he's able, and I have to be there when he does, to know that he's okay and to help him if he's not.

Turning in the water, I dive through the oncoming wave. No matter how aggressively I beat my hips, my tail can't propel me forward in a storm like this. Every finger length is a well-calculated gain. I use the rushing water to my advantage, pulling myself along the rocks when I'm thrown too near to the cliffs, and hiding in crevices when I need to plan or rest.

I run through the power in my tides five times before reaching the cove. The sky has darkened to a perfect black, the sun gone behind the horizon. The wind still blows fiercely. A burst of lightning outlines the cliffs, followed by a roll of thunder. The elevator clanks against the rock, lopsided.

Putting my tides back onto my brace, I wait for the next wave and ride it toward the dangling clamshell. At the last moment, I catch hold of it, clinging as the wave crashes into the cliffside, the clamshell grating against the rock.

I hit the lever. Nothing happens. Then the metal squeals and the clam jerks upward, slipping from my hold. A screech rises in my throat. Throwing my body into the air, I catch the lip of the clam between my arms. I refuse to let go.

Gathering my strength, I pull myself higher, tossing my torso over the side of the clam. My breath comes in gasps, fighting for enough air to sustain my aching muscles. The clam rises in jerky motions, slowing and then jumping upward. I nearly drop every time it springs, my heart rising into my throat.

The waves rush farther and farther below. The slick metal offers no hold for my wet hands. I clench my fingers until the ridges bite into my scales, shark teeth holding me in place, agonizing.

The wind picks up, tossing the clam from side to side and driving rain into my eyes. As I near the top of the cliff, it slams me against the rock. Bits of the cliff crumble, falling toward the sea and vanishing.

Blood pounds in my ears, and I can smell its metallic tang from somewhere beneath my hip. I chance a look down, my head spinning from the height. A fresh wound rides up the side of my tail, scarlet tinting the water that streams along my brace. My fingers slip and I dig them in harder. Everything but the cut hurts. My shaky arms feel torn from within, my hands marred and scraped.

A terrible ache fills my skull, and my vision wavers. It would be so easy, so easy to drop. To let it all go.

The very tip of Dejean's house peeks over the edge of the cliffside. I won't fall. I'll reach the house—I'll be there for Dejean, and for Murielle and Simone too.

Another gust of wind assaults the clamshell. I swing

toward land and let go, hoping for the best. The air rushes over me, my stomach rising into my throat. I sail past the cliff, tumbling over mud and rock. The force of the jump and the slick ground send me barreling halfway to the house before I finally slow to a stop.

I lay there, concentrating on breathing in and then out again. The pain throughout my body fades into a worn, stiff ache. I must be bruised all over.

The house appears empty, no foreign machines out front, no townspeople howling for siren blood—at least not anymore. No Dejean, and no Murielle or Simone. But they might be on their way now.

Pushing myself onto my elbows, I crawl toward the house. Mud coats me from the back of my head down to the tip of my tail. The relentless rain washes some of it off as I lie before the back door, staring at the knob. My vision wavers the longer I look up, my bleeding tail pulling me into the dark.

But I refuse to fade out here, with my tub one stupid human wall away.

I force my chest up until the blackness takes me, floundering for the knob. The back of my hand whacks into the metal, and I grasp the handle and turn it. It opens.

Limp with relief, I drop my head to the ground. Slowly, my sight returns. A groan rolls out of me as my eyes land on the tub. I want to be in it. I want to relax onto the sponge and sleep for a week.

Crawling my way into the house, I knock the door closed and wiggle into the tub. The mud drifts off as I soak there, listening to the beating of the rain and the whip of the wind. I should check on my tail wound; the tub water smells faintly of blood. But it can wait a moment. *It can wait . . .*

A crash from the front door startles me awake. I jerk to attention, my head spinning. My gaze moves to my tail. The wound sealed while I dozed, but enough blood seeped out that my head still spins, my limbs heavy. Another bang echoes through the house, and my heart speeds up.

Dejean? He wouldn't use the front door, nor would Murielle. Simone then, perhaps? Or it could be the storm, tossing a tree branch into the windows. But a darker fear looms in the back of my mind. Kian's first mate, Theirn. There was the chance he escaped before the sirens arrived. He could have taken notice of Dejean and hunted out directions to his home.

I swallow my fear as I wait, the rattling of the storm fading and returning in a chaotic rhythm as the wind shifts direction. The crash comes again, accompanied by the snapping of wood. The rain suddenly sounds near and vibrant, a torrent rushing in from the front of the house. Footsteps follow, light leather boots. My body fights me, unsure whether to sink into the tub or hide among the junk. I'm not given time to choose.

A figure appears in the dark entry to the room, lit by a burst of lightning from behind. A cloak covers them, similar to Simone's, but a smaller, featherless hat sits upon their head. The fabric falling around their leather boots twirls in the wind, and a feminine snort breaches the crashing rain.

"There you are."

My heart stops. *No. Not here. She can't be here. She can't—*

I hiss at Kian. The sharp, fierce sound boils out of anger and loathing, but it drains away quickly, caught by the strangling sensation in my chest and the trembles running down my spine. Seeing her again feels like having every good thing stripped away. A dreadful doom smothers me. Even with the nightmares and the ghosts, somehow I had forgotten that I feared her so completely, that her mere presence hurt this much. The terror must have been a part of me then, a constant force clinging to my soul. But now I've known something better.

I will not let her take me.

"Get out," I snarl, though my words mean nothing to her.

She laughs, and the faint lines of a smile show on her lips as another strike of lightning flashes at the front of the house. "You're bold again. How cute." Her voice implies something different altogether; a malicious jibe encased in bitterness, a sound that matches the familiar pain of her fist against my face. She takes a step toward me.

My body freezes, unresponsive to the panic that runs through my mind. I have to move. I have to get away from her. Forcing my muscles to work, I slip to the back of the tub.

Kian walks smoothly toward me. She hums and flicks the light switch near the door. Only three of the glass lamps shudder to life, and they drift in and out, matching the reverberation of the storm. In their faded glow, the sharp lines of Kian's features stand out, her black hair pulled into a low bun at the nape of her neck. The jagged scar across her left jawline casts a weak shadow on her skin.

"Look at that. Gayle's trying to help you swim again, isn't he? It's a fun little contraption, I'll give him that." She stalks to the edge of the tub, stopping there to look me over. "I hear he let you back into the sea," she muses, as though talking to herself, as though I'm not worth a reply. "How did he manage to change you? He must have exploited my previous attempts. But no . . . no, that's not right, is it?" Her eyes move over me once more, and bounce along the tub, to the sponge Dejean sleeps on and the tank where he keeps my fish. "He built off my work, yes. He used your weakness to convince you he cared. He offered you more than I did, and you thought it meant something. He manipulated you. Clever."

"No." I flinch away from her words as though they can physically harm me. She spouts only lies, trying to stir up my doubts. Dejean would never take advantage of me. He's not like Kian. He cares. And Murielle—she's kind and vibrant and honest. Mur wouldn't go along with something like that.

They're my pod.

I won't let Kian turn me against Dejean, but there's still a tingle in my back of my mind, telling me she's right, that I'm alone, unwanted. It's the same voice Dejean hears, taunting and demeaning. No matter how strongly I know the truth, I can't ignore it. It tugs at my nerves even as I bash it down. Glaring at Kian, I wrap my arms around myself.

She narrows her eyes. Laughter spills out of her, harsh and cruel. "Do you actually care about this man?" she asks. "He may treat you better than you deserve, but he holds no real affection for you. He's lost people to your kind, just like all sailors."

"No." I shake my head furiously. *"That's nothing but an assumption."* Dejean doesn't begrudge me like the other humans.

"You think I'm making this up?" Kian lifts her brows, and her scar twitches. "I saw his father die in the same siren attack as my own parents." She snarls her last few words, stepping around the side of the tub with the poise of a predator.

Part of me almost believes her, as irrational as it is. *What if it's not so irrational after all?* The little voice in my head sparks up again. Maybe he held it back because he didn't want to raise my suspicions. Because he didn't want to risk losing control over me.

But Kian's claim can't be true. Dejean would have told me if he had lost his father to sirens, wouldn't he? Dread curls in my gut. He never spoke of his father, even when he mentioned his past. Maybe it's true. Maybe he was hiding it from me.

My attention snaps back to Kian as she continues around the side of the tub. I move away from her in shaky, stiff motions, my body refusing to work as it should. *"Get out,"* I repeat my earlier words, low and panicked this time.

"You don't want me here, I know," Kian says. "And I will leave. But not without you." She doesn't follow me around the edge of the tub. Instead, she squats down, drawing something out of her pocket. "You remember this, don't you?" Between her fingers rests a little rectangle. She flips the top of it open, and a spark of lightning jumps between two wires that stick out like spines.

I can feel the blood drain from my face, a tingle running along my skin. I thought she had lost it after the first week.

"This voltage won't kill you, of course. But you know how unpleasant its shock can be in the water." She smiles in an all too familiar way that makes my insides turn to ice.

I can't stay in the water. Though she holds it far above the tub, the excruciating shock of the lightning already tingles on my skin, threatening to draw my gills closed and force the air from my lungs, to make my organs curl and burst. But moving to the floor means letting go of my only advantage.

My hands shake, and I can't pull my gaze away from Kian's sparker. Every muscle in my body clams up, resisting motion, my scales clinging to the water. But I move on fear alone, edging toward Dejean's sponge. I watch Kian, wait for her to lower the sparker to the water, to tell me how stupid I was to think I could escape the punishment. Her arm dips. Panic floods through me and I move faster, yanking myself out of the tub in a gasping rush.

Kian grins, letting the spark dance between the wires of her device again. Shuddering, I turn my face away and dig my hands into Dejean's fabric. The tub's water still clings to me. The thought of losing it makes my scales itch, but it's nothing compared to the burn Kian's sparker can inflict when I'm wet. Twisting along Dejean's sponge, I let the water seep away.

Kian shoves the sparker back into her pocket with a snort. Her smile quickly forms again, vicious and terrifying. She prowls toward me.

Scrambling onto my elbows, I snarl at her. My vision swims, black spots invading from the sides. I drop back onto the sponge, trying not to look vulnerable. One corner of my wound seeps fresh blood, soaking through my damp brace. I feel faint again; from fear or blood loss or both, I don't know. My gaze shifts to the little drawer furnishing beside the back door, but Kian steals my attention.

She moves toward me, her brows pulled together. "You don't have to fight this," her words are unreasonably soft, the sort I've not heard from her before. Somehow this is worse than her usual tone, like an endless void stretching beyond my reach, cutting me off from the rest of the world. "You don't need to resist me," she says. "I can be kind too, if you give me a reason."

I don't know what her concept of kindness is, but it is not the same as Dejean or Murielle's. It isn't real.

For once my anger adds to my fear, rising a deafening hiss in my chest. I bare my teeth, tensing every muscle in my body. But darkness still clings to the edges of my vision, weighing me down, slowing my movements. If I'm to fight, I need to be awake. Kian stands between me and the furniture with the little drawers. If I can only get close enough . . .

Shoving off Dejean's sponge, I burst toward it.

Kian tackles me as I leap, forcing me to the ground with her hips. We roll once. I snap at her skin, but it slips out of reach. I try to dig my nails into her arm and she twists like an eel, moving from my grasp without letting me go. The world drifts in a fog of color and darkness, the flickering of the lights and the beating of the rain adding to the dreamlike haze.

Kian's elbow rams into my shoulder. A burst of pain follows, and my vision grows darker as I fight to breathe. She slams me against the ground and twists until she's on top of me. Her hands come to my mouth and nose, squeezing them shut. I grab at her arms, but I don't have the strength left to both claw her and gulp against her hold at the same time. My chest tightens, lungs empty, and my gills burn, pleading to be used. But I have nothing to push through them, nothing to offer.

The abyss of darkness rises around me, pulling me down. My body seems to give away, my back crumpling into the floor as the ceiling spins into itself. My fingers trail over Kian's wrists, but they're too distant, almost intangible.

"Give in," Kian whispers, her words echoing. "You can make the pain go away."

I squirm harder, my body crying out for something, anything to keep me conscious for one more moment. Compared to this pain, any version of kindness Kian might offer seems reasonable. The inner voice taunts me, competing with my mind as I scream for air.

Dejean isn't here. Dejean doesn't care. He's using you, just like Kian. The thoughts feel smothering, the world beyond them fading in and out, a blurring mess of truths I can't reach. The rush of the ocean echoes in my head, blood pumping through my ears as I drift off. The sea. I love the sea. And I love Dejean, whatever his reasons for helping me. He's been kind, and asked nothing in return. He is not Kian.

I let myself go limp, closing my eyes.

Kian's hold on me loosens. Air returns to my chest, and it's all I can do to breathe in tiny, subtle gasps. I relax further, as though I'm struggling to regain consciousness. My senses feel dazed enough that I think perhaps I am, but the fierce sting from my gills makes up for it, like a vibrant slash of color in a sea of gray.

My fingers brush the side of a metal object; One of the tubes that makes faraway things close. I give myself another few breaths. Grabbing the tube, I smash it into the side of Kian's head. She howls, her body falling away from me as she brings a hand to her head.

I lunge at the drawers. My vision slips, my fingers bashing into the wood. The ocean pounds through my ears again, but I hear the grinding of my nails beneath it. I grab the top two draws, yanking them free. Their contents spill onto the floor with a distant clatter. I think some of them hit me, but I feel the effect after it happens, an awkward disconnect between my blurred vision and my other senses.

Kian's boots echo: behind me, around me, through me, I can't tell anymore. I swear I feel her breath chill my neck, but it's only a stray gust through a window banging open. I grope across the ground, my hands hitting trinkets and bandages and little circular bottles. I knock over a small box, and round pills spill out, about the shape and size of the blood replenishers that saved Dejean after Storm bit him. Shoving two in my mouth, I swallow them before they can disintegrate.

I feel no different.

Kian's boot slams into my ribs, shooting knives through my chest. I fall onto my side and wrap my arms over my head, pain spreading from the area in flaming pulses. She repeats the kick twice more, working strangled cries out of my lips. Once she stops, I whimper and go still.

Kian's hand grips the back of my neck, pulling me upward. She scoops her other arm under me, and my head spins as she lifts. It's the same position Dejean carries me in, but from him it feels safe, considerate, dignified. Kian's grip is like a cage, her every movement bruising. I think she leaves my tail to dangle, but I'm not sure. I can see nothing but a blur and flashes of the house in between darkness.

I make out the shifting lines of the front door, and suddenly the rain pelts me like tiny wet rocks. Thunder cracks in the distance, but the shadowed form of the house's peaked top hides the flash of light that follows. I want to reach for it, to pull myself back somehow. But I manage only a weak lift of my fingers before the darkness takes me again.

I hit the seat of Kian's land machine with such a thud that my senses return for a moment, blood pounding in my head. Kian looms over me. I struggle as she wraps a box of wire over my mouth, knocking her back with my hands. She grabs those next, locking them in a set of metal cuffs.

A new dose of fear washes over me as they bite into my skin, cold and heavy. I won't go back there. I won't let her chain me to that tub again, away from the ocean, away from my pod. But I don't know how to fight her like this, barely hanging on to consciousness. It's all I can do to keep from blacking out.

Kian leans forward, brushing a thumb along my forehead. "If you had been obedient to me, as you are with Dejean, you could have had everything you wanted. We could have both won," she says, her words soft yet seething with bitterness. She shoves my head away. "But you were selfish. You made me work for it," she spits, turning.

The rain clashes against the top of the metal machine, covering her footsteps. I drift, woken by one door slamming closed and the other yanking open, as though both happen simultaneously. Time means little. The machine roars to life, rolling back before shooting forward. It bumps along the ground, tossing me in the seat. I do my best to close my eyes and ignore it. I will survive this. It's just a ride, like the one I took with Dejean the day he first brought me to his house.

But it doesn't feel as simple as that. It feels like my muscles are being peeled off the bone as each joint shakes apart. It feels like my ears are being pushed to their limits with the shrill noise of the machine and the clatter of the water falling from the sky. It feels like fear.

Very soon, I dry out. I itch and burn all over, the raw rims of my gills agonizing. Even the saltless rain outside calls to me. I close my eyes and try to fix my attention on an escape plan. Nothing will stick in my mind long enough to make sense. When I can think, I'm pulled back to the pain spreading throughout my body everywhere above my vacant tail, darkness stretching between one moment and the next.

Lights appear, hazy behind my eyelids. I force them open to the blurred lines of buildings. Glowing yellow orbs hang from poles along the street, forming halos out of the pouring rain. *The harbor?* The streets are empty of life, but for a single form standing in the shadow of a tall truck, one arm dangling. I squint, looking for a face in the darkness. Instead, it's the void that comes for me.

I jerk awake again, my head clearer this time. Tree branches and black clouds cover the stars, my muddled surroundings an endless stream of thick foliage. Gone is the harbor. We're going somewhere else, deeper into the island, or perhaps all the way across it.

The searing pain of my dried-out state distracts me from all rational thought. My gaze wanders to Kian, a tremble running down my shoulders. I need water. I feel as though I'll crack into little pieces and disintegrate if I'm not given something soon. She knows this; she must. She pushed me near death from the lack of it before.

A whimper rises in my throat, and I stare at Kian in desperation. She gives me a look I can't read in the darkness. Her hand appears out of nowhere, knocking into the side of my head. My vision wavers, pain sparking everywhere at once. A cry rises in my chest, but it comes out hoarse and rough.

The next moment, a slow trickle of water drips across my face from a cup she holds above me. I tip my head toward it, closing my eyes. A bump from the car sends the rest of the water splashing onto my head. I gasp in relief. It doesn't take away the pain, but it's enough for now. I go limp against the seat, letting my consciousness drift.

I jerk awake as Kian rolls the machine to a stop and shuts it off. Outside, the trees give way to sand, and sand to sea. The waves crash with the ferocity of an attacking siren pod, sending foam far up the beach. A large dinghy rests just out of the water's reach, four people keeping it still. Beyond the wall of rain, the faint silhouette of a ship bobs in the harbor, the distinct shape of the stacks on the stern and the elegant curve of the bow painted into my memory forever.

A pit forms in my gut, like a blow to the stomach.

The *Oyster.*

[14]

THE OYSTER

If I want to hold on,
> *Is it best to tighten my grip,*
> *Or to let go?*

METAL SCRAPING METAL startles me as Kian exits the machine. The wind slips through the open door, blasting me with a bucket's worth of saltless water. It vanishes again just as quickly, returning to its incessant pounding on the walls of the machine.

Darkness threatens to creep back in. I focus on my breathing, trying to keep the taunting void of unconsciousness at the corners of my vision. Dejean hovers before me. A rush of joy rises in my chest. I reach out to him with my chained hands, the weight clinging to my trembling arms. My fingers go straight through his cheek, and he vanishes.

My hope plummets. A trick of my mind, that's all it is. Dejean's on the other side of the island, with Murielle and Simone. My helpless mind spirals through terrible questions. Does he worry over my safety? What will he think when he finds me gone? Will he wonder after me at all?

Time passes slower than usual as Kian walks around the machine, shouting instructions at her crew. I see Dejean again, in the waves, in the rocks, in the trees. In the first he's distraught, and in the second he fumes with anger, but I cannot make out the expression on his dark face as he stalks toward me through the forest, only the stiff arch of his shoulders and his powerful, staggering stride.

I shy away from Kian as she opens the door on my side of the machine. She picks me up roughly. My stomach turns, but I don't protest. If I have any hope of escaping, I need to conserve my strength until I'm above deep water.

She carries me to the grounded dinghy and sets me inside. Pain laces up my back from the bruises, but the gentle drop hurts little compared to her usual punishing slam. She underestimates me. My soul pulls toward some dark abyss, its jeering rush spinning my head. Perhaps she's right. I don't feel like a terror of the sea when my desperate cling to consciousness flails more than it succeeds.

But with the visions of Dejean fading, my focus sharpens. Pushing through the haze, I curl onto my side and poke my head over the edge of the boat. Theirn catches my eyes with a firm look.

"Stay quiet. She's . . ." he pauses, seeming to search for words. "In a mood."

I give him a very tiny nod. We may be enemies, but we both know how dangerous Kian grows during times like these, to humans as well as sirens.

Theirn returns the nod. "I'm sorry," he adds. "That captain, Gayle—you seemed happy with him. But I couldn't . . ." His face falls and his words fade into the rush of the rain in the wind and the pounding of the waves.

A part of what he says tugs at my heart. But the pity he harbors won't stop him from knocking me straight back into the darkness if he thinks I mean to escape. Theirn or not, I have to get away. I'll have to time this very carefully.

Two women work on the other side of the boat, preparing the steam machine that will push it forward. I've never seen either of them before, but the third member's voice rings like an echo in my ears.

Chauncey.

He stalks toward Kian as she rummages through the driving machine's main compartment. "You have your ship and your fish. Pay up." The storm conceals his face, but he hovers a hand over the hilt of his thin sword.

Fury hits me with a blast of wind off the unforgiving sea. Dejean left the *Oyster* in Chauncey's care, to sail up to Luciole Rock. Yet he ran instead of protecting his first mate, and here he stands, the *Oyster* floating just off the coast.

"Traitor," I hiss under my breath, my word lost in the storm. Dejean and I have no sign for it, and it tears a bitter hole in my heart at the thought of needing one.

Kian hardly pauses from her work, snapping over her shoulder, "You promised me the siren, but you failed to deliver."

"There were complications!" Chauncey exclaims, stopping beside her. "But I got the *Oyster* out of the harbor without stirring up trouble. That's worth half of what you agreed on, at least. Hand it over."

In the darkness, Kian goes still with the chilling quiet of a predator preparing to attack, to kill. Then her shoulders relax and she laughs a high, sharp sound that matches the storm. "This is a good day," she says, motioning at Theirn. "Toss him his reward."

Theirn lifts his brow, but says nothing. I flinch out of the way as he reaches past my head and grabs a bag from the chest beside the mast. He hurls it at Chauncey. The traitor struggles not to let it slip through his fingers in the wet and the wind.

As he tightens his grip on the bag, Kian yanks his sword out of its holder at his belt and sticks the sharp end through his stomach. She twists and then tugs upward. His guts spill and he crumples to his knees, his eyes wide. None of Kian's crew so much as flinch.

A peculiar satisfaction grows in my stomach. Chauncey deserved this. Though his damage is already done, I'm glad he's no longer a threat. But now the scent of his blood whips toward me in the winds, mixed with the sharp, briny smell of the sea. I chance a whine, trying to catch Kian's attention without appearing too assertive.

Chuckling to herself, she yanks somethings hot and bloody out of the hole she made in Chauncey's stomach. She cuts it up into finger-sized pieces and shoves it through the bars of the little cage she muzzled me with before the ride here. My instincts fight, fear tugging me away from her, but I force myself to take the meat. My weakened body needs this blood, and even the smallest slices taste fresh and potent and wonderful. A kidney, I think.

As though triggered by the nutrients, the pills I took at Dejean's house kick in. The last curls of wooziness retreat from my mind. My muscles still ache, tender with bruises and shaky from use, and the pounding of my ribs and gills refuses to subside, but I move easily once more, as though a weight has been lifted off my body. Maybe I can get out of this after all.

But Dejean appears again, stalking at the edge of my vision, and my hope fades. I'm still hallucinating. Whatever trick this is, it hasn't rid my mind of the fatigue-induced intrusions. I go limp, peeking out over the side of the boat. The world seems to collapse, a chaotic gale encircling me as a weary dark cloud settles within.

"Go away," I mutter at the hallucination of Dejean, *"I am alone."*

He ignores me, creeping his way around the side of Kian's driving machine, the storm obscuring his movements. With three great strides, he reaches Chauncey's lifeless form. He yanks the man's sword free of his flesh and the body rolls, face down.

My breath leaves me. This Dejean is here. He's here, and he's alive. He came for me. His genuine presence fills a hollow deep in my chest, and I want to go limp all over again. The feeling lasts only a moment, though.

If Dejean is here, then Kian can hurt him.

Raising his stolen sword, he charges at Kian, stumbling through the sand. Her blade blurs as she draws it from her side. It meets with Dejean's, the sound lost in the roaring of the wind. They fight as dancing fish, darting at each other once, twice, three times, then retreating. The rain turns each movement to a blur, all noise muted beyond recognition. Dejean attacks like an injured dolphin, lurching in and out with a vicious cleverness, while Kian becomes a shark, lurking with perfect strength and attacking with equal ferocity.

One of the unfamiliar sailors stands awkwardly, her hand on a dagger at her hip. The other continues her work, shooting Kian and Dejean just as many nervous glances as she gives the storm raging in the waters beyond us. Theirn draws his pistol, aiming at Dejean. He wavers, wiping rain from his eyes, his dark braids whipping around him.

No.

With all my strength, I launch out of the boat and drive my metal cuffs into his face, tackling him to the sand. His pistol fires into the air. I go to bite him, but the cage around my mouth knocks against his neck. I rip my fingers into his shoulder, but my bound grip barely tears his clothing. In one giant heave, he tosses me off. He slams me into the sand, pressing his hands to my shoulders.

I shriek at him, struggling against his weight, but he drives his knee into my hips, stilling most of my movement. Snarling, I meet his gaze with a glare. My muscles go still at the forlorn expression on his face, his thick brows low and his full lips in a tight line. His head shoots up as Kian shouts.

"Prepare the boat!"

I follow Theirn's gaze to find her still locked in her fight with Dejean. He backs up more than he steps forward, each block slower than the last. I must reach him, help him somehow. With Theirn's concentration torn between Kian and the dinghy, his grip on my shoulders loosens. I shove my hands into the center of his chest and twist out from under him.

He grabs for me again, and I swing my hips, flinging my tail at his side. It falls like a solid weight, but the unresponsive flesh lacks the power of flexed muscle. It smacks against him sluggishly and he wraps his arms around it. I slam my cuffs into the center of his throat. Choking, he drops my tail and crumples to the side, supporting himself on his elbows.

I roll. The sand gives way beneath me. Along the line of my hips, I feel the spray of the waves, drawn there by the gale. The ocean seems to pulse with energy and freedom, calling me to come. It's so near. In a few short moments, I could vanish into it and be lost from Kian forever.

But I glance toward Dejean, and the sea fades to the back of my mind. He stumbles as he backs away from Kian, his movements askew, wobbly, and contorted. His fall from the cliff impaired him. Like this, Kian will win. Kian will win. Then she'll kill.

Dejean's feet slip out from under him, sprawling him onto the wet ground. Drawing a deep breath, I release a curdling shriek, my whole body quavering. I wait long enough to catch Kian's gaze before twisting and scrambling toward the sea. The poles on my brace snag on the sand, but I let them. If I escape Kian, she'll turn and attack Dejean out of fury. But once her hands are on me again, she'll be too proud to let me go. I hope.

I hope, and don't look back.

The screeching of the wind masks any footsteps. Hands latch around my neck, sudden and terrifying, sending a shock through my spine. I wilt into the half inch of water beneath me, pain numbing my senses. My vision falters, and suddenly Kian looms above me, lifting me up. I struggle against her with as much ferocity as I can manage, slipping out of her grasp. She prepares to hit me, or perhaps to tear into my gills again. But then her gaze flickers to Dejean, struggling to stand, Chauncey's sword still in his hand.

"Theirn!" She calls.

Leave Dejean. Please.

As though hypnotized by my plea, she shouts again. "Theirn! Help me carry this damn fish or you'll be swimming to the ship."

Her first mate appears by her side faster than the ominous boom of far-off thunder. Together, they take hold of my tail, lugging me toward the dinghy. My chest drags, sand rubbing into my gills. I try to scream at them, but the sound comes out as a grating whimper. Dejean follows us, tottering but pulling himself forward.

"Stay—be safe," I sign to him, making the motions as best I can, upside down with my wrists chained together. Because I don't think he'll listen otherwise, I add a hasty, *"Find me."*

For a moment, I worry he didn't understand, that my signs were too muddled. But then he nods, mouthing something I can't make out in the rain. Something we must not have a sign for.

Theirn and Kian heave me into the dinghy, and Kian presses me down, throwing a net over my body. I toss it off twice before she manages to wrap me up, half of the netting falling overboard. Before Kian can retrieve it, one of the women fires up the machine and we burst into the sky with a rumble and a clatter.

The dinghy tips as something tugs on the net wrapped around me, pulling it taut over the side of the boat. Theirn throws his weight against the other edge, and it almost flies straight for a moment, before the wind tosses it into disarray. We're like a flower petal riding an ocean current, thrown to the whims of the storm.

At first, I hope for the chaos to win, to fling us to the mercy of the water below. But a creeping fear sinks into me, weighed down by the metal around my wrists. The waves rise like solid mountains of water, and the speed of our rickety boat as we skid through the air just above them feels as though any crash would cause instant death. Theirn holds the side of the dinghy in a death grip, while Kian pins me to the wood below. The woman manning the machine presses flush against the side of it. The last crewmate holds to the mast.

"Distance?" Kian shouts.

"About a hundred sherlots, captain!" the mast woman cries back.

As she speaks, the boat takes a sudden dip, twisting in the wind. Her grip on the mast comes loose, and the wind yanks her up. She spirals through the air, over the side of the dinghy, and vanishes into the darkness. No one speaks. The woman at the back hunkers herself down further, gritting her teeth as her face goes white. She doesn't turn the boat to attempt a rescue, and Kian doesn't order her to. In this way, maybe humans truly are very similar to sirens.

My stomach turns the longer we churn through the storm. I hold in my nausea, ignoring Theirn as he chucks up a mess of browns, which disappear into the wind as soon as they leave his mouth. My raw scales grind against the wood. Misery sweeps through the scrapes and I almost wish for the release of unconsciousness when the woman at the machine finally calls to Kian.

"We're approaching! How should I bring us in?"

"I want a clean landing, on the deck," Kian replies.

The woman's face pales further. "Captain?"

"A clean landing."

I arch my back, trying in vain to see over the edge of the boat. Landing on the deck, in these winds? I don't know how the humans direct their boats so precisely, but even leaping from sea to ship in a storm like this would become a trial of luck. Landing a dinghy can't be any easier.

My chest catches as we dip down. I want to close my eyes, but they refuse, as though my life will flash away if I blink. My lungs stall. The dark sky flies over my head, rain pounding in torrents. Theirn leaps toward the mast, letting out one of the sails. It billows and catches, and the dinghy shudders, yanked backward by the sudden drag. Gale winds rip at the sail, drawing it off the mast. As it tears away, the boat slams down onto the ship's deck.

It ricochets. Kian grabs me out of the netting and jumps from the dinghy. We tumble across the slippery wood, skidding to a halt. The little boat grates along the length of the deck. As it knocks through the railing on the other side, Theirn launches himself out. It vanishes into the sea, the last crew-mate still huddled beside its grinding steam machine.

Kian lets me go. She stalks toward Theirn in a series of predatory steps that make my blood run cold, barely staggering even as the ship heaves over a massive swell. Theirn bows before her, letting her knock him across the side of his head with a fist. His braids fly about, torn by the wind, and he shakes, trying to hold himself in place as the deck moves beneath him. But he doesn't look up.

You could have had everything you wanted, Kian's words echo in my mind. *We could have both won.* But this is what obedience to Kian looks like. Pain.

I shiver as violently as Theirn. My gaze falls to the sea and a fierce yearning tugs me toward it. Using the wetness of the wood beneath me, I slide along the deck. The water looms up before me, nearer and nearer, but then the ship keels and my destination rises instead, tossing my weight back. Kian catches hold of my tail, yanking me in the direction of the hatchway to the lower decks.

With a shriek, I seize the sides of the door frame, digging my nails into the wood. Kian pulls harder and my fingers skid feebly. My arms drop to my sides. The streaks of silver lightning that run across the sky fade as the doorway gets smaller, the flickers of swaying yellow lanterns replacing them. My tiny sliver of hope dissolves in an instant. I couldn't escape Kian before. How will I manage it now?

Dejean. Dejean will come. Someday. After this storm works itself out, and he returns to the *Tsunami*, he'll hunt Kian down and together we'll be rid of her once and for all. I just have to stay alive until then.

The ship creaks and thunders as the sea bites at it, but from the inside, tossed about in a dark container, the raging storm is a distant, unknowable thing. Kian drags me to the next set of stairs, bits of wood driving into my flesh. She wrenches me over her shoulder and lugs me the rest of the way. I go limp. Protesting will do me no good.

Her cabin looks the same as ever, though her trinkets and papers slide about with the roll of the ship. Waves crash against her large windows, engulfing them before letting go with such force that the dark expanse of the sky covers the entire space, cracks of lightning shooting through it at random. Kian rips my focus away as she tosses me onto the ground in the little side room.

The water at the bottom of my old tub forms a shifting puddle the size of my palm. The weight lays off to the side, a terrible, ugly block. I refuse to look at it. Instead, I glance at Kian. Trying to appear as small and weak as I can, I dangle one of my arms over the side of the tub and motion to the water. I force out a whimper that stings my gills, and hold back my cringe.

Kian looks from me to the tub and snorts. She strikes her heel carelessly into my tail. Whirling, she slams the door closed, locking me within. I feel nothing from her kick, but the effect must be there, like the pounding in my head and the sting in my gills and the shooting pains from my ribs. Everything hurts, unrelenting and consuming.

I hate Kian.

My nails grate into my palms and I release my grip with a yelp. I refuse to do her work for her. Draping my torso over the side of the tub, I scoop out the bit of stale water from the bottom, dripping it across my face, my eyes closed. When I finish, I slump there, filling my chest with slow lungfuls of scorching air. I won't let Kian win. And I won't wait around for Dejean to arrive in a week. I can free myself.

Kian already made a mistake; she left me here without chaining me to the tub. There must be some way I can use this to my benefit.

I jump at a loud thud from the port window. My breath catches painfully as I squeak in shock. Dejean hangs outside the little circular piece of glass, holding himself up by his better arm. Around his waist hangs the net Kian wrapped me in, swirling in the wind. He looks alive, but his face pinches in pain, his eyes listless.

"Dejean!"

I throw myself over the tub and grab the corners of the port window. My fingers slide against a little latch. I fumble with it. The boat tips, Dejean's face rising toward the sky. The window flings open just as the ship keels the other way. I grab Dejean's restricted arm and the front of his shirt, pulling him forward. Only his head and one shoulder will fit into the tiny circle.

"Perle—"

A wall of water slams into his back. It shoots through the cracks around his body, rushing into the little side room as though fired from a gun. As the ship tips away, it vanishes, leaving us both drenched and gasping, water a hand's-length deep sloshing beneath me.

The thin coat of the sea dripping down my scales brings me new life. I strengthen my grip on Dejean. He can't take many more of these waves, but I won't let him go until I know he'll be safe.

"Perle," he repeats himself, his voice tired and weak with relief. "You're not hurt?"

"Not badly," I say, shifting my hold in order to sign the word *no* with one hand, ignoring the pain in my ribs. I follow it with a simple, *"But you are. You shouldn't be here."*

"I'll be all right," He brushes away the question, just as I did. "There's a knife in the sheath on my arm. Take it."

"But—" I have to stop my signing and hold him with both hands as another massive swell knocks into our side of the ship, adding to the water on the floor.

"Take it," he insists. "I'm climbing to the top deck. I'll find you. Get out of here and meet me at the stairs."

"I don't like this." He fell once already. In his weakened state, he looks at me as though he can't quite distinguish my face from the wall at my back. I'm not even sure he remembers what he just said. But I can't hold him here until the end of the storm. If he's going to climb, he should do it now, while he has some strength remaining.

The sea calls to me in violent, yearning bellows as I yank Dejean's knife loose. If I remove my brace, I might squeeze through the port window, vanishing into the storm. Then what? Lay on the ocean floor, chains too heavy to swim in, doomed to die there knowing I'm free, while Dejean is trapped on Kian's ship, or worse, dead? My sea will wait for me.

The knife feels odd in my hands, a strange human contraption made to kill faster and stealthier than tooth and nail. I think of the fishing spear and pretend it's the same. It's not for Kian anyway.

"Perle?" The confusion in Dejean's voice breaks into my thoughts. "Let me go."

"I don't want to." I shake my head fiercely. I don't want to let him go. I want to keep him close, to sing to him until he smiles and the twinkle returns to his eyes, to tell him my fears and hear him say that he'll stand by me while I face them. My chest tightens, my fingers responding in a like motion.

Dejean flinches, but he gives me a soft smile. "It's just for a moment. I'll be with you again soon."

It's all I can do to nod. I wait for the next swell to end, the room filling a fraction further. Carefully, I let Dejean go. He pulls his head out of the window, his restricted arm hanging awkwardly at his side. And he climbs.

My stomach ties itself into knots as he moves up the side of the ship, much too slow and much too fast all at once. When his foot vanishes out of my view, I shove my head through the window. As he reaches for the main deck, a wave knocks me back, filling my nose and mouth. Fighting to bar it from my lungs, I slam the window closed.

"*Be safe,*" I whisper the words over the sound of the simple lock clicking shut once more. With shaking hands, I cut the leather tying the cage over my mouth. I consider opening the window again just to toss the cursed thing out. But Dejean will be here soon.

I try the knife on the chains around my wrists, but the thick metal refuses to break. Turning my attention to the door, I glance over the lock. Murielle would know how to pick this. Or one better, she'd know how to take the door off its post. I narrow my eyes at the thing. *Maybe that's it . . .*

Moving to the side of the door, I drive the knife around one of the metal spikes holding the hinges together. I force it upward until it springs off. The door creaks. I set onto the other hinges. As the last one comes apart, I throw myself back, the door collapsing inward. Scrambling around it, I shove the knife's hilt in my mouth and crawl toward the front of Kian's cabin.

Her trinkets fly at me as the ship keels, but I shove them off. A stray song blocker clatters across the wood, toward the bed. A shudder pinches my gut. This ship must sink, carrying whatever store Kian has of the blockers to the sea floor, her and her crew with it. If we can't manage that tonight, we may never have another chance.

Soft footsteps echo from the stairs beyond, too light and precise to be from a fatigued Dejean. Panic tenses every muscle in me, and I throw myself into a roll. I tumble across the room, the tipping of the ship carrying my momentum. Diving behind the huge desk bolted to the center of the cabin, I grab my tail and yank it close to my body.

Through the crack beneath the desk, I can just make out the bottom of the cabin door, and the gap that marks the side room. With the door fallen in, it creates an empty hollow, a scar in the wall.

The little light on the underside of my tides catches my

gaze, a beacon in the night. A beacon for Kian. I cover them with a palm, but one rattles from within. Ripping off its back panel, I press my finger to a loose metal bit, just beneath two colorful wires attached to a little square of bright, boxy designs. Murielle mentioned something about these. Something dangerous.

My soul seems to rip from my body as the door to Kian's cabin swings open. I hold my breath. Her boots pound like a hurricane, the chaos outside a mild breeze in comparison. Forcing my eyes away from Kian, I turn to the giant windows at the back of the cabin.

The waves pound against the glass, the world obscured by water. But something catches my eye; a flash of teal. A murky brown streak follows it, then a glimmer of gray. The world goes quiet as death.

[15]

THE WEIGHT

The longer I bear it,
the heavier it becomes.
I let go.

MY EYES JUMP from the sirens whipping through the waves to the blocker now sliding toward Kian's door. On a higher deck, Dejean struggles to reach me, defenseless against the songs of my kind. I stretch for it instinctively, stopping just before my fingers leave the cover of the desk. It continues to slide, passing me by. With a soft click, it hits Kian's boots. Panic wells in my chest as she reaches down, clashes of wind and water the only sound breaking the tense silence.

Silence.

It washes over me then, a stifling, clinging uncertainty. I saw Teal out in the waves. That was no hallucination; my eyes are tuned to spot sirens. But no song drifts into the cabin, not even the low rumble of a pod preparing their chorus. An eerie hush reigns, filtered by the muffled storm and the creaking of the ship. Even the crew above us works noiselessly.

The thump of erratic footsteps breaks the quiet and the cabin door swings inward. Dejean's boots come into view beneath the crack of the desk.

The meager glimpse blisters my soul. I have to see him. Clenching the open tide in my hand, I poke my head out. Kian slips her gun from the little carrier on her belt and aims it at Dejean.

He lifts his unrestricted arm high into the air, his other hand raising as far as it can, palm out. His weight bears heavily on one leg, and he wavers as the ship careens. The indecision on his face unites exhaustion and fear. His eyes drift around the room, barely focusing. But they find me.

I sign to him, *"Stay,"* adding quickly, *"Get her talking."*

An idea forms in my mind, but I don't know how long it'll take me to rig it. Tackling Kian here and now would be easier. I could knock her to the ground, driving Dejean's knife into her heart, and hope her gun doesn't go off in the process. My plan offers a more permanent solution though, if only Dejean can stall. I shove the knife into a notch in the deck and begin to work.

"Please, I have to know Perle is safe." Dejean sounds desperate. Pleading. Scared.

Kian laughs, a sharp, terrible sound. "You named the fish," she says, all humor vanishing in an instant. "You can't possibly care about them! You think they won't turn on you? The moment you stop benefiting them, you're dead. You drop that charade of kindness and they'll rip your throat out."

My hands stiffen. Slowly, I glance out.

A pinch in Dejean's forehead draws his brows together, his gaze dropping to the ground. When he finally looks up, he focuses on Kian. "It's not a charade." He says it with certainty, as though he knows nothing truer.

My wonderful human.

Kian's lips twist and the jagged scar that runs across her jawline trembles in the low lamplight. "You don't know, do you?" She lowers her gun ever so slightly, taking a step forward. "I was there, the day the sirens killed your father," she says. "He was torn apart by a pearly white siren, just like that one you so accurately named. It gleamed in the moonlight, ripping out his insides like they were candy."

The confidence slides off Dejean. He stumbles once under the tilt of the floor, his unrestricted arm stretching out to the side to catch him. His eyes fall to me, shock and turmoil lighting in them.

I yank my head back into the safety of the desk before Kian can follow his gaze. *Don't think about him.* I shake my head, gripping my tide. *Concentrate.*

"I've picked up more sirens than you could count in the last year, colors from across the spectrum," Kian continues. "But that fish is the only one with the iridescent white coloring. What do you think that means?" Her question requires no reply, because the answer comes in the tremble running through Dejean, his feet slipping once more.

"How . . ." He clears his throat. "How do you know?"

Pain blossoms deep within my chest, a gnawing that swells as it bites down, threatening to eat me alive. One thought echoes in my mind. *Kian was right. Dejean won't want me now.*

But I force the thought down, binding up my pain with one sharp grimace. It doesn't matter what Dejean thinks, or why. All that matters is sinking this ship and rescuing him in the process.

I focus on my tides, on the final wires I'm rerouting. My metal cuffs clang softly together as I connect the second wire to the first wire's place. It sparks, a pure, engulfing blue piercing through its core. I hurl it toward the back of the cabin, just above the stacks rumbling a few decks below.

Kian takes another step toward Dejean, shadows flickering across her scar. "I watched. I—"

A burst of thunder cuts off her words as the tide morphs into pure, blue light. There's not enough time for a solid thought to form in my mind, but the torrent of dread that runs through me is prompted by a question I wish I'd asked. To me, an explosion is the burst of power from a wave, and crash of steam out a stack, the flicker of lightning across the sky. It occurs to me now that Murielle's human explosion may be something larger and more powerful than that, something that would wreck us along with the ship.

Panic rips through me in time with the growth of the

tide's glow, swelling outward in a perfect sphere of crackling lightning. I hear nothing as it comes for me; not the wind or the sea, not even the sound of my own heartbeat. I try to lift my hands to my face, to shield myself in some way, but compared to the expanding flare, my motions are like the growing of coral amid the darting of fishes. Then, a hand's width from my tail fin, the massive orb of light stops.

Its sound changes to a dull thrumming, splintered rays of white running through it in crackles. It turns in on itself, as though sucked back by a turbulent whirlpool. In one last swirl of light and a flash of blue, it returns to its original shape; a small lifeless blue stone, the metal of the tide that once contained it now blasted apart or burnt away. The stone hovers in the air for a breath before dropping.

Time and life return.

The parts of the ship the light touched have vanished—wood and metal and glass and fabric gone as though they never existed. In their place lies a gaping spherical hollow, cutting out part of the deck for two floors in each direction as well as a great chunk of the ship's stern. Wind rushes in, followed by rain.

A blue siren washes through the opening in the deck beneath us, emerging with a sailor between their teeth. The shouting from above echoes screams from below. The ship tilts and spins, floundering among the crashing swells. It'll sink, sure as the sun will rise, but the cavern I made in its side still sits above the waterline, waves crashing through it with each swell. We may yet escape this.

I cling to the side of the desk, sticking my head out. Kian's gaze fixes on the gaping hole in her ship, unblinking as she clings to a furnishing attached to the wall, her pistol gone. Dejean clutches the other side of the desk, a million emotions fighting for control of his face.

"You . . . blew a hole . . . in . . ." Awe fills his features for a moment before slipping into anger. "You could've killed yourself!"

"*Blame Murielle,*" I hiss, only bothering to sign her name alone. It shuts him up, and I fling my chains toward him as best I can without sliding out from the side of the desk. "*A little help?*"

"I'm never trusting you with anything again," he mumbles, grabbing my wrists. One look at the lock and he shakes his head, glancing back the keys hooked to Kian's belt.

The shriek of a siren pierces my ears as Gray falls from the deck above, a pirate squirming beneath the clench of their teeth. They both slam into the edge of the cabin's floor and drop out of view. Kian chooses that moment to launch at Dejean.

My heart ricochets through my chest. She slams him against the side of the desk, and the wood creaks as they wrestle. I grab for Dejean, but the arcing of the ship throws their locked bodies across the room.

"What have you done!" Fury strains her voice, and she punches the underside of his jaw with such force that his head raps into the deck.

I throw myself at them, using the roll of the ship and the rain-slick floor to my advantage. "*I did this.*" A protective rage turns my words to a snarl. I grab her, sinking my teeth into her arm. Warm blood seeps through my mouth as she screams a low predatory sound. She jerks and knocks me off with an elbow to my bruised ribs. Twisting, I grab onto her leg.

The ship rocks fiercely and a violent groan runs through the decks. It comes to a sudden halt, the wood vibrating beneath us as it screams. The ship goes still. *A rock.* Without the forward power of the stacks, we ran straight into it. The rocky projection's smaller crags bite into the edge of the deck beneath us, glimmers of white water crashing off it as a wave hits and then rolls back, revealing the broken body of a large, dark-colored siren and a trembling human clinging to the stone.

Everything in the cabin shifts from the vessel's sudden stillness. Trinkets fling across the space, and the metal Kian weighed my tail down with during my captivity grinds along the floor. As I slide, I grab a ring hooked into the deck, clinging to it with such might that my fingers go numb.

Dejean scrambles for a similar hold. He misses. Flying past me, he hits the wall of the cabin without a sound. He crumples to the floor, the key to my chains grasped in his limp fingers. The air goes stale.

"*Dejean!*" I lift my voice against the noise of the storm, but a gale rushes through the cabin, drowning out my hoarse cry. He stirs, his eyelashes fluttering. Some of the tension releases from my chest.

It returns in a rush as Kian lunges toward him, the knife he gave me clutched in her hand. I fling myself at her, catching her by the legs. A voice in the back of my mind tells me to be cautious. In her unstable state, she'll stab me just as soon as look at me. But I must keep her away from Dejean, the need as imperative and urgent as the rapid pumping of my heart.

She twists toward me, but the ship shudders again. We roll, and my hip knocks against a large, metal object. The weight. The straps Dejean and Simone used to lift it float back and forth in the thin layer of water covering the floor, still attached. I snatch them.

Ducking away from Kian's blade, I tie the straps around one of her ankles, binding her to the metal. The crude knot won't hold forever, but when she lowers her guard to release it, she'll have my teeth at her throat. She kicks at my stomach. The strap holds, jerking her foot to a stop and drawing a pained grunt from her lips. With one hand, she brings her knife toward the strap.

Fire in my muscles, I fling myself on top of her, shoving into her wrist with both my palms. The bulk from my chains works to my advantage and the weight of them overpowers her, pinning her hand against the deck. The knife clatters away, vanishing into the sea. If I can get my jaws around her throat . . .

But shifting my weight will remove my hands from her wrist. I must be quick. As she struggles against me, I bare my teeth and hiss, preparing to make my move.

Kian forms a noise that sounds more siren then human. "Do it." Her scar wrinkles as her mouth pulls into a snarl. "Finish the job."

I want to, desperately, fiercely, the terror and anger I've built deep inside churning up in a rush. But the look in Kian's eyes gives me pause. It reminds me of Storm, of the hurt and hatred so many sirens harbor for the humans, a loathing buried deep within. The ripped edge of her normally tight collar billows in the wind, exposing the side of her neck; skin I've never before seen.

The sight jolts my insides. Scars, like the one on her jawline, old but still generous. They run in long stripes from her neck far down her chest, the skin around them contorted and stretched. The teeth of a siren.

I saw his father die the same time as my own. Torn apart by a pearly white siren, she'd said. *She'd never implied they'd tried to eat her too.*

But something had.

The boat creaks a thunderous sound. My head snaps instinctively to Dejean, and Kian's free hand slams into my gills. Choking, I crumple on top of her, blinding pain shooting up my neck. The world turns violently as she throws me off. My head knocks the deck. From the hole in the back of the ship, the blurry form of a tan siren leaps toward me. I kindle a spark of hope, but a swell catches them, dragging them deeper into the deck below.

Kian crashes down on me with the force of a wave.

"How can you be so kind to him, after what you did?" she shouts, slamming my face into the deck. Her mouth brushes my ear. "You should've finished the job."

"*It wasn't me!*" I whisper the words, wanting to scream

[211]

them, wanting to be sure they were true. I never murdered the human children . . . did I? It seems like such a ridiculous question, something I should have been paying attention to all my life. But I don't know. *I don't know.*

My panic fades into an empty reconciliation. Kian's a monster, yes; Kian and Jaquelin and Storm and many others. And so am I.

But not anymore.

The violent sound of snapping wood pounds through my head, and the ship seems to drop out from under me. My back hits the cabin deck as it jerks to a stop again, sharp pains shooting up my shoulders. The support won't last long, though. The crumbling *Oyster* will sink, whether I manage to remove my chains or not.

Twisting my whole body at once, I slam my cuffs against the gash I bit into Kian's arm. She grunts, her hold on me loosening. Another hit makes her crumple, and I roll out from under her. Water shoots into the cabin, scooping me up and slamming me into the wall beside Dejean.

I grab onto the open cabin door to keep from being carried toward Kian on the retreating backwash, clinging to Dejean with one arm. He looks dazed, his body cocked awkwardly. It seems to be all he can do to hold to me as the ship sinks lower once more.

"*Dejean.*" I don't scream or cry; I just speak his name, drawing on everything he means to me. A dim smile softens his face, eyes almost sparkling. He opens one of his hands to me, revealing a key clutched so tightly it's formed its shape in the skin of his palm.

I take it, unlocking my chains in a rush. They fall away and hit the deck with a sharp clank. The sound turns to a rattle, a low, terrible vibration that seems to shake every bit of the ship. Through the gap in the end of the cabin, a stream of sirens vanish into the sea, fleeing. And for good reason.

The ocean beyond us is calming; the rain gone and the

wind a low whistle. But the ship is coming apart all the same.

The deck slides as the *Oyster* sinks. The end I blew open goes first, dipping straight into the water as the side of the cabin where Dejean and I sit lifts precariously. Kian shouts at me, her words muddled, her eyes wide. She claws at the straps I used to tie her to the weight, but the metal block slips faster than she can manage. It plunges into the rising water, dragging Kian with it.

Before I can stop myself, I roll across the deck. I catch hold of the edge of the desk with one hand and grab Kian's wrist with the other. She grips me tightly in return, terror almost masking the bitterness in her gaze. The sea smells so strongly of blood that the scent washes over me with each gust of wind. The water creeps above Kian's hips and up her chest.

There is one thing I know for certain: I don't want to help her, but if I don't offer her a choice, I'll regret it. So many have already died from the enmity she feels, sirens and humans alike. The tang of the blood turns my stomach, reminding me of those I've killed myself. I remember every angry line of Storm's face, but the humans' features are drowned in the sea of indifference I once held. They were just invaders, murderers with no hint of honor, and an easy meal. Yet it's their pain I feel now: Dejean and his mother mourning a man who never harmed me, and a young girl with a neck and chest torn apart.

I can hate Kian. I can make certain she never ruins another life, siren or human. But she still deserves a choice—the choice Dejean gave me—to let forgiveness change her, and not death.

"I can help you." She won't understand my words, but I whistle them in a soft, questioning tone.

The last flicker of light from inside the ship shimmers off the scar on her jawline. "*Now* you think you can be nice to me?" She gives a bitter, low laugh, void of humor. "I know what you're doing. I know your kind. You're no different from humans," she snarls. "Both of us are monsters."

I tighten my grip on her wrist as the water licks at her chin. *"We don't have to be."*

A spark flares in Kian's eyes. Her nails dig into my wrist.

I shriek as she claws her way up my arm, drawing blood with each new grip. *Let go of her, let go of her.* But I can't.

With one last burst of motion, she reaches for my gills. Her fingers tighten around them. Pain blooms in their wake, turning my vision to stars. My piercing screech breaks through my skull. I throw her off.

As her hands fall away, the ship drops completely into the water, plunging us toward the depths. Kian sinks downward through the opening in the side of the ship, dragged by the weight at her ankle. She tries to bend, to reach for the straps, but the force of the water presses against her. Bubbles cascade from her mouth, creating a ring around my vision.

She chose this. Perhaps much of the pain she inflicted was a result of her past, but the targets of her rage stretched far beyond the pearly siren who scared her as a child. Beyond sirens, beyond her enemies, all the way to her own crew. Perhaps my offer came too late, but I doubt she was ever willing to accept it at all.

The ship slides away behind me, leaving the contents of Kian's cabin drifting through the calming waves as it spirals deeper. Sirens dart around it, a few picking at corpses, others watching me with curiosity. None of them touch Kian. Somehow, they know better. They know this is a death she chose, drowned by the same weight she had pinned to my tail not so long ago.

Beating my arms slowly, I watch Kian drop, her hands outstretched. Her body grows smaller and weaker until the dark waters consume her. She's gone. Captain Kian, my night-terror, is nothing more than a corpse, soon to be pinned to the bottom of the sea. It should bring me joy, or contentment, or in the least, relief. But still, I feel nothing, as though the world is no different than before.

Hurried shrieks and hisses catch my attention as a fresh batch of sailors swims from the sinking form of the ship. Sirens pick them off, one by one, filling the water with small clouds of pink. They keep away from Dejean, either because they recognize him from before, or the equally likely case; he looks half dead already. Drawing my remaining tide off my brace, I hold it between my hands and burst toward him. It takes me three tries to aim right, but I reach him, scooping him up and shoving us both to the surface.

We break the waves. Immediately, we sink back down. I keep us above the water-line with the tide's power, but each blast grows weaker. Dejean coughs once, drawing in air. Though the waves are small and fragile in the wake of the storm, the incoming swell still shoves us back down. I beat my hips but the shifting water engulfs us relentlessly. My arms shake once more, the fatigue returning in the wake of Kian's death.

Panic tightens my gills. I search for a siren who will help me support Dejean. Instead, another human appears, his braids swirling like tiny eels around his head. Theirn grabs Dejean and drags him to the surface.

I follow, pumping my arms steadily. *"Theirn!"*

He stares at me, a mix of surprise and fear on his face as I whistle the tune of his name for the first time.

"You killed her."

"She died," I correct him, but I know my nod is all he'll understand.

Sorrow droops his features, but he returns the motion. His attention shifts to the barely-conscious Dejean. "If he's going to live, we need to get him to the shore."

"You'll help?"

He must understand something from me—my confusion, my suspicion—because he says, "If I support Dejean, the sirens will leave me alone?"

I nod again. *"Yes. I think."* I'm glad he can't interpret that last part.

Theirn takes it as an affirmation. Holding up Dejean as best he can, he swims toward the distant beach.

Dejean awakens just enough to kick his legs. I come up beside him, wrapping his restricted arm around my back. His fingers tighten against my side. He says my name, and I smile at him.

The shore sits a long way off, but between my tides and Theirn's help, we'll make it.

[16]

TIDEMARKS

What could I ever know but these:
  I love the sea; I always will.
  And one more thing.

THE SAND WARMS beneath me, its caress better than any sponge. Somewhere behind the trees, the sun rises. It fills the sky with its brilliance, turning the leftover clouds pink and purple. The wind off the sea still whirls, hurried and wild, but the calming waves crash through their normal dance across the slope of the beach, drifting in little peaks and valleys. No trace of the *Oyster* remains, and the siren pod who attacked it has vanished as well. With Kian and her blockers no longer a threat, they've likely split up and moved on, off to find their old territories or mark new ones.

I run my hands through Dejean's curls, tenderly weeding out the snarled clumps. His eyelashes flutter as he continues to drift. Lingering hints of distress cling to my stomach with sharp teeth, but the healthy color of his face and the steady rise and fall of his chest comfort me. He seems relaxed, and he managed a few words to Theirn as we neared the beach before collapsing onto the sand, his head in my lap. The quiet is a necessity. We all need the rest.

Theirn sits a little ways off, his head on his knees. In the glimmer of the morning light, the bruise Kian left along his jawline turns his dark skin puffy and purple. He stares at the sand, silent. I don't know why he spent so long watching Kian hurt me, or why he let her inflict a similar life of pain on him. Nor do I know how I would broach the topic, even if he could somehow understand me.

The gentle crashing of the waves has nearly lulled me to sleep by the time Dejean shifts. He opens his eyes and tries to sit up, but I make him lie still.

"How do you feel?" My signs match my tone, soft and a little worried.

"I think my head is trying to pound its way out of my skull, and the rest of me feels like I've been thrown about by a hurricane all night." He shields his eyes from the rising sun, squinting at me. "My ears are ringing just a bit, but I think I'll live."

"You'd better." I glare at him for good measure.

He chuckles. His eyes sparkle, and relief floods through me. He's still my Dejean. He'll be just fine.

"How did you get here?" I ask. *"How did you know Kian was taking me to the Oyster?"*

Dejean's brows knit. A glimmer of morning light shines on the waves crashing along the shore, their water a gentle lap by the time it reaches us. "I . . . think I saw you, in town . . . somehow. It's not hard to follow people here. There's only so many roads through the jungle. I stole a ride . . . a car or a truck, maybe? I can't remember all the details from the night, just flashes: you on the beach, the *Oyster* going down." He sounds ashamed to admit it, as though he expects me to be angry.

"I thought you might not. You didn't seem all there." But he was there for me. Even half-conscious and in pain, he still came when he knew I'd be in danger. My awe fades to worry. How much of Kian's speech does he remember? I have to know, yet it takes me a long time to shore up my courage. *"Why didn't you tell me about your father's death?"*

He hums quizzically in the back of his throat, but his features droop. "It was a long time ago," he whispers. "I wasn't on the ship; I didn't see it happen. I knew it was a siren attack, but I never thought for a moment you might have been the one who killed him. There are so many sirens in these waters." He presses a finger and thumb to the corners of his eyes, drawing in a long breath. "I know now that the attack—all attacks, outside of Kian's—have been bloody, painful misunderstandings. It hurts to dwell on. But I refused to blame you, and I didn't want to bring you into it."

I realize my heart pounds to a rapid beat only as it finally starts to slow. Dejean's reason is silly, but I understand, somehow. It's easier to pretend we have nothing against each other, to claim the war between my kind and his doesn't extend to us simply because we moved past it. *And still . . . "You should have told me."*

"I know." He follows his words with a quiet, "I'm sorry. I was afraid that it would come out wrong, that it would change the way you think of me, or . . . or the way I think of you, if you knew I had your ghost in my past, same as Kian."

An empty feeling sucks at my chest as I realize his fears were right. When Kian first mentioned Dejean's past, I doubted him. My gaze slides over his face, picking out every little wrinkle, every harsh line. I can see his doubt too, subtle and overpowered by the other, stronger things he feels for me. But still there.

"Was it you?" He says it so softly that I think it might be my imagination.

"What?"

"Was it you who ate my father?" Not a hint of accusation hangs in his voice, but it hurts all the same. "I know you've killed many humans, and I don't hold that against you, but I'd like to know."

I try to draw up memories, frantically searching for a face from a sea of blank features. If I can't remember whether I tried to eat a small human girl, how could I pick a man I have no reference for? It's a fruitless attempt.

With a start, I realize it isn't necessary.

"It couldn't have been me," I tell him, my relief changing the pitch of my whistling and lightening my hand motions. *"I*

know the rate at which humans age, and I'd have been very small at the time, perhaps not even born." It seems obvious now that I think about it. Humans wouldn't know how sirens mature, but some of us watch the land-dwellers grow, happy to leave them be so long as they keep to their sand and trees. *"The siren who killed your father—"* and scarred Kian *"—was probably the parent who birthed me. They had the same colorings as I."*

Dejean nods, pushing himself to a sitting position. I mourn the loss of his warmth, its absence as shocking as the sting of a ray, but he wraps me in his mobile arm and pulls me against him. I melt into his side, the pain in my ribs masked by the comfort his closeness brings.

"You know, even if you were that siren, it was at a point when you didn't know any different. You did what you did because you thought you were protecting your territory from humans who ignored the paths you set for them."

I whistle a gentle, wordless noise. *"Do you think we could teach them; the humans and the sirens? Teach them to communicate? To work together?"*

"We won't know unless we try." Dejean traces his fingers along my shoulder, drawing a happy tremor through me. "Do you think it would help? There are plenty of human groups who still hate each other even though they speak a common language."

"We won't know unless we try," I say, repeating his wording as best as my signs can manage. *"I don't think there's anything we could do to eliminate the fighting entirely, but it would be very good for some, and that's enough."*

"How would we manage it?"

"We'd need to travel." That would be best for us anyway, being on the sea. The cove and the cliffs are home, but sirens are made to swim deeper waters too. I love the wide open between the islands just as much as Dejean. *"But I don't want to leave our territory open. It'll take time to build a large enough pod that some of us can depart for a season, so we*

should stay at the house for a while first. Keep an eye out for anyone who might be willing to join us. The delay would give everyone time to rest. Just the thought of my tub makes me want to sleep for a week.

"I'll ask Simone if she'd like to take command of the *Tsunami* for a couple runs," Dejean says. "She could bring Murielle with her. There's some good pirating waters near the coast where they're planning to take their honeymoon."

"You'll want to return to pirating eventually, won't you?"

"Well . . ." He hesitates. "I got into that business by accident, and I think my old captain would support this venture. It could make the seas safer for other pirates and merchants alike." He chuckles, his shoulders trembling. "You never know; blends of human crews and siren pods might form along the way. Maybe we can start a special brand of pirating."

"You're terrible." The warm swell in my heart seeps into my voice and softens my hand motions. I pause, scanning the horizon. *"If any of the sirens Kian sold off are still held captive, we should search for them."*

"They might not be near the sea, you know."

"I know." A shudder runs through me at the thought of traveling farther onto land than Dejean's cove-side home. *"But if I don't look for them, who will?"* He opens his mouth, and I cut him off with a grin and a whistle. *"Other than you."*

He smiles. "Mur can probably build you something for navigating across the ground. Some kind of little water-filled vehicle you can drive yourself."

"I'd like that."

Dejean replies with a soothing brush of his fingers along my arm.

No other words seem necessary at the moment. It's surreal to look out over Kian's grave and plan a happy future. But I wouldn't want anything else. Except maybe a fresh dolphin liver.

As we sit in relaxed silence, the tide rises enough to soak

my tail. I can't feel its gentle touch, the waves stopping before they reach my hips, but it turns the warmth of the sun from scorching to lazily pleasant. Somewhere far off, a human machine chugs away.

The sound grows steadily closer, until both Dejean and I turn to look at the trees. A boxy driving machine bursts down the road, swerving to a stop at the edge of the beach. Murielle flies out of it with a crooked yet energized limp, her hair a metal-raining cloud behind her. Simone follows at a slower pace, surveying the area as she approaches. Her eyes lock on Theirn, still huddled in place, but Dejean shrugs to her and she leaves him be.

"We thought you died!" Murielle shouts, tackling us with such force that I tumble onto my back, taking Dejean with me. She wraps her arms around us both at once, so tightly that I yelp. "Shit. Shoulda asked if you were injured . . ." She lets us go, looking embarrassed.

Grinning, I ruffle a hand through her fluffy hair. Her affection brings a smirk to my lips, and seeing her safe and happy takes a weight from my heart I didn't realize I still carried. I give a little wave to Simone.

She smiles at me before aiming a glare toward Dejean. "You! How dare you leave town in the middle of a storm and not tell us where you're going?" Her palm raises as though she's going to smack him in the back of the head, but then thinks better of it.

"I didn't have the time! And you would've come with me," Dejean says.

Simone grits her teeth, her fingers tightening. "By the looks of you both, you could've used the help."

"We're alive." He shrugs his good shoulder. "And Mur stayed out of the fighting. I knew she'd be by your side no matter what you did, so I decided it was better if it took you a while to get here."

"Ah." Her face softens. She leans forward, giving Dejean a little squeeze on his scarless shoulder before carefully detaching her protesting fiancée from our bodies and scooping her up. "This doesn't mean I've forgiven you," she adds, settling into the sand at Dejean's side.

Murielle leans against Simone, poking Dejean's leg with the tip of her boot. "Bet she'd accept an apology if it came in the form of a wedding present."

Shaking his head, Dejean laughs, his voice blending with the melody of the waves.

The sand shifts as Theirn finally moves. He doesn't stand though, just changes positions, covering the sides of his face with his hands. I don't want to feel bad for him, but I do.

A small, round shell bounces off my shoulder, and I snap my head around to find Murielle grinning at me. "How'd those little powery pulser things work out for you?"

"They worked beautifully, but I lost one of them blowing up the Oyster.*"*

Murielle's face goes blank for a moment before lighting up like the blinding morning sun, her grin stretched across her entire face. Simone can't have any idea what I said, but she sees Murielle's expression and groans. It's Dejean who speaks, though.

"That . . . that was you." His words come out too flat to be a proper question, as though he's trying to convince himself of something he already knows. Or, more accurately, something he's forgotten.

"You were upset with me then, too," I tease him.

He groans, dropping his forehead onto my shoulder. "I hope I shouted some sense into you."

I bare my teeth playfully. *"For that, you would have to have sense in the first place."*

Tightening the arm still around me, Dejean grumbles a soft, "You be nice, Perle." Murielle tosses another shell at us, but this time it hits Dejean instead. He growls under his breath, snatching it out of his lap and chucking it back, a smile pulling at his lips. "What, Mur?"

"Did you get any of Kian's blockers?"

Dejean glances at me, and I shake my head. *"The crew who wore them were picked apart by sirens, and the rest sank with the* Oyster. *They're resting on the sea floor somewhere, but I doubt any human could find one."*

Murielle sighs, going dramatically limp in Simone's arms. "Would've been nice to glance at one before you two went and destroyed them all." She doesn't seem put out. The blockers might've been unique, but I suspect she has enough to play with in the scrap around Dejean's house alone.

Theirn interrupts our conversation by pulling himself to his feet. He walks toward us slowly, one fist balled tight.

"What does he want?" Simone sounds ready to drive a sword through the center of his chest.

I silence her with a dismissive wave. *"Theirn?"*

He looks at me oddly, as though his mind refuses to process my existence. In a jerky motion, he crouches down and shoves his fist at me. I lean back on instinct, but he only opens his fingers, palm up. In it lays one of the blockers, glowing faintly.

I'm not certain he'll let me have it, but when I don't take it right away, he dumps it into the sand at my side. Picking it up hesitantly, I roll it between my fingers. The small frame squishes enough to sit comfortably in an ear, with small, sound-admitting spaces cut through the glowing and mechanical compartments.

Closing my hand around it, I turn my attention back to Theirn. *"What do you want from us?"* I sign, giving Dejean time to translate.

Theirn's mouth opens, only to hang there vacantly. His brows come together, and he looks as lost as a fish on land. He drops his gaze to the ground, digging the toes of his bare feet into the sand, his shoulders caving. The hair along his chin masks his age, but looking closely, he can't be any older than I.

"He has no one," I sign to Dejean. He catches the thoughts I'm not sure how to voice.

"He's here and he accepts you," he says softly. "We could use the help." With his hands alone, he adds a quick, "Are you all right with him around?"

I pause to consider it. If Kian had lived, I could never have been comfortable near her. But Theirn only scared me because of his relation to Kian, and he hurt me far less than she hurt him. If he wants to be done with that lifestyle, I can adjust. I'd like to see what sort of a man he'll become when he's no longer crushed under Kian's constant influence.

"Tell him he has a place in our pod, if he wants it." I add quickly, *"On a trial basis. If he doesn't behave himself, I'll eat him."*

"Perle says you can stay with us if you have nowhere to go. For the time being, at least."

Theirn's head shoots up, and his mouth opens again, but it takes a moment for anything to come out. "Thank you. That—" He stammers, looking embarrassed. Finally, he repeats the, "Thank you," and tips his head. Some of the tension drains out of his shoulders. He takes a few steps back, shifting between his feet, and settles onto the sand again, not quite close, but much nearer than before.

Murielle snatches the ear piece out of my hands while I'm distracted. I glare at her, baring my teeth, but I want to know what she thinks of it too much to try and take it away. She spins it around in her fingers. Yanking a tiny, stray tool from her hair, she picks at the thing, pulling it apart. Her grin grows wider the longer she works.

"It's made of the same stuff as the little energy shooter aids," she says. "The insides're incredibly detailed. Even if a few of them did get out, some's gonna have a hell of a time trying to reverse engineer this, much less design it again from scratch." Whistling, she cradles the glowing bit in her palm and holds the rest at eye level. "Whatever you gotta say about Kian, she was a damn genius."

"It took her years." Theirn speaks softly, not looking at us. "Drove her mad, all that time focused on building something that would let her hunt sirens. But she was so proud of that design, once she finished. She—" He stops himself, curling his legs up to his chest again. We sit quietly, but he says nothing more.

A strange pressure builds in my chest. Kian became a monster, but she had been more, once. Perhaps she let her anger and bitterness force her too far into the darkness to return, but that didn't stop Theirn from caring about her, even in his fear. I won't excuse Kian's violence, and I won't pity her. But I'm glad Dejean and I have the chance to reach out to others with similar wounds, both human and siren, to stop their hatred before they use it to lock themselves on a destructive path.

I catch Murielle's attention with a wave of my hand. *"If you get rid of the rest, you can keep the glowing bit."*

"Thank you, thank you!" She bounces in Simone's lap, making her fiancée grunt and grab her shoulders to keep her still.

"Ask Theirn if anyone else has the plans for Kian's ear pieces."

Theirn shakes his head once Dejean finishes translating. "No," he says. "She wouldn't share it. She used the designs as a bargaining chip, but she would never have given them up. Letting go of something she'd spent so long on wasn't in her nature."

I release a breath of relief. While I don't trust Theirn entirely, in this I think he's telling the truth. Nothing else would fit with what I know of Kian.

Leaning against Dejean, I follow the line of the crashing waves. The water beneath us seems to retreat, the tide running its course. In the distance, the blurred shape of a far-off island mars the horizon. A flicker of black in the nearest waves catches my eye. It vanishes and appears again, just above the white water.

I lift my voice in a greeting. A small, black siren sticks their head out of the water, returning my call with a fainter, melancholic sound. *Abyss.* I nudge Dejean in the side and sit up properly. Abyss lingers out among the waves, making a series of mournful tunes.

"You can come here," I tell them. *"The humans won't hurt you."*

Every jerky motion and nervous glance screams their reluctance, but they come, letting the wave carry them in. Grabbing onto my tail, they wiggle up onto the wet sand beside me, small and wary. And alone. Red is nowhere to be seen. After all the trouble Abyss went through to protect them, I can only think of one reason for that. A sharp pain swells in my chest.

"You lost them. We helped, but you still lost them."

Abyss lays their head in their arms, their dark body drawing in the light. *"They would've been gone much sooner, if you hadn't helped."* They pause, trembling once. *"Can you . . . can you thank your human for me?"*

"Of course."

Dejean already looks at me intently, and I explain everything to him, my signs soft. His face drops, his lips turning down, but he nods. "Poor thing."

"Are they all right?"

Theirn's question surprises me, almost as much as the worry behind it. I let Dejean relay the situation. The corners of Theirn's face sink as he drops his head. He seems to know that it's partially his fault for handing out the ear pieces to Jaquelin's hunting party, though I suspect offering them had been a ploy by Kian to drive me out of hiding.

Abyss scoots onto their elbows, staring at him curiously.

An awkward softness takes over Theirn's features. "Is there anything I can do for them?"

His words mix with Abyss's song-like voice. *"Who is he?"*

"He's . . ." Kian's old first mate doesn't quite seem to fit. *"He's with us. You can come too, if your old pod left. We have a nice cove, and a little house. It's a good place."* A home.

"Yes." They don't look away from Theirn as they speak,

their voice little more than the whisper of the wind. *"Yes, I'll come."*

"Abyss is going to be staying with us too," I sign to Dejean. *"Tell Theirn he'll have plenty of chances to help them."*

It takes Dejean three tries to translate Abyss's name, but Theirn looks very happy when he finally completes the explanation. Murielle gives Abyss a wink, and Simone sighs. She dumps Murielle out of her lap and stands, offering her fiancée a hand up. They walk down the beach, slow enough that Murielle's limp almost vanishes, their hushed tones too muffled by the waves.

Theirn shifts for a moment before following their example, meandering off the other direction. He picks up an intricate shell from the sand and, noticing Abyss looking at it, offers it over. Cautiously, they roll toward him. Taking the shell from his hands, they begin pointing out sections of it, not caring that Theirn has no idea what they're saying. He doesn't seem to care much either.

A swell of hope rises in me at the sight. Maybe someday they can help Dejean and I share our language with the rest of the sea, as we will with them.

Taking great care, Dejean draws me closer to his side. "Perle?" He waits for me to acknowledge him before lifting his hand enough to make that soft, fluid sign I saw from him back at the cave. "I love you."

It might be the first time the phrase leaves his lips, but it comes as no surprise. His love is one of the few things I'm sure of. I release a long, contented breath, leaning my head against his shoulder to watch the waves. *"I love the sea,"* I say after a while, *"But I love you almost as much as I love the sea."* If I had to choose one, Dejean or the ocean, I no longer know what I would pick.

No—perhaps that's a lie. I would pick Dejean. The sea wouldn't feel quite like home anymore without him in it.

My heart sinks after a moment. *"Don't humans equate love with mating?"* I ask. *"I love you, but I don't feel those impulses with you. You have legs. And toes."*

Dejean's brow shoots up, but a joyful laughter rises out of him with such force that I can feel the trembling of his chest. "I don't feel that either. If I'm honest, I don't even feel that about humans. Never have." He pauses, looking nervous. "But, I would like to kiss you."

I remember his lips pressed against my fingers, and my chest grows warm. *"I'd like that."*

Cupping the side of my face, he leans forward. He presses a kiss to the center of my forehead, a soft, perfect touch that takes my breath away. Feeling a little dizzy, I wrap one arm across his chest. My stomach rumbles.

"Dejean?"

"Hm?"

"I'm hungry."

He laughs again, his eyes sparkling. "I think that means it's time to go home."

Home. With Dejean. With Murielle and Simone. Now with Theirn and Abyss as well.

Lifting my head, I press my lips to his cheek.

"Yes. Let's go home."

REVIEWS FEED WRITER'S SOULS
(AND THEIR STOMACHS)

If you enjoyed this novel, please consider telling other
readers by reviewing it on Amazon or Goodreads!

ACKNOWLEDGEMENTS

I have been blessed with many pearls in my life—as well as many sparkly-eyed pirates—and without each and every one of them I would never have made it even half this far.

I owe my thanks:

First, to my mom, who is the most spectacular mother anyone could ask for, and whom I should have trusted fuller and sooner than I did.

To my entire family, for their undying support and ability to listen to my constant updates on my writing progress.

To my critique partners and beta readers and the avosquado writers support group *(all hail the great avocado in the sky!)*, but most especially to Jillian, Christina, Audrey, Rai, Katelynn, Emily, Sierra, Hannah, Alixander, and Tara. It takes a village to raise a child, and this was my child. Without their honest feedback and unending encouragement, I would still be crying over the rough draft.

To my editor, Courtney, not only for her great work and for being a joy to work with, but for her excitement over the story itself.

To the first storyteller, the great *I Am*, for being also the first love, the first forgiveness, and the first saving strength, without whom I would be nothing at all, much less a writer.

And of course, to Szilvia once again, who somehow tricked me into turning *"I HAVE THESE TWO NEW BABIES WHO I AM IN LOVE WITH HALP"* into a proper novel.

Learn about D.N. Bryn's future releases
and sign up for the newsletter at dnbryn.com

CPSIA information can be obtained
at www.ICGtesting.com
Printed in the USA
LVHW031948090120
643080LV00008B/1223/P

9 781721 833412